RECALL

AN ASH PARK NOVEL

MEGHAN O'FLYNN

PYGMALION
PUBLISHING

Distributed by Pygmalion Publishing, LLC

IBSN (paperback): 978-1-947748-89-7

WANT MORE FROM MEGHAN?
There are many more books to choose from!

Learn more about Meghan's novels on
https://meghanoflynn.com

For those who wish they could forget.

1

"How'd you hear about this place?" Eden stepped through the half-cocked gate, squinting at the halo of orange around the single streetlamp in the center of the cemetery—brilliant compared to the olive-black under the giant willows that hung recklessly over the entrance. The headstones glowed as if they were hot. Dangerously hot.

"Don't worry about that." Sammy smiled, that quiet, almost shy smile she'd fallen in love with in ninth grade, though she knew he was neither quiet nor shy. He cocked his head—he looked just like Kevin Hart when he did that—and she finally forced a grin, though the night felt like it was pressing against her back. Behind her, the dark was thicker still.

"Come on," he said.

Eden skirted a broken beer bottle and followed him past the rows of placards proclaiming everlasting love, each plot more overgrown and neglected than the last. Dead tulips lay on their side on top of one headstone, the petals flattened with rot. The night had fallen silent despite the charged bustle just a few streets over, the girls in the three-inch heels—"Hey, baby, looking for a date?"—the hushed desperation of the sleeping homeless, the night-shift workers pushing through the masses to get home with bags of takeout tucked under their arms, steadfastly pretending to be blind.

"You sure this is safe?" A chill crept up her spine despite the warm late-summer air. Here, even the wind seemed muted.

"Of course. Not like the killer is still here." Sammy laughed. "You ready?"

She raised her eyes. The mausoleum, stones of smoky gray that had probably once been white, stood in silent vigil, the door splintered along the side from long-ago vandals. Her breath hissed through her teeth—too loud. Loud enough to wake the dead. "So this is where…"

He smiled, that smile again, and edged his way through the shattered doorframe. "This is it," he called over his shoulder. "You look hard enough, and you can still see Meredith Lawrence's blood."

Meredith Lawrence was the most famous person to die here, the first victim of the notorious *Looking Glass* killer, but she was far from the only victim. Eden swallowed hard and ducked inside the building after Sammy, suddenly far more keen to step over the threshold than stand alone in the open air.

She blinked. Dark in here, damp, tinged with iron and mildew so thick she could feel it—heavy, almost meaty on her tongue. Something skittered in the back corner, a harsh scratch-rattle, too loud to be an insect, but she couldn't see beyond the orange-yellow rectangle from the streetlight outside the open doorway. A rat? She hated rats. *Please be a rat.*

Sammy turned to her in the dim and pulled something from his pocket…his cell. She squinted in the sudden glare of his phone's flashlight, directed at the enormous stone slab that ran along the back wall like an altar.

"See?" Sammy stepped closer to the altar stone, his voice high with an almost childlike excitement. "Right here!" He ran one slender finger—a piano player's finger—along the edge of the stone slab, the place where the *Looking Glass* killer had tied his victim. But blood? The slab, like the walls, was gray and rotten looking as a dead tooth—no bloody remnants of the words the killer had scrawled on the back wall, no poems. Nothing of interest that she could see.

"I heard they never found him. The *Looking Glass* killer." Sammy whirled on her, his eyes bright, hand still resting on the stone slab.

"I think they did," she said. Hadn't she read that?

Sammy shook his head and turned back to the wall. "That was a ruse. They want us to think they got him, so everyone feels safe, but…"

She rolled her eyes. She knew better than to argue with him about his obsession, and maybe he was right, anyway. Most of what she knew about the *Looking Glass* killer was probably more urban legend than anything else.

"Can we go now?" she asked, and though she tried to keep her voice even, it came out a little tight, a little strangled. This was the third crime scene or "haunted house" they'd been to in the last two months; their last excursion had taken them to an abandoned property no one had bothered to clean, the scene of a particularly nasty murder-suicide— blood on the walls, blood soaking the floors, and the flies…*god*.

He turned on her, cheeks hollow and ghoulish in the flashlight's harsh shadows. "Are you kidding? I've been looking forward to this for weeks!"

"I know, but…" The hairs on the back of her neck prickled in the warm breeze from the open door. And was that the rat again, scratching from the corner? "I just don't want to get hacked to pieces."

Sammy sighed and ran his hand along the back wall—the wall that had once been streaked with Meredith Lawrence's blood. Caressing it the same way he caressed her back or ran his fingers through her hair. "Not like the killer's here now, Eden, just his…essence."

"Killer essence? You're so weird," she said jokingly, but she shuddered anyway. And beneath the anxious vibration of her heart, her stomach turned—guilt. He was right. He had been waiting a long time.

Snap!

Not from the back corner like she'd thought, but Sammy didn't appear to notice, busy as he was examining the wall. She whirled on the broken door, listening hard—her breathing, Sammy's breathing, hissed through the air, her heart thrumming through the veins in her throat. Nothing more, no other sounds, but her rib cage had become a vise. "Seriously, let's go, okay?" She tried to keep her voice from shaking. "I'm tired, and we have, like, an hour to drive."

"Fiiiine." Sammy grunted and clicked off the flashlight, plunging the room into darkness. She blinked hard, trying desperately to force her eyes to adjust to the hazy orange film from the streetlamp that had lit the room earlier, but the dark seemed thicker now, more domineering—she could see nothing but the black.

"Sammy! Where are—"

A hand grabbed her waist and she shrieked.

Sammy laughed. "Just me, just me." He pulled her into his arms and pressed his lips to hers, and the damp mildew smell vanished as the scent of his soap filled her nostrils—spicy, almost flowery. She relaxed against him…but only a little. Why was it still so dark in here? But her eyes were slowly adjusting; already, she could see the outline of his form, feel the heat of his skin—warm. Safe.

"Come on," he said. "Come sit on the slab."

"On the…are you fucking kidding?"

"No one's here."

"I'm not worried about that." But she was, a little. That snap could have been a murderer coming to kill them like poor Meredith Lawrence. *No, that's the horror movies talking.* If there was one thing Sammy loved more than true crime research, it was movies about serial killers, the more gruesome the better. Perhaps she should mind that they spent so much time on his pursuits, but if she was really honest, there was something about the pounding in her temples even now, the jitter of nerves in her belly, that made their dates more interesting than pizza with some idiot jock. And certainly better than the clichéd dinner and a movie her parents thought they were enjoying. He was the most interesting boy she'd ever known.

"I guess I can take you home…" Sammy ran the tops of his fingers under the hem of her shirt, skirting along her backbone and sending little ripples of excitement through her nerve endings, melting the ice that had stiffened her spine since they'd arrived.

She stood on her tiptoes to whisper in his ear: "Maybe we should go back to the car."

He edged his fingers into the front waistband of her shorts and undid the button. She stepped back toward the stone. Maybe it was just an urban legend—maybe nothing had ever happened here at all, and, even if it had, it was so long ago. And the cemetery owners had surely cleaned it up, right? That's what they did with public property, after the police took all the gross stuff into evidence. And heck, she and Sammy'd had sex in the gooey mud beside the boathouse upstate, same spot in the dirt where three people had been shot to death. No way the police had cleaned that up completely.

Eden backed against the slab—thank god her eyes were working again—and hopped onto the stone. Orange light seeped through the broken door. She closed her eyes and leaned into Sammy, listening to the heavy thud of her heart and the soft whisper of his breath against her ear.

Snap!

She froze. "Sammy, did you—"

Sammy toppled backward—no, not toppled, *flew*, ripped from her grasp, the pads of her fingers burning, pain radiating from her twisted wrist. Her limbs felt disconnected from her brain, because someone else was there now, a man, a huge man, the subtle glow of the streetlamp hidden behind his bulk, and he had Sammy in the middle of the tiny room— had Sammy on his knees on the cold mausoleum floor, holding her boyfriend by the…face? Yes, hands on either side of his head. And the stranger was muttering in a low whispery growl, some other language, one she'd never heard before, but it was like in the old horror movies Sammy watched—was he summoning a demon? *Are we sacrifices?*

Oh god, all the horror movies were right, and Sammy was right, too, about the black guy dying first, because Sammy was the one on his knees. But the big-breasted blonde never lasted long either. Eden was next.

Her mouth went dry. Ribbons of panic sliced through her throat, cutting off her airway.

She wanted to cry out, to tell him not to hurt Sammy, to say that they'd do anything, anything at all if he'd just let them go, but her tongue was a weight, cold and dead against her bottom teeth.

The stranger was silent; no more strange words. Not even breathing hard. Maybe not breathing at all.

Then Sammy screamed once, kicked his legs; a quick jerk

of the intruder's hands—*crack!*—and Sammy's head twisted, too far, too far, his screams degenerating into thin wails, like a mewling kitten. Weak. And then Sammy wasn't moving at all.

The giant man straightened and stepped closer. *"'Ana last aleadui."* She strained her ears, trying to decipher the words. Was he mumbling? Or was it coming from someone else, someone she couldn't see?

"I—I...don't know what you want." Her voice echoed against the walls, her heart a frantic animal trapped beneath her ribs.

"'Ana last aleadui." It hit her ears like a growl of thunder—hushed, threatening, but somehow distant. The man stepped nearer still.

Eden skittered away on top of the slab until she felt the back edge—nowhere to go, just this little space between the slab and the wall where once poems had been scrawled in blood.

"'Ana last aleadui." This time the voice seemed to come from somewhere behind the man, hitting her ears oddly, harshly. Too low.

"Please don't kill me," she whispered. Sammy mewled. *Alive, he's alive!*

The stranger's breath hissed, too close. "You'll live for now," he said in a voice like silk, and she jumped at the loudness of it—not at all like the growly rumble she'd heard before. "You'll live for now, if you run." He moved away suddenly, his back against the side wall, deeper into the shadows, and the square of orange light returned, flooding in behind him, so bright now, revealing the concrete floor—*Sammy, he's not moving, and his neck,* fuck, *his neck.* The man raised one thick arm. Pointed to the door.

Eden clambered off the stone slab and pressed herself

against the wall opposite where he stood. Ten feet away. One step forward and—

She edged closer to the door, eyes on the stranger, stepped over—*oh fuck, oh fuck*—Sammy's body and she thought she heard him wheeze her name, but the crazy man was there and he was closer—he was almost touching her.

"Run," the man whispered.

She did. She left Sammy there, the only boy she'd ever loved, jumped over his legs like he was a bundle of old clothes, and burst through the splintered mausoleum door into the muggy night air.

The streetlamps glittered sickly orange against the dew-soaked grass like bloody tears.

2

_____

Even at six in the morning, Rita's diner was alive with the sounds of clanking silverware, the laughter of strangers, and fluorescents bright enough to sober the drunks in the back booth. Even the red vinyl gleamed.

New place. Same old atmosphere. Except...

Edward Petrosky frowned. Across from him, Linda sipped her coffee, her bow lips the same as they'd always been, save for the laugh lines that had crept in around the edges. The crow's feet at the corners of her hazel eyes were new, too, like little reminders of all the times she'd smiled. It suited her—like the fine cracks in the ceiling above your bed that you recognize, unequivocally, as home. Or maybe Linda just *felt* like home. Over the past year since he'd caught their daughter's killer, Petrosky and his ex-wife had cautiously chatted on the phone a few times...though he'd never been a phone person. He still wasn't entirely sure why Linda wanted to eat with him this morning, even if it was just breakfast before work. Things would never go back to how they used to be before they'd lost Julie—before the divorce.

What are you doing, Petrosky?

He speared a patty of turkey sausage, wishing it was pork. Turkey was supposed to be part of his heart-healthy regimen, but this left a little circle of grease on the plate—he'd already dripped some on his jeans.

"Is your food okay?" Linda asked.

"Yeah." *I should have ordered bacon.* He smiled awkwardly and shoved the bite in his mouth just as his cell vibrated in his front pocket, followed by someone rapping about... *What the hell is an ass master? Goddammit, Jackson.* What was it with his partners and his fucking cell phone? He should get rid of the damn thing.

Linda raised an eyebrow and nibbled her toast as he snapped the cell to his ear.

"Wake up, you old bastard." Regina Jackson, his partner, had a voice that could rattle the surliest perp, but she saved the singsong teasing for him because she knew it grated on him more than just barking out instructions.

"What the fuck did you do to my cell?" he said around the sausage—just as greasy as bacon, for sure. He liked it better for that.

She laughed. "Ah, 'Ass Master'...that'll wake you up in the morning. You dressed yet?"

He swallowed, glancing at the navy jacket on the bench seat next to him, the holster with his service weapon hidden beneath it. "I am. Eating breakfast at a lovely little diner, in fact."

"Sure you are."

He cleared his throat and frowned at his water. Some asshole had put a lemon in it. The silence stretched.

Jackson sighed. "Get your ass over to Whispering Willows."

The cemetery? "What've we got?"

Linda watched him and said nothing, but he knew that expression; he'd seen it enough times during the decades they'd been married: *Off on another police call?* This really was just like old times.

"Couple of college students thought they'd tempt the horror movie trope and go exploring."

"Fuckers think they're invincible." He pulled the napkin off his lap, careful not to get grease on his blue button-down. "Stupid white kids."

Linda appraised him with her hazel eyes and brushed a stray hair from her forehead—brown with white streaks, but not salt-and-shit like his; more like veins of precious metal running through stone. He liked that on her too.

"Victim's black this time, but I think you're right on the invincibility thing." Jackson's voice had grown solemn. "And this time, the kids were wrong."

WHISPERING WILLOWS WAS as he remembered it. Busted iron gate that no one had ever bothered fixing, grave sites littered with broken bottles, cracked syringes, and the occasional bouquet of dead flowers. The willow trees for which the cemetery was named bordered the entrance and ran along the back side, branches so long they brushed the ground. A good spot for a killer to hide if he knew a bunch of kids were headed here.

Jackson stood in the center of the cemetery in front of the mausoleum flanked by two other officers, one thick-necked blond-haired beat cop with acne scars from chin to hairline, and a thinner, sinewy brown-skinned man with enormous eyes that popped like a bullfrog when he saw Petrosky approaching. Jackson glanced his way, sun shining off her buzzed black hair. The sharp lines of her khaki suit jacket cut the background behind her.

"What've we got?" Petrosky said, in a voice just short of

snapping. Jackson said he snapped too much. Not that he cared what she thought, and she sure as hell deserved it after that stunt with his phone, but he looked away when she raised an eyebrow at him and glowered at the beat cops instead.

The blond cop straightened to attention like he was preparing for an army march. "Homicide."

"No shit," Petrosky said. "Got anything else for me, Sherlock?"

The kid's jaw dropped.

Tough one, eh? Petrosky locked his eyes on the frog-eyed cop. "I hear you got one dead college boy."

Bug-eyes nodded. "Yeah. And a female witness with a twisted wrist. We were out on patrol—"

"You were patrolling here?" They made occasional runs back this way, but most of the disturbances happened at least three blocks west. Where the non-embalmed people were.

"Yeah, it was a fluke, I guess," Bug-eyes hurried on. "First time out here all week. We heard her screaming from in front of the gate. Officer Babcock stayed with her while I ran back here to the building, but the kid was already dead."

Petrosky frowned. "Why call sex crimes?" He and Jackson didn't usually get called in on routine homicides.

The man blinked his giant eyelids. "Well, I guess they were going at it when the killer walked in. And...dunno. Sounded like the killer...like he might have a fetish or something."

A fetish for...dead folks? He sniffed, glared once more at Blondie, and turned to the building.

Jackson shook her head as they ducked into the mausoleum. The walls were darker than he remembered— dirtier—though the stink of blood had not changed from the day he'd walked in on the *Looking Glass* case. He could almost see the poem scrawled in uniform, dripping crimson letters on the back wall.

"Someone spit in your eggs, or what?" Her voice was tight.

"The dead kid on the floor isn't enough to irritate you?" Petrosky bent, crouching over the gray tips of his sneakers, frowning at the thick musky stink that intensified the lower he got to the floor. No mistaking that odor—like an open sewer pipe.

The kid was on his belly, head twisted around unnaturally far, looking over the back of his own shoulder blade. The bones in his cervical spine bulged beneath the thin skin of his neck, his brown eyes wide like he was shocked anything terrible could happen in a run-down cemetery in the middle of the night. Arms splayed, but seemingly unbroken. Damp had soaked through the back of his pants—dark. He'd shit himself. What a way to go.

"Samuel Amos, eighteen," Jackson said, voice tight. "Attacked from behind, neck broken. He was still moaning when the girlfriend ran off for help—one Eden Johansson. Not sure if the killer incapacitated him then waited for the girl to leave before wrenching his head around farther or what. We'll have to get the specifics from the ME."

Petrosky shifted closer to the boy's shoes; brown loafers of soft, shiny leather. Expensive. The kid's hands—his nails —were clean, too clean for a college kid exploring a ceme-tery in the middle of the night, but the pads of his fingers were black from touching the walls, or from falling. Minimal scuff marks on the floor. He hadn't had time to fight back.

He eased backward. The kid's eyes followed him.

"This is some *Exorcist*-level bullshit right here," Petrosky muttered, but gooseflesh crawled up his arms. He could almost feel his old surfer-boy partner behind him, snapping pictures. *Suck it up, California, this is the job.* You never knew when the people you loved were going to leave you.

Or worse.

Jackson didn't respond, not even to tell him he was a jack-bag or whatever insult she might dream up. He met the boy's glassy dead eyes—*sorry about your luck, kid*—then pushed himself to standing. "Let's go talk to the girl."

"Woman," Jackson said, heading for the door. She gestured to the grove of willows that lined the back of the cemetery—to the ambulance barely visible beyond the thin striations of willow fronds.

"Fine. But I'm sure I've got at least forty years on her."

Jackson snorted, the noise mingling with the sound of their feet thumping against last year's dried leaves and the occasional shushing of his pant legs on the tall grass as he skirted the headstones. The sun hitting his face was jarring. Too bright for the occasion.

"You've got at least forty years on damn near everyone," she said, voice still tighter than usual.

He glanced in her direction. She kept her eyes on the path ahead, but he could see the purplish tint beneath her lower lids. "I don't have forty years on you," he said.

"I'm only twenty-nine."

"You've been twenty-nine since I've known you."

They stepped out into the road; well, more like a dirt path, barely wide enough for the ambulance—an older model, faded and dinged. Eden Johansson sat with her legs dangling off the back of the cot, eyes staring blankly into the distance, but she blinked when Petrosky and Jackson emerged from behind the tree branches. The dreadlocked EMT standing at the side of the ambulance straightened, too, tossing his cigarette away—probably annoyed that he had to wait for the cops with a girl who wasn't really hurt, but he was still a fucking hypocrite. Petrosky's mouth watered anyway. Jackson elbowed him and glowered—*nope, you quit*—and he refocused on the girl sniffling on the ambulance cot. The *woman*.

"Can I go home?" Eden Johansson said in that hushed little-kid voice that people got when they were scared. Julie had used it when she'd done something wrong. Petrosky's heart ached. Less ache than in years past, but still. "I just want to go home," Eden said again.

Petrosky scanned the street—no sign that anyone was observing them, not that he'd expected the killer to stick around. Beyond the vehicle, the road split, one fork snaking back toward the cemetery and the trees, the other side easing into a flat open area, once a pavilion for mourning families, now grown over with Kentucky bluegrass and pigweed.

The EMT approached, smelling gloriously like mentholated tobacco. "She isn't physically hurt, but I figured you'd want to take her to the precinct."

"She's not a prisoner," Petrosky said, mentally adding "assclown" even though he absolutely did need to talk to her, and the guy had done nothing wrong except tease him with the now-dissipating cigarette smoke.

Eden eyed Petrosky warily, but she didn't flinch as he climbed into the back of the ambulance. He stifled a groan. His knees ached, and the flesh on the backside of his legs burned; three skin grafts after a bust this past year and the nerves were still angry. *Worth it.* He'd pulled a teenage girl out of that fire. Layla still called him sometimes to update him on her life—school, friends—and it always made him smile.

"Tell us what happened," Jackson said, climbing up like a fucking gymnast to sit across from him.

She tugged at a tendril of blonde hair with shaky fingers. "I told the other guys already."

"Humor us," Petrosky said. "Please."

She did, in halting sentences. Going to the mausoleum to see an old crime scene. Getting a little freaky. Then…the hulking killer, the twist of Sammy's neck, her stepping over her boyfriend's body and running for her life. The killer had peeked out after her, she said, maybe to determine which direction she was going. Thank goodness he'd decided not to chase her. From the grass stains on her bare knees, she'd spent just as much time stumbling as she had flying through the weedy grass. Though, from both her account and that of the responding officers, the police were on the scene within minutes. So how the hell had this fucker gotten away?

"How tall was he?" Petrosky asked now.

"Huge. Like a monster."

"Did he have to stoop to get into the mausoleum?" The doorway wasn't all that tall—six feet tops, just over Petrosky's own head.

"I…no, I don't think so. He was standing upright."

Less than six feet. But taller than Eden Johansson, who was no more than five-three.

"But he *was* huge," she insisted.

"Stocky? Muscular? Or just chubby?"

"Definitely muscular." Eden chewed her lip, eyes on the doorway. "Can I have a smoke?"

Petrosky inhaled—the driver was at it again. "That shit'll kill you." He turned to the door. "Hey, Cheech! You mind?"

From around the side of the vehicle came unintelligible muttering, then silence. But the air cleared.

Petrosky met Eden's eyes once more. "Did he say anything?"

"He was mumbling," she said. "Sounded like gibberish, just kinda…blabbering. I remember thinking it was like…another language. The one they use in old movies."

Old movies? Petrosky cocked his head.

"You know, like *The Exorcist*." Her eyes filled. "Sammy loved that movie."

The Exorcist—that had been Petrosky's first thought when he saw the kid's head turned halfway around. Had this been some kind of...ceremony? That didn't seem right. No candles, no bloody writing, no green vomit or praying or priests...that they knew of. The killer had snapped the boy's neck in seconds. And it didn't appear that he'd touched the body afterward, though they'd have a better read on that once the forensics came back.

"*The Exorcist*...you think he was speaking Latin?"

"I think so? I'm not sure. Really, he was just mumbling nonsense."

Petrosky nodded, waiting for Jackson to cut in like she usually did. Crickets chirped from the tall grass outside. He glanced across the way at his partner—scribbling in a notepad, her face a mask, dull and unreadable. She'd been a little distracted lately, or at least quieter than usual, but he knew better than to pry into other people's shit. Might even be this case. She'd lost a teenage son five years back, gunned down in the street by an off-duty federal agent. Just a few years younger than their vic.

Jackson wrote on, face blank. Like a fucking professional.

"Do you remember what he said? When he was mumbling?" Petrosky drew his eyes back to Eden as she shrugged.

"No, I don't speak that language. It was so weird, almost like the voice was coming from somewhere else. Like it wasn't even him talking."

Huh. "Did you see anyone else while you were walking through the cemetery? Maybe when you were running away?"

She shook her head. "Just heard that other...voice. But it was dark, I guess, so I couldn't really tell if his lips were moving. Maybe he just sounded different when he was saying that other stuff."

The guy could have been hallucinating—Petrosky had seen more than a few people arguing with themselves. Everyone battled their demons, but some folks did it out loud.

"And then at the end…" Her eyes clouded. "He told me to run. In English. And he said I was going to live, but only for now."

Only for now. Maybe this was planned. The killer could be coming back for her. But why would he let her go talk to the police and then murder her later? The thrill of the chase? Thin, but Petrosky had seen weirder in his years on the force —and more sadistic. But in most of those cases, the victims had been mixed up in something they shouldn't have.

He kept his eyes on her as he asked: "Did anyone know you were coming out here?"

"I don't think so. But I guess Sammy probably put it online." Fresh tears welled in her eyes.

Petrosky swallowed the sigh that had crept into his throat. Kids and their fucking social media. Not that bad people doing bad shit was the fault of the victim, but Jesus Christ, victims didn't need to make themselves *so easy* to find. Outside, the world beyond the ambulance breathed, the hushed rustle of the leaves like muted whispers from the dead. Was the killer out there somewhere, hiding, watching? Surely he hadn't anticipated the police presence this morning —maybe he'd been about to chase her when the officers had squealed up. And if the killer's plans had been foiled, he might come after Eden Johansson again.

"I'm going to have someone drive you to the precinct to sit with a sketch artist," Petrosky said. "Then they'll take you home, stay with you to make sure you're safe while we look for the man who did this. You comfortable with that?"

Eden bit her lip but nodded.

"Good." He turned to Jackson, who was frowning, maybe skeptical that Eden needed a detail, but he'd do it himself if no one else would. "Go get those two goofy fuckers from the cemetery, would you?"

Eden snorted, almost a chuckle, her eyes still rimmed with red. But the snorting…that seemed promising.

"Can you be more specific about which goofy fuckers you want?" Jackson said as they climbed from the ambulance.

He narrowed his eyes.

She didn't bother looking his way. "You ain't gonna stare me down, you cantankerous bastard. I don't care how many years you have on me."

There she is. Maybe she'd just stayed up too late watching reruns of that dragon show. "Fine, I'll get them myself." He glowered at her and headed back through the willows before she could see him smirk.

3

"WE DON'T KNOW for sure who the killer was after," Petrosky said, keeping his voice low, mellow, though he wanted to get the hell out of there—to do something useful. Sitting in the chief's office was like being stuck with the principal, even if Chief Carroll wasn't berating him about his shit grades. Petrosky didn't care about bureaucracy or budgets; he wanted a detail on Eden Johansson until he was sure she was no longer in danger. "Our suspect could have been after the girl the whole time. Maybe stalking turned to killing when he saw her with someone else, or he'd planned to chase her before the cops rolled up." *He said I was going to live, but only for now.*

"Wait...stalking? You think this is jealousy?" Chief Carroll raised an incredulous eyebrow, and he suddenly wished Jackson occupied the empty seat beside him, even if she didn't seem to agree with him any more than the chief.

"Jealousy is a lame reason, but it's common." He shrugged. "He could have stalked her, intending to rape her, and the boyfriend got in the way, or maybe he's a voyeur, jacking it in the shadows until the jealousy got too intense." He blinked at

Carroll's narrowed eyes, the tight corners of her mouth, then finished, "Or he might be a sadist, could just enjoy watching their fear as they flee past their dead boyfriends."

"Not '*their* dead boyfriends.' It was one woman, Petrosky. And one victim. Singular."

But there might be more if they didn't stop the killer up front. Maybe there had been other victims already.

"I think Eden Johansson is in danger," he said. "An organized killer watched them, stalked them, and waited until they were too engaged to notice him sneaking up in the shadows. There's no reason he couldn't be watching her now."

Carroll crossed her arms. "Sounds like we don't even need the shrink this time."

Of course they needed the shrink. The killer had been mumbling gibberish; it was highly probable this wasn't a stalker situation at all, that the girl was in no danger, that their killer was a raving lunatic blathering about nothing— that this was a crime of opportunity. But if he told Carroll that, she'd pull the detail. Then it was all on them if Eden died like her boyfriend.

"Whatever, the shrink can't hurt." He ran a hand down his lower face, like he was trying to help gravity bring his soft jowls to the floor. "And we don't know much yet, that's true," he conceded. "Samuel Amos's parents came down to make the identification, but they refused to answer more questions until tomorrow morning. And I've already got Eden sitting with the sketch artist. We'll see what they come up with."

Carroll sat straighter in her seat. "Did you just say you don't know much?"

"I'm saying we have more ground to cover."

"What I'm hearing is that you think I'm right."

"No, I didn't say—"

"Yes, yes you did." Her brown eyes glittered as she leaned

back in the chair and sighed. "Get the fuck out of here, Petrosky. Find this asshole so we can pull Babcock and Khoury off detail."

"Who?"

"The goofy fuckers from the cemetery," Jackson said from the doorway. She leaned against the jamb, arms crossed.

"Ah, yes," Petrosky said. "Ebony and Ivory."

Jackson raised an eyebrow. "I thought *we* were Ebony and Ivory."

"Fine. Bug-eyes and Captain Shock." That blond kid had looked surprised as hell—had Amos's body been his first corpse?

Jackson shook her head. Carroll rolled her eyes. Petrosky headed for the door with a backward wave at his boss.

WHILE THE ROAD that fronted the cemetery was usually abandoned, the blocks surrounding Whispering Willows were littered with sleeping bags and tents and makeshift refrigerator-box homes speckled with last week's dirt like the well-loved playhouses of blanket-clad children. In the winter, the downtown shelters were filled to bursting—fewer out on the road—but during the summer months, the sidewalks turned into a hippie village ripe with body odor and broiling urine. He'd never been a patchouli fan, but damn, this place needed it.

The sketch Eden had given them—generic white guy, straight nose, wide-set eyes, high blond eyebrows, thick neck, no tattoos—went nowhere quick. Not a shock; he'd surely be in hiding the morning after he killed a man. Two women sharing a bottled water squinted extra long at the image and shook their heads a little too hard, but even the promise of a fifty didn't get them to cough up a name, or the place they'd last seen him. Maybe they didn't know—their suspect could have simply wandered by once or twice, or maybe the sketch just happened to look like a million other guys. The CrossFit era was ushering in more and more men with necks the size of their heads; men who were too bulky to use an airline bathroom.

The shelters led to more of the same, and the local hospitals were no better. With the muttering, they couldn't discount drug-induced rage or hallucinations, and the superhuman strength common to some stimulant drugs might make it easier to break a neck with bare hands. But the hospital staff stared at Petrosky like he'd asked them for a dick pic when he inquired about recent discharges and showed them the sketch. They left empty handed. This guy probably wasn't a recent discharge anyway—the shrinks wouldn't have let him go if he was still actively hallucinating, and the last place a killer would voluntarily go was the hospital. And whether their suspect was hearing things or not, talking to himself or not, he was functioning well enough to sneak up on a couple and twist a motherfucker's head halfway off then hide from the responding officers. Not that the perp wasn't batshit crazy—self-preservation could trump mental illness—but he wasn't so far gone as to be unaware of the world and his place in it. By the time they headed for lunch—an Indian place Jackson insisted was "better than whatever unseasoned pile of blandness you were hoping for"—Petrosky was nursing a throbbing headache and craving a cigarette. After an entire morning scouring the streets around the cemetery, they were no closer to finding their killer; even if there might have been witnesses, no one in that neighborhood wanted to talk to the cops. He watched the lantern above the table, the little pinpricks of light that cast dizzy spots on the walls as the lantern twirled in the gentle breeze from the air conditioning. "They couldn't afford real lights?" he muttered after they'd ordered.

"Your night vision going already?"

"I just think a place ought to have proper lighting."

She snapped the napkin into her lap, lips tight. "Like all dive bars you're used to?"

Petrosky frowned. He'd been clean since he'd arrested his daughter's killer. Over a year now.

Jackson's eyes widened. "Sorry, below the belt. I've just been a little...distracted and—"

He looked back up at the ceiling, the lights spinning like the bedroom after a binge. He might have fewer skeletons to silence these days, but they still came out and poked him sometimes. "Don't worry about it."

"No really, I didn't mean—"

"I said, let it go. No hard feelings." It wasn't like she was wrong, even if it stung. He kept his eyes on the whirling light. Maybe he should ask what was eating her. But she obviously didn't want to talk about it, and he hated when people did that shit to him, butting into his personal life, trying to fix it. Even if sometimes...he needed it.

He dropped his gaze to his partner, watching her chew the inside of her cheek, watching her glare out the window. "Jackson?"

She looked over, but not at him—the waitress was back. He hadn't even noticed her approaching. Morrison would have said the interruption was the universe telling him to pause and think it through. He didn't believe it, but... He closed his mouth.

Jackson's cell rang as the waitress was setting down the curried chicken Jackson had ordered for them, the dish fragrant with spice and salt, and weirdly...orange colored. Man, he'd kill for a burger. She picked up her fork, listening to the cell, and mouthed "Scott."

Evan Scott had moved down to Ash Park from Vermont with Petrosky's encouragement—he'd been instrumental in helping Petrosky find Julie's killer. Scott had a master's in forensic science and a bunch of other fancy-ass degrees and was a whiz at technology even if that wasn't technically in his job description. Kid was a fucking genius. Hopefully, he could find what they were missing.

Jackson "Mm-hmm-ed" her way through a few more minutes, mouth twisting harder with each second, then finally re-pocketed the cell. "Bad news," she said, stabbing a piece of chicken. "Looks like we've got a repeat offender. Scott's still working on getting the other case files together —one seems to be missing half the paperwork, a filing error or something. But what we have is enough to think there are at least two other related cases: Two other couples getting freaky, killer sneaks up behind the man and snaps his neck."

I knew it. Take that, Carroll. And it took a ton of force to snap someone's neck—it wasn't like in the movies. Their killer had to be built like a semi-truck.

"One of the murders took place on the street out behind the cemetery," Jackson continued, eyeballing the rice. "Left the guy screaming his guts out, but he was dead before any passersby heard him—the woman with him, his wife, didn't even call it in. The other murder was a block or two past Whispering Willows, up one of the alleys. Both reports say that the killer was talking to himself." She reached for her water. "But there's a catch. Guy's been out of commission for the last five years."

"That we know of." Petrosky sampled the chicken and it scorched the inside of his mouth—spicy. He choked out: "There could be other crimes that weren't reported, or victims that he hid some—"

"We would have found the bodies. This guy didn't even

try to hide Samuel Amos, and he let Eden Johansson run right to the cops. He's not worried about getting caught."

"We don't know if he *let* her run to the cops. He might have intended to chase her, but wasn't expecting the police to drive by." Petrosky blinked water from his eyes. Food this spicy was just stupid, but...his nose was clear. And it was savory, salty, definitely better than the hippie mushroom coffee his old partner'd tricked him into. "Did he chase the others? Tell the other women to run?" His fork paused over the chicken; he scooped rice into his mouth instead, hoping it would cool the burn on his tongue.

"Not sure yet," she said. "We'll check."

Yeah, they would. "Scott's probably halfway through the old case files already. Kid's thorough."

"High praise coming from you," she said, forking a bite of veggies. *With* the rice. "Scott promised he'd have copies of the full case files in the next few days," Jackson said. "So far, the witnesses are a no go anyway. The wife of the man killed behind the cemetery died in an auto wreck—she was drunk, ran into a tree—and the investigation showed no connection to the murder. The witness to the other killing, the one in the alley, vanished into thin air right after it happened; they found out her ID was fake after they interviewed her."

He followed her lead and dipped his chicken-rice combo into—*is this yogurt?*—and chewed, thinking. That area...the witness from the alley was most likely a working girl, not a girlfriend. Eden Johansson and Samuel Amos were not the usual expected visitors. And if a john died in the throes of passion, the working girls were the ones who looked suspicious, the ones who got arrested; they wouldn't call the cops if they could help it. "Well, if anyone can track our rogue witness down, it's Scott." He sniffed. The chicken—his nose ran, his eyes watered, but the yogurt helped.

Jackson nodded agreement as he stuffed another bite into

his maw. "In the meantime, we can look into that five-year hiatus," he said around the rice. If the killer had been locked up somewhere, their job just got a hell of a lot easier, but any lapse could prove useful. Coming out of murder retirement was usually triggered by something. A trauma? Loss? *Maybe they just got tired of fighting the urge to be a fucking psycho.* He set his fork aside. "You want to take the prisons, see who was locked up after the last attack and just got released? I'll go sweet-talk the mental hospitals out of a list of their recent discharges."

Jackson shook her head and dabbed her nose. "Those long-term facilities are private and will tell you to fuck all the way off."

"What can I say?" Petrosky smiled. "I like a challenge."

4

THE BULLPEN BUZZED with the electric energy of six other cops running on caffeine and adrenaline, and the manic rustle of paperwork. Located on the second floor of the precinct, their workspace was really nothing more than an L-shaped room split by a support pillar and populated by rows of rectangular desks topped with ancient PCs and stacks of case files that would never be completed if they had a million years; for every case closed, there were ten more criminals in the wings.

Petrosky leaned back in his chair and sipped sludge from a paper cup, wishing he had a fucking donut. While he'd warmed up to the Indian food, it was not better than a Rita's chicken sandwich as Jackson had promised, and it definitely wasn't better than the ice cream she'd refused to stop for on the way back to the precinct. And they'd needed dessert after dealing with the hospitals.

The few inpatient facilities had yielded nothing of interest. Though the shrinks had agreed to examine the police sketch, no one confirmed that their suspect had been a patient, and one said the sketch matched any of a dozen men they'd discharged in the last year, though none of those had been admitted for hallucinations. Back at the station, another hour gave them fifteen possibilities from the prison list; out of those, only one even came close to Eden Johansson's description. And he'd been picked up in Indiana on a drug charge Saturday night. He was sitting in the precinct there at the time Samuel Amos was killed.

Jackson tossed a manila folder onto his desk—the possibles from the halfway houses and group homes in the area. "A couple of maybes," she said. "Almost all have a history of substance abuse, and Eden said he was muttering gibberish... maybe he can function, but isn't all the way there, you know?"

He nodded and took the folder. People with mental illness tended to be treated like criminals. Some self-medicated because of the bullshit prescription drug prices, and some panhandled because they were too ill to hold down jobs or afford their meds, but most saw the inside of a cell before the inside of a hospital, and they had nowhere to go upon release except a halfway house or a group home. And not all group homes were tight with their records; he'd once had a case where their perp used an alias and paid cash to avoid detection.

Petrosky flipped to the picture of the guy Jackson had put on top, his partner's way of saying "this is my number-one suspect." The license photo was ten years expired, but the guy looked good for it. Right build. He'd vanished after the last killing five years ago, too, and he had... Petrosky looked up. "Schizoaffective disorder?" What the fuck does that mean?"

"Hell if I know; that's a question for the shrink." Jackson picked up his half-full coffee cup, sniffed it, and winced. "But he left the halfway house last night just before lights out—before the killings—and didn't return until this morning.

Owner has no idea where he went. And with his five years away...he might have a few bodies in another part of the country."

Petrosky held up the photo and met the man's blue eyes—angry looking with pupils sharp as daggers. As you'd expect from a man who'd snapped a teen's neck just for being in the cemetery. "What brought him back to town now?"

"Death in the family earlier this year. His sister, I think. Managed to get a bus ticket here for the funeral and then..." She shrugged.

Petrosky tucked the photo away. "Losing a family member might trigger a little madness."

Jackson smiled, but her eyes were dull. Tired? Or...shit he shouldn't have mentioned losing family—Jackson had lost as much as he had. "The halfway house is only three blocks up from the cemetery," she said. "And the head resident says he's a mumbler."

Petrosky stood. "Let's go see what he's mumbling about."

CLAYTON BARNES WAS a hulking beast of a man with golden stubble and pale eyes, the bags beneath his lower lids deeply maroon and swollen. Stocky, with a neck like a wine barrel, and six-four easy, but it was possible he'd crouched a bit to get into the mausoleum—easy to misinterpret movements in the dark.

Petrosky cleared his throat. "How are you today, Mr. Barnes?"

The man raised an eyebrow. The homeowner had insisted Barnes had been no trouble until now—went to therapy, maintained his personal hygiene, followed the rules—but the blank stare in this guy's eyes sure didn't scream "model resident." Smoke leaked from his wide nostrils, a cigarette dangling from his thick lower lip. Not even dangling; stuck to his flesh with saliva. Still burning.

Petrosky watched the butt of the cig, waiting for it to drop to Barnes's bare knee and light his leg hair on fire, and more than that, wishing he could bum one. But he'd promised Shannon, his deceased partner's wife—promised for her daughter, who called him "Papa Ed." Shannon liked to remind him that he had things to look forward to, and that if he got cancer, she'd slap him silly. That seemed fair.

Jackson shifted in her chair, the folder with the artist's sketch of their perp in her lap. Barnes's eyes were too close together to match the sketch exactly, but Eden had only gotten a quick backwards glance as she'd fled, and even in good light, witness accounts were rarely perfect.

Barnes scratched one fleshy ear then ran his fingernails up through his buzzed platinum hair, the stubble grating against his nails with an irritable hiss. He dropped his gaze to his knees as if he, too, were waiting for the cigarette ashes to light his leg aflame.

The healed wounds on the backs of Petrosky's legs ached. He let his eyes rest on the man before him. "Mr. Barnes, can you tell us where you were early this morning?"

"Sleepin'." He scratched at his neck, closed his eyes a beat longer than a blink, and muttered something Petrosky couldn't hear.

"That's strange, Mr. Barnes, because the owner of this home says you were nowhere to be found between the hours of nine last night and seven-thirty this morning."

Barnes's lips wrinkled as he dragged on the smoke, then relaxed again as it dangled once more from his mouth. "I came back for breakfast." Inhale, puff, release, dangle. The ashes finally fell onto his knee, and promptly went out—anticlimactic. Barnes didn't flinch. "Pancake day."

"I'm not worried about your food, Barnes, I'm worried about where you were."

Jackson was staring beyond the man, at the paneling. Maybe she'd be taking notes if the guy was giving them any-fucking-thing at all.

"Ain't your concern."

"I think it is." Petrosky leaned so close he could smell the man's sweat, musty and far too sweet—putrid. "If I didn't know better, I'd say you were doing something illegal."

"Say what you want." Barnes coughed, didn't even raise his hands to cover his lips, then blew a lungful of smoke in Petrosky's face.

Petrosky wiped spittle from his cheek, but his mouth watered. Why did all the most delicious things try to kill you? "How about this: did you learn how to twist a man's head off in the army?"

"Say what?" Barnes raised his head to meet Petrosky's gaze with another heavy blink.

"There was a murder in the cemetery last night. That's what I'm worried about, Barnes. I don't care if you were off getting stoned, if you were paying someone to work your knob, if you were—"

"They care. The home."

"They care that you left, Barnes. You think you'll still be allowed here tomorrow?"

His gaze dropped back to his knee. His shoulders slumped. "I went for a walk. Got lost. Can't kick me out for that."

"Can they kick you out if I arrest you?" But Petrosky already knew the answer; most of the homes required that residents remain abstinent from drugs and free from run-ins with the law.

"I didn't do nothing," Barnes muttered to his toes, then raised his head and scratched at his ear. Again. "You can't—"

"That sheen of sweat on your upper lip, it's not just from the heat," Petrosky said, lowering his voice. "You can't even hold onto that cig right. And all that itching you're doing...I can't imagine you got crabs or lice without the home noticing." He pulled out his cuffs and rose. "Oxy? Am I close?"

"I'm in pain, man." But Barnes sat straighter and glanced behind him, probably looking for the group homeowner, his knee knocking the side table and rocking the ashtray he wasn't bothering to use. "I'll tell you, okay? I don't want trouble." He put his hands up in a "whoa boy" gesture. Ashes fell from his cigarette onto his thigh. This time, Barnes winced and brushed them away.

Petrosky eased himself back down into his chair. "So where'd you go?"

Barnes sniffed. "I was walking, like I said. I...I have a guy, over on Shane Road." Panic brightened his vision as he lit on the cuffs, still clenched in Petrosky's fist. "I've got pain, okay? Shrapnel still stuck in my ass."

For just a moment, Petrosky felt the dry sand in his nostrils, the warm heat of the desert sun on his skin—then it vanished. "I understand, Barnes. I did my time in the military too." It was a fucking miracle anyone still volunteered; Barnes had served, and he couldn't even get treatment for service-related injuries.

"Listen, I'm not worried about the drugs," Petrosky said. "What the pharmaceutical companies do, fucking everyone over, that's the real crime."

Jackson shook her head, but Barnes finally met Petrosky's eyes and nodded, one corner of his mouth turning up; the corner with the cigarette. The butt wiggled. "Yeah, man. You're right on that." He shifted, straightening up tall, even bigger through the shoulders than Petrosky had initially thought; shit, Barnes might have needed to squeeze into that mausoleum sideways, and even Petrosky's fat ass could walk through—sixty pounds lighter than he'd been a year ago, but he still had enough chunk to worry his doctor...when he bothered to go.

"So you headed to Shane's..."

"Yeah, picked up my...stuff. Walked back up the block, to the alley back behind that Chinese place. No one asks questions there."

Petrosky knew exactly where he meant: four blocks from Whispering Willows, long, dark, full of dumpsters like most of the alleys out that way, and lots of deep back doorways. He'd broken up more hooker-john "dates" out there than he cared to remember—and cleaned up three bodies.

"Doesn't take all night to score a few pills," Petrosky said. *Or to ride out your high.*

"I...snorted it." Barnes bit his fleshy lower lip, narrowly missing the cig. "Then I fell asleep for a bit; only time I get real sleep, only thing that makes that pain stop. Woke up and wandered a little, finished the rest, passed out again."

Petrosky watched him take the cig from his mouth and hold it between his index and thumb. For Barnes to be lucid now, he was probably stoned—or sleeping—at the time Samuel Amos was killed. And Oxy was a downer. It wasn't impossible for someone on Oxy to claim a victim or two, but their killer...he'd twisted someone's head half off for fuck's sake.

But Whispering Willows was between this home and the alley where Barnes claimed to have slept—just because he was unlikely to have committed the crime didn't mean he hadn't seen something useful. "Did you walk past the cemetery at all?"

The man's eyes jittered in their fleshy sockets. His hands shook against his knees. Cigarette ash fell to the floor. Nervous as hell, and not just about the drugs.

What do you know? It was a hell of a coincidence for their prime suspect to have come across the real killer, but these little forgotten sections of the city were smaller than anyone on the outside understood; only so many places to go, only so far you could travel. "What'd you see out there, Barnes?"

Barnes shook his head, muttered something unintelligible, then: "I didn't see anything in the cemetery. But there was a guy…came running out from where all those trees are. Back behind it."

The willows. Where the ambulance had been parked—the only direction the killer could have run since the police had come in from the front. Petrosky's heart ratcheted into overdrive, throbbing in his temples. "What'd he look like?"

"Little fellow. Shorter than me."

"That ain't saying much, guy." But while the killer might be shorter than Barnes, was there any way he'd describe the man from the sketch as a "little fellow"?

"Yeah, you right about that." Barnes smiled, a tentative smile, almost suspicious, but better than a scowl.

"What else do you remember about him?" Jackson cut in, tapping her pen against her notepad.

Barnes glanced at her, then back to Petrosky. "He was… darker-skinned. Arab maybe. And he had a little dog in his arms, like a…hot-dog dog." He raised an eyebrow. "You think it was a terrorist thing?"

Petrosky shrugged. "Attacking a college kid in an abandoned cemetery isn't really the terrorist MO. But maybe they're starting to recruit Dachshunds. Time will tell how efficient that is."

Barnes's smile fell. He sniffed, then crushed his cigarette into the ashtray. "Well, either way, he didn't look right. Went tearing out from behind those trees like he stole something. And I didn't want any part of it." He scratched behind his ear again, and this time when he pulled his fingers back there was blood under his nails.

Petrosky leaned back in his seat. This darker-skinned man definitely wasn't who Eden had seen kill her boyfriend, but maybe he was a witness. "You talk to him?"

Barnes shook his head.

"Get a good look at his face?"

"Black hair. Brown skin. No beard…I don't think. That's about it. Far enough away that I couldn't see his face real good." He pursed his lips, muttered something, and sucked a wad of snot into his throat.

Hopefully they could track this dog-walker down—hopefully Barnes was telling the truth—but something was still eating at Petrosky. It was awfully coincidental that the killings had stopped after Barnes had disappeared; that Barnes and their killer had a thing for talking gibberish. "What about the last five years, big fella? You vanished pretty completely."

"I was at the VA upstate. Getting treatment for"—he pointed to his temple with one bloody fingernail—"this. You can check."

"We will." It would be easy enough to verify hospital admission dates with the guy's consent. Petrosky squinted at Barnes as the man tapped another cigarette from his pack and stuck it to his lip. Their perp might be hearing voices, might be talking gibberish, but Barnes wasn't the one who'd killed Amos—Petrosky could feel it in his gut.

Even if his gut had been wrong before.

5

THE BULLPEN STANK of day-old Italian food and older coffee this morning, but at least it was quiet; only two others in the room besides him and Jackson, and they were sitting at their desks beyond the pillar.

"It's all too fucking clean," Petrosky snapped at the forensics report in his hand. No fingerprints. No hair. No saliva. Just dirt and grass. "How the fuck does he walk in there and not get a single piece of himself on anything?"

But Petrosky knew well enough: Gloves. Or he hadn't touched anything aside from his victim—no usable prints on skin if that was all he'd grabbed. This guy felt more organized than a man wandering around muttering to himself and waiting for the perfect opportunity to murder. That was bad news for them—an organized killer was much harder to catch.

Petrosky slammed the folder onto his desktop beside his half-eaten chocolate cruller. Across the way, Detective Decantor raised an eyebrow, but the big man knew better than to say anything. The guy was probably just irritated that Petrosky had interrupted his reminiscing about some random pop star, or maybe the Kardashians, who Jackson had informed him were "kind of a big deal." Petrosky didn't get it. Even Decantor couldn't tell him what they'd done outside of "be famous" and Petrosky had seen one of their pictures—no one should be all up on their own sister like that, no sir. That shit was illegal in most states.

"At least there were boot prints in the grass," Jackson said, leaning toward him over the opposite side of the desk—*my desk, dammit*—to squint at the file. Her silk sleeve tickled his hand. She'd hung her coat on the back of her seat. "Or one anyway. Wish we could tell more on the boot type, but the bottom was so worn the treads are practically flat. We've got a size, though: eleven."

With the worn boots...maybe homeless. "Right size foot for a little Arab fellow," Petrosky muttered. But small prints for a monstrous killer.

Jackson pursed her lips. "You really taking that guy seriously? He was just looking to pass the buck."

"Maybe, maybe not. We can't ignore it." He drummed his fingers on the desktop. The dog-walker surely lived near the crime scene. Did their killer? Three murders within a couple blocks wasn't an accident, so either the perp lived close by or was just hunting near the cemetery. But why there? And this time the victim was the son of a councilman—the publicity alone would push him underground, or make him leave the state altogether.

Jackson sighed heavily and reached across Petrosky's desk for—

"Hey!"

She shoved the half donut into her mouth. "I know we can't ignore it," she said, voice harsh around the pastry that should have been his. "I just hope this 'Arab guy' is a witness to the crime, not a scapegoat." Pain flickered in her eyes—her child had died a scapegoat, shot walking home from a friend's house for the high crime of being black.

She blinked hard and wiped sugar from her lips with the back of her hand before Petrosky could respond. "Let's keep the investigation quiet. The press gets wind of it, in the current political climate…" She shook her head.

She didn't have to tell Petrosky not to talk to the press. Those fuckers were the last people he'd call if he could help it —especially if there was a chance they'd stoke the public into an uproar. He eyed a donut crumb near her clavicle. "I only eat one of those a week, Jackson, and you just—"

"I'll buy you another one." She looked at her watch. "Come on, it's time to go see McCallum."

The stairs down out of the bullpen were dark and just as aromatic as the bullpen itself, but the air was thinner, lighter. Or maybe it was the lack of people that made the pressure between Petrosky's shoulders ease.

"So how's Linda? Friend of mine said he saw you at the diner yesterday morning." Jackson glanced over her shoulder at him. "It was Linda, wasn't it?"

He sighed and listened to the dull thwack of their footsteps against the stairs—his rubber soles squeaking just a little more than her boots. He pressed his lips together.

"I knew it!" Jackson exclaimed. "Good news travels fast."

"Leave it alone, woman."

"It's cool if you have a girlfriend, even if she is your ex-wife. Maybe I can help her move in…again." Jackson heaved open the exit door, and warm sunlight spilled into the corridor, assaulting the tops of Petrosky's ears. Polish folks and sunshine did not mix.

"It was one breakfast, Jackson, and she's absolutely not moving in."

"Don't be so quick to—"

"She's allergic to dogs."

The sun gleamed off the tips of her short hair as they crossed the lot toward McCallum's squat brown building. "Come again?"

"She was fine for forty years, and now she can't even be in the same room with a canine." And his Great Dane wasn't going anywhere; Duke had been a gift from a woman he'd helped once—a woman who'd helped him. He'd made her a promise. And from the nod Jackson tipped him as she pushed open the door to McCallum's office, she understood that all too well.

"My goodness, look who it is!" Past the waiting area, McCallum's inner-office door was open, the man himself behind his desk, rolls of belly pressing against the shiny mahogany. His olive green jacket boasted leather elbow patches, which could be a sign of frugality or an intellectual fashion statement.

"You get a new desk, Doc?"

"Of course. All this government wealth, why not?" McCallum chuckled in a very Ivy-League Santa Claus way. Petrosky couldn't help but smile. He'd always liked the doc, even when the man was being a real bastard in an effort to help. But thanks to McCallum, Petrosky's alcoholism and his self-destructive tendencies—okay, *most* of his self-destructive tendencies—were behind him…for now.

"Been too long since you've come down here." McCallum leveled his stare at Petrosky, curious without being accusatory, very shrink-y. Like he could read your mind. Petrosky and Jackson slid into the high-backed chairs across from McCallum. Jackson's phone buzzed. She ignored it.

"So what do you think, Doctor?" Jackson said. "You review the files I dropped off earlier?"

McCallum nodded. "If the witness statements hold up, and the man was talking to himself or to someone no one else could see, you might have any number of conditions at work." He laced his fingers over his rotund belly. The man was no twiggy little pop star and Petrosky dug that about him.

"Conditions like…" What did that Barnes guy have? "Schizoaffective disorder?"

McCallum shook his head. "Doubtful. Even if he was muttering to himself, your suspect's actions were not disorganized nor hesitant—at least not from the witness statement."

"But if he was muttering gibberish—"

"Some conditions lead people to say words other than the one they mean; they might latch onto rhyming words, or even string together a jumble of seemingly unrelated words, but they don't lead people to magically speak Latin."

"Well, we don't know for sure it was—"

"Plus, those with severe and persistent mental illnesses are more likely to run in panic than they are to attack, you know that." McCallum shifted in his seat and folded his fleshy fingers on the desktop. "And your killer let the witness go."

"But some of them…they're paranoid right? Delusional? What if the killer was hearing a voice that said Samuel Amos was dangerous, or a voice that wanted him to kill both Amos and Eden Johansson?" *He said I was going to live, but only for now.* "He murdered a man in cold blood, muttering all the while—there has to be a reason." At least he hoped that were true; it would help them figure out where to look next.

McCallum cleared his throat. "I'd put my money on a psychopath trying to talk himself out of hurting people before someone with a condition like schizophrenia or schizoaffective disorder. Someone organized, but fighting their urges." McCallum leaned forward, his eyes gleaming. "You have other cases—he's clearly done it before. Maybe it got messy, or he was almost caught. It is possible he actually managed to suppress those urges for the five years between killings. Maybe this self-talk was his way of increasing self-control."

"So what happened for him to snap now?" Jackson asked. "He'd need a trigger, right?"

Her phone rang again. She pressed it to her ear and whispered into the receiver as McCallum said, "Sure, a trigger is possible, but if he's been repressing his urges for that long, it might not be anything exceptional; watching a scary movie could do it."

Petrosky shook his head. "Fucking Stephen King."

Jackson was still muttering into her cell, her shoulders tight now. *Uh oh.*

"I'm more frightened of the evening news." McCallum grinned with his entire face. "Listen, if it turns out we have someone hearing voices and responding with violence, the plan to locate him might change, but you're already looking at the group homes and hospitals. And anti-social personality disorder, psychopathy, is a spectrum. There are as many psychopaths as there are people with bipolar disorder, but most of them are just...numb. Unfeeling, but not violent."

But their killer *was* violent. Whether or not the suspect had tried to fight those urges, he'd quietly and efficiently murdered a young man with a twist of his hands. Had murdered at least two other people before that.

"Fuck." *Jackson.*

Petrosky looked up as she pocketed her phone. Her face was drawn.

"We've got a problem," she said. "A big one."

6

THE HOUSE BELONGING to Samuel Amos's parents had morphed from a clipped-lawned, I-have-a-gardener-and-you-don't abode, into a shitshow of denim cut-offs, camera phones, and picket signs. And Confederate flags. Jackson tensed from the driver's seat as she hit the siren, earning an angry glare from a white man holding a sign that read "Terrorists Get Out."

Heat rose in Petrosky's chest. "What the fuck is this?" Jackson had filled him in a little on the way over: an article had hit the internet this morning claiming that Eden Johansson had incorrectly identified a white male as the attacker when the real culprit was some version of Middle Eastern. Clearly, Barnes had been talking.

Jackson parked her Escalade in the street across from the Amos house, narrowly missing a man wearing a lumberjack-style plaid shirt despite the heat. Her jaw was hard as stone.

It made no sense; even if Eden Johansson had identified the wrong man—which she hadn't—why the hell would thirty men be picketing outside the victim's home? He narrowed his eyes at a little fuck with a sign reading "Muslims Kill Americans." *Crusaders of the Republic, my ass.* "They're probably here because they don't like mixed-race couples. We should get them some white bedsheets and a burning cross so they can get properly attired."

He joined Jackson on her side of the car, and they headed for the house together. "Bunch of sore losers, that's what they are," he muttered. "And they've got the wrong flag."

Jackson turned to him. "What?"

"They need a white one, for surrender, like the Confederates back in the day." He forged ahead, preparing to bulldoze his way through, waiting for someone to elbow him in the ribs so he had an excuse to toss a motherfucker in the back of the car wearing a fancy new set of silver bracelets, but the crowd parted—too easily. Their voices quieted as the men backed up, hands at their sides or folded in front of them; not a one had hands behind their backs which might have given Petrosky reason to haul them out of line. And now that the path ahead was clear, he could see the empty green grass, where the crowd thinned to nothing at the curb. They'd been careful to assemble in the road instead of on private property. *Guess we can't arrest them for trespassing.*

But though the crowd had gone silent as they passed, the frenetic energy made Petrosky's hackles rise, especially when they registered Jackson. He could feel the tension radiating off her sinewy arm—the tautness of the muscle.

"We'll get rid of them anyway," he said. "Get them back to dating their own right hands where they belong." Here, in a gated community forty-five minutes outside of Ash Park, rules were more stringent—the No Solicitation sign at the front of the neighborhood was evidence enough of that. "No one needs to deal with this bullshit."

They emerged from the cloud of body odor and Pabst Blue Ribbon and—oddly—coffeehouse cappuccino to see the officers from the cemetery, Blondie still looking shocked in the middle of the lawn, the more composed Bug-eyes standing on the front porch. The crowd found its voice again as Petrosky stalked up the concrete steps. "What the fuck are you doing here?"

Those big eyes got even bigger, something Petrosky wouldn't have believed possible. Khoury, that was his name, but ... "Why aren't you with Eden Johansson?" Had Carroll pulled the detail already?

"We are...I mean, Eden Johansson is here. Her parents and Amos's parents...I guess they're best friends or something. She lives right up the road." He gestured vaguely past the crowd to the left of the Amos house, and Petrosky raised a hand against the sun. There was a smaller, but equally restless crowd in front of what must be the Johansson home.

"Why are there Nazis in front of her house?"

"Nazis? They're protesters, sir." But from the look on Khoury's face, he didn't believe that any more than Petrosky did.

"Call those fuckers whatever you want, just fill me in."

Khoury's jaw hardened. "The group seems to think she's wrongly accusing a white man when the evidence says the killer was Muslim."

Same bullshit rumor they'd heard, but how the fuck had it gotten out? They'd interviewed Barnes less than twenty-four hours ago and they had yet to locate the dog-walking witness. "Why would Eden falsely accuse anyone?"

"Yet another liberal conspiracy?" Khoury shook his head. "Eden Johansson's mother is part of some anti-gun organization, and Amos's father is a councilman—a good guy. Well-known for his more progressive ideas. He's made great strides in urban planning, protected the poor folks when some company wanted to bulldoze the section-eight housing."

"You seem to know a lot about him, Khoury."

"I grew up here. I still follow local politics."

Petrosky appraised him, the honest, steady gaze in his giant eyeballs. And nodded.

The foyer was at least twenty degrees cooler than the outside, and devoid of humidity. Petrosky hadn't registered that he was sweating, but now the back of his shirt collar plastered itself to his neck—sticky. He wiped his forehead and peered into the living room, where Mr. and Mrs. Amos sat on a black leather loveseat, the Johansson family on the matching sofa across from them. All of them engaged in a staring contest. Shocked still, or maybe numb. A wooden table with a full pitcher of iced tea sat between them. Only Eden, sandwiched between what had to be her parents, looked up as Petrosky and Jackson entered.

This was the worst part, talking to the victim's family. Probably why he tended to put it off.

Mr. Amos finally turned as Petrosky and Jackson stepped around the set of wingbacks holding vigil between the couches like navy-clad priests. Amos's black facial hair, run through with white, cleanly edged his brown cheeks, the lines of his beard so sharp they looked drawn on. The hair on the top of his head was equally manicured, closely shorn, as neat as a just-trimmed hedge. But his face gave him away; the pain there was overt and striking. Dark half circles puffed beneath his eyes. "Are they right? Is Eden…did she make a mistake?"

So much for introductions, though they'd all surely prefer to cut to the chase. Go back to drinking. Or whatever other people did to dull the pain.

Mrs. Amos grabbed her husband's hand and settled their locked fingers in her lap, the light blue of her silk dress making their knuckles stand out in stark contrast—the grasp of pain over a clear summer sky. Petrosky knew that grasp, knuckles clenched so hard they lost circulation. He'd pushed

Linda away more times than he wanted to admit. But not Mr. Amos; he squeezed her hand and leaned into his wife.

"I know what I saw," Eden said quietly. "He wasn't Muslim. Even if he like…talked like one."

What the… Petrosky's shoulders tightened. "Talked like one?" She'd initially said the man was speaking gibberish and then told her to run. "Did he have an accent?" But he'd asked, he was sure of it. She'd said the words sounded…like *The Exorcist.*

She pursed her lips. And shook her head. "Well…I mean, when he told me to run he didn't have an accent."

"What made you say he did, honey?" Mrs. Johansson had her daughter's milk-pale complexion but her lips were painted as red as blood. Perfectly outlined. Everything about Mrs. Johansson was perfectly outlined, right down to the pleats in her black skirt.

"Maybe he was speaking that language when he was mumbling," Eden said. "Muslim."

Petrosky squinted; Muslim wasn't a language any more than Mexican was.

"You said Latin yesterday," Jackson said, her voice low. "Now you think he was speaking Arabic?"

"I don't know, I just…I mean, I think so."

Jackson stepped up beside Petrosky, tapping her phone. "Can you recall exactly what he said?"

They'd asked her that too, and Eden had told them she didn't know…no, she'd said that she didn't speak the language. That she couldn't understand.

Jackson extended her phone toward Eden. "Even if you aren't sure what they mean, if you repeat the words he said, we can try translation. This app should help us narrow down the language too."

"Um…something that started with a *ch* sound? And then…*aleadui*?" She frowned. "I'm pretty sure that's what it was, because later, after I got home, I was thinking it sounded like singing. Like a-la-doo, you know? But he wasn't singing. Just mumbling."

Jackson took the phone back, and Petrosky peeked over her shoulder. The *ch* sound wasn't going to give them shit. But *"aleadui"*...

"Enemy."

In Arabic. No translation in any other language.
Well, fuck.

"Are you positive that's what you heard?" Petrosky asked. "That word?"

"I...yeah, I'm sure."

So their killer, their white-skinned, blue-eyed killer had been speaking Arabic? Was he saying he thought Samuel Amos was the enemy? Had to be—he'd let Eden walk out even if he had hinted that he might come back.

Eden wrapped her hands around her biceps and shivered, trembling like the leaves on the willows had been—fragile. "I still don't think that other voice was...I mean, it really was like two people talking. They sounded totally different. I'm just not sure it was him."

"Sorry?" Mrs. Amos frowned and leaned forward, toward Eden, her eyes mere slivers of darkly lit glass beneath her eyelashes; tears had long since washed the makeup from her face. "What do you mean, dear?"

"Well the other voice didn't sound like him, like the guy... who hurt Sammy."

Ah, yes, the whole two-voices thing. "You said you looked back when you were running away. Are you certain you didn't see anyone else?" They'd found no other footprints, nothing to indicate a second man on the scene. Then again, they had no forensic evidence from their suspect either, save for that single worn boot print. The killing had been...meticulous.

She sniffed. "I didn't see anyone, but it was really dark on the side of the building, the...mausoleum. I think there used to be a streetlight over there, but it must not have been working when we were...when I was there." Her lip trembled. "Maybe the person who killed Sammy...maybe he broke it on purpose."

They'd look into it, but half the streetlights in that neighborhood had been busted out for no reason beyond the thrill of vandalism. If their killer had gone so far as to break a streetlight for cover, it was more likely a planned attack, but he may not have cared who he killed so long as the victim was part of a couple—like the previous killings. Maybe he liked an audience.

"So, they're right."

Petrosky startled—he'd been so focused on Eden, he'd completely forgotten Eden's father; Mr. Johansson was so generic as to be invisible: light skin, gray suit, gray hair, gray eyes, little gray spectacles. He turned those silver eyes on Petrosky. "All those...*idiots* outside, they're right, there was someone else there and she...we..."

Petrosky had never thought that tears could be gray, but the liquid Mr. Johansson blinked away definitely appeared stormier than normal. A yell—maybe a chant—rose outside, then settled. *Shut the fuck up, assholes.*

Petrosky's jaw tightened. "No, Mr. Johansson, they are not right." *They will never be right about anything.* "We have no reason to believe that Eden was incorrect in her sketch of the killer, but, as is routine in all criminal cases, we're still looking for other witnesses to the murder." He turned at a tiny sound from the other side of the room.

Mrs. Amos's eyes had filled, and she touched her bangs, her hair coiffed and shiny black and perfect as if it had no idea of the horror unfolding around it. "*Murder*. God, I know, I know that's what it was, but hearing it… I'll never get used to that, I won't." She dissolved into tears, and Mr. Amos put his arm around his wife as she buried her face in his shoulder.

"We're sorry for putting it so bluntly," Jackson offered. "But we have to ask these questions."

Outside, someone yelled again, and a clamor of agitated voices responded—obscene in the face of grief, the sorrow in here thick as smoke. His jaw ached, and he tried to relax his mouth before he cracked a molar. The confusion outside wasn't going to help the Amoses open up. Neither, he thought, would having an audience.

"Can we speak alone, Mr. and Mrs. Amos?" They had some difficult questions to get through today; the family had requested privacy immediately following the identification, but he and Jackson couldn't wait any longer despite the family's pain. Grief was part and parcel in the business of death.

"No, these people"—Mrs. Amos gestured to the Johanssons—"they're like family. Please."

Petrosky nodded, though he didn't understand, not at all. He hadn't wanted to leave his room after Julie was killed—refused to speak to Linda even when she'd sobbed through the door that she needed him. Maybe if he'd been better, they'd have stayed together…the way Samuel's parents probably would.

He and Jackson exchanged a look and settled into the pair of button-upholstered wingbacks perpendicular to the couches. "Tell us about Sam," Jackson said, and he was struck, not for the first time, by the hard edges in her voice—empathy laced with a pain too sharp to swallow.

"He graduated top of his class," Mr. Amos said. "Wanted to be a lawyer, like his old man." One side of his lips curled into a smile, then dropped again.

"Did he have any unusual friends? People who might have been angry with him, might have wanted to hurt him?"

"Wait." Mrs. Amos straightened. "I thought this was a random crime. You think this is…that it was on purpose? That someone was after our Sam?"

Jackson raised her hand. "No, we don't, not necessarily. We're just trying to figure out what happened, and any information about who he was could help. Even things that might seem insignificant."

Mrs. Amos pressed her lips together in a tight line.

Mr. Amos shook his head. "There's nothing that I can tell you. He was a good kid, a really good kid."

The silence stretched.

Eden cleared her throat. "We didn't know anyone like that, people who were mad or hated him or anything. We didn't hang out with anyone weird." But they were weird enough, going off to a mausoleum in the middle of the night.

"Did you know he was planning to go to the cemetery?" Petrosky asked Mr. Amos.

Mrs. Amos swallowed hard and sniffed. "No," Mr. Amos said.

"I didn't tell anyone." Eden leveled her gaze at them, less shaky now. "But with the social media thing…" She shrugged, but she was far more chatty than anyone else in the room—and more likely to give them the background they were after. Friends often knew teenagers better than their parents did, as hard as that was to accept. Julie's face flashed in his mind, and he shoved the image away.

"How long have you two been dating?" Petrosky asked.

"Practically forever. Years."

An awfully long time at their age. But despite this romantic track record, her eyes were clear—all the Johanssons were dry-eyed, somber but stoic. Even the Amoses had stopped crying. *This isn't going to work.* He and

54

Jackson would have to call each of them separately at a later date, when they felt free to let their guard down—when they didn't have to keep up appearances. Maybe when the shock wore off. Even Eden was looking at her father now and not at Petrosky or Jackson. Whatever she said here, in the presence of Samuel's parents, might not be the whole truth. And they were all so damn...dull. Quiet. *Off.*

Petrosky stood. "Can we see his room?"

The Amoses exchanged a glance, and Mr. Amos's eyes narrowed. Mrs. Amos bit her lip.

Interesting response. Sometimes people didn't want to disturb their loved one's things, but Samuel's parents looked...nervous.

Mrs. Amos finally released her husband's fingers—probably sweaty as fuck by now—and recrossed her legs. "It's just...he was already starting to pack his things. Moving out in the fall."

"I understand ma'am, but if we could see what he left behind..."

The Amoses frowned, but Mrs. Amos stood, suddenly, like she'd sat on a wasp. "I'll show you. Just please don't touch his things. I don't think I can handle...anything else being taken."

Jackson raised an eyebrow at him as they followed Mrs. Amos upstairs and down the hall. *Something is wrong.* His shoulders tingled. Mrs. Amos waved at the door. But then she made her way back toward the stairway, leaving them in the hall like she couldn't even touch the knob let alone cross the threshold. And as soon as Petrosky ducked inside, he knew why.

"Holy shit," Jackson whispered.

The room was a cave, painted black as night. But unlike the stars Petrosky had helped Shannon stick onto Evie's ceiling, the walls were covered with crime scene photos that rivaled any investigator's tack board, each set arranged like a pyramid. Photos of the house or scene on the top, images of the murders themselves beneath, then murder weapons, vehicles, burial sites, and…

His mouth went dry. On the right wall, the mausoleum glared back, that same mausoleum where Samuel Amos had died, and below it, a glossy color photo of Meredith Lawrence's corpse tied to the stone altar, her abdomen split down the center from ribs to groin, intestines coiled around what was left of her belly and spilling onto the concrete floor. And on the mausoleum wall, the bloody words scrawled by the killer in Lawrence's blood—part of a poem from *Through the Looking Glass*, which was how the *Looking Glass* killer had gotten his name.

Had Morrison taken these photos? It was possible. But the thought of his ex-partner, his dead partner, Evie's father, a man who might as well have been his son, was a knife in his chest, hot and painful. No wonder Shannon hightailed it to Georgia. Had to be hard to stay in the place where your husband was brutally murdered. Maybe as hard as patrolling the streets where you'd found your partner's corpse.

"No one thought to mention that Samuel had crime scene photos from the same place where he was killed?" Mrs. Amos had seemed pretty avoidant of the kid's room, but his parents had to know. Had to. Not like the kid had hidden the pictures.

"How did he even get these?" Jackson leaned closer to the wall, her nose almost touching the photo of a man with blood soaking the floor beneath his severed neck. "Some of these look like they're from the case files—they shouldn't be public."

Petrosky cleared his throat and sucked a breath through his nose. "The age of social media, right?" One lousy cop or a file clerk looking to make a few bucks, and private files weren't so private anymore. "Maybe Samuel paid for inside information and got a little more than he bargained for." He turned away from the photo of Meredith Lawrence. His vision had begun to blur. "Samuel Amos went to the mausoleum to see the place in person; clearly he was obsessed with this stuff, going to old crime scenes, looking at these pictures and…" He touched a red string that Samuel had attached from Lawrence's photo to another of the *Looking Glass* victims: Jane Trazowski. Another woman, glassy-eyed, eviscerated. Lots of red string around the room. Lots of victims Petrosky didn't recognize, cases that weren't his. "Our killer said Samuel Amos was the enemy," Petrosky said. "Maybe that's because the kid was onto him…or them. Maybe little Sammy closed some random cold case but hadn't had a chance to tell us. And if Eden is right, if there really was a second voice, a second man in that cemetery, one partner could have been playing lookout while the other killed Amos." He rifled through the desk drawers: pens, blank yellow sticky notes, lip balm. A rosary, of all things. But nothing to indicate the kid had solved a crime—no envelopes, no *ah-ha!* moments, no IT WAS HIM in red marker. Just the remnants of a life. "We'll ask about his laptop, the phone records. Maybe he was lured out there. All this"—he waved his hand at the photos of the dripping mausoleum wall, at Lawrence's bloody guts—"it feels like too much of a coincidence."

Jackson nodded. "We'll poke around the precinct too, see if we can figure out where Amos got these photos. Probably be good to get this whole room catalogued. Parents won't like it but…you know." She shrugged and looked down.

He did know. Lots of things in the coming weeks that the Amoses would hate, lots of desperation, lots of nostalgic items to cling to now that they couldn't hold their kid, but nothing was going to bring him back. Nothing would bring

Jackson's son home either. And Petrosky still had Julie's night-light in his bedroom. At least he no longer fantasized about painting it with his brains.

A shout from outside drew his attention to the window, glass framed by thick black curtains now pulled back to that weird gauzy shit, same as downstairs. What was it with these curtains? Half-assed approach. Either open the window or close it up. Petrosky moved aside the filmy cloth and peered down at the people milling around with their signs. A man on the sidewalk snapped pictures of the house with his cell. "Fucking social media," Petrosky muttered. "Should we get Scott on it, see if he can figure out where the false-accusation story came from? Shit, maybe one of these assholes killed Samuel Amos just so they could blame a dark guy, then tossed the story around on their internet pages." That was an insane theory, and from the look Jackson shot him, she knew it too.

Someone else yelled from the lawn, and this time, a chorus of voices answered, cursing, screaming.

"What the fuck? Don't they ever stop?" Babcock and Khoury were both on the walk now, corralling protesters who had apparently thought they'd get a little closer for a better shot of the house—at least this room probably looked normal from the outside.

A man looked up at them, a skinny twat with a Confederate flag T-shirt and a mullet. Petrosky flipped him off. His mouth opened in a shocked, racist O.

Some other flag-wearer threw his arms in the air in front of Khoury, screaming, pointing at the window, yelling in Khoury's face. They should get down there, maybe call for backup. "Can we shoot one of them, at least?" Petrosky said. "It's been a long day, and it would really help my mood."

Jackson finally laughed, but her face clouded when she peeked over his shoulder at the scene on the street. "If only."

7

———

PETROSKY WATCHED the setting sun glare pink off the metal bumpers in the merge lane as Jackson eased her unmarked onto the interstate. They had one suspect, possibly two, and the Arabic speaker believed Amos was his enemy. The question was: why?

He ran his beefy palm down his face, inhaling the sultry stink of the coffee-shop espressos Jackson had stopped for. Even the cup—red and shiny—was pompous, like it knew something he didn't.

A shiny white Jeep cut in front of Jackson's Escalade, earning a loud bleat from his partner's horn and a handful of colorful curses—a few more than usual.

"You okay, Jackson?"

She glanced at him and sniffed. "Yeah, those bigots just pissed me off." But the sadness in her gaze told him the protesters weren't the whole of it.

"You're the one who didn't want to shoot them," he said instead of pressing. He turned back to the window and watched the bumpers, then the white Civic creeping up on their right—swerving, just a little. "Hopefully, Scott's doing okay."

They'd called Scott to come in and catalogue the bedroom. Scott was always game for field work—in Vermont, he'd been a rookie detective, but what he really wanted was more time to examine the evidence, the closer the better. And he wouldn't be ham-handed with the Amos boy's items. They needed to keep their relationship with the Amoses and the Johanssons on the up-and-up with some semblance of mutual trust in case they needed more information, especially since everyone in that house had seemed off…maybe even a little secretive.

"I'm more worried about Babcock and Khoury," Jackson said.

The white Civic came level with his window, and Petrosky watched as the woman in the driver's seat penciled eyeliner onto her lids using her rearview mirror. "Eh, if the crowd gets too crazy, I'm sure Babcock will just bulldoze over them, hit them with that giant neck of his. Or have Khoury look at them extra hard."

He put his badge to the window, then reached over and tapped Jackson's horn, keeping his eyes on the woman in the car beside them. She startled and turned to them, a furious expression on her face. Petrosky smiled as her jaw dropped, her half-lined eyes widening; one of them had a streak of black nearly to her eyebrow.

"You get her to fuck it up?"

"Two points for me. I think that's twelve now."

"You're forgetting about the guy with the electric razor."

"Oh yeah. Kid shaved half his goatee off." That guy had been younger than the eyeliner woman, though not as young as… The chuckle died in his throat as Samuel Amos's glassy dead eyes rose in his memory. He blinked. The car beside them slowed, and when the makeup woman was beyond his line of sight, Petrosky said, "So, Amos was obsessed with homicide."

"You're obsessed with homicide too," Jackson said, her eyes on the rearview.

"I get paid for it."

"Not much."

"Fair enough."

Jackson tightened her fingers around the wheel. "Let's say Amos's homicide obsession led to something, that he stumbled upon the identity of a killer. Why wouldn't he call the police?"

"Maybe he didn't have proof yet. Wanted to play vigilante."

Jackson raised an eyebrow at him.

Petrosky ignored her. "It's also possible he didn't actually have the evidence the killer believed he did, or that some of the images hanging in his room contained a clue that Amos never noticed. All it takes is a killer getting antsy." A killer with knowledge that Samuel Amos had the photos in the first place. But neither Amos's parents nor Eden had known where those pictures had come from; they'd asked. And Amos probably would have told his girlfriend if he'd solved a real-life crime. They'd asked about that too. Nada.

Jackson reached for her coffee, but instead of lifting the cup, she traced the lid then tapped on it with her fingernail. "He could also have been obsessed with homicide for darker reasons. We've both seen that before."

Petrosky squinted at the setting sun. Samuel Amos's room was like that of any of a dozen serial killers Petrosky had chased. And though Eden had denied it, Amos could've had twisted friends Eden had never met—maybe an older friend who had killed two other men more than five years ago. Would Amos have known if one of his buddies was a murderer?

Thin. It was all so fucking *thin*.

Tap, *tap*, *tap* went Jackson's fingers on the coffee lid. Anxious.

"I like Amos figuring out who this perp was better than him being sick and twisted too," Petrosky said. "Gut feeling. And what better motivation for the killer to come out of retirement than the fear of prison?" But if Amos had known about this guy, why the fuck would he make himself the perfect mark?

"Mm-hmm." Jackson's eyes were on the rearview—mouth tight. She was not okay. Not at all.

"I know, I know," he said slowly, watching her. "Let's just hash through all the crazy things it could be. Helps me clear my head."

Her eyes flicked from the windshield and back to the rearview. He turned around in the seat and narrowed his eyes at the blue Taurus riding their back bumper.

"Is that the one we parked behind at the Amos house?"

She squinted. "Sixty-five percent sure. I didn't see it coming out of the neighborhood, though; noticed it about ten miles back when we were getting on the freeway."

"Pull off here."

"So we can get shot on a side street?" she said, but her blinker was already on.

The Escalade's oversized tires ground against the exit ramp, pavement marred by hundreds of crumbling patch repairs. Petrosky watched the Taurus in his sideview. His gun sat heavy against his lower back.

The car followed them up the ramp and hung a right after them at the first set of streetlights.

"Maybe we should just ram his ass," she muttered.

A gas station loomed ahead, lights glowing from the minimart inside, but no other cars idled at the pumps. Jackson whipped the SUV into a spot near the back and leapt from the driver's-side door, hand on her weapon, as the Taurus turned far more slowly into the spot beside them. Petrosky climbed out too, staring down the man who emerged: deep cherry-wood skin, brown eyes so dark they were almost black, hair thick and black like Khoury's and gelled to perfection, a helmet that didn't move in the slightest even as he shut his door. And his face…familiar.

Petrosky released his service weapon and pulled his hand from beneath his jacket. "I know you. Right?"

The man smiled. "We've met. Last time you told me to get the fuck out of your crime scene."

Jackson stood near the Escalade's back bumper, her hand still on the gun beneath her jacket.

"Reporter," Petrosky told her.

The man extended his hand toward Jackson and smiled again. "Reyansh Acharya, at your service."

Jackson straightened and stalked up the narrow space between the cars, eyes spitting fire. "Why the fuck are you following us?" She poked him in the shoulder with one extended index, and the guy stepped back against his Taurus. "You have no reason to—"

He put his hands in the air. "I just wanted to see what you guys were up to."

"Real fucking incognito," Petrosky snapped.

"Listen, there are tons of articles out there, about the killing in the cemetery. I'd like to get the truth about it. The real story."

"Why would you be after the truth when fake news sells so well?"

"It matters, Detective." Acharya raised an eyebrow. "Rich black kid, son of a public figure, wrong part of town, and now the civil disobedience, the picketers in front of the houses—"

"The picketers are stalking a grieving family because they

think our witness is wrong about the killer's ethnicity," Petrosky said. "We sure as shit didn't tell anyone that. Did you?"

"Of course not." He straightened. "And the Crusaders have been after the Amos family for years. Running articles, trying to discredit the councilman every time something comes up for a vote."

Petrosky frowned. Khoury seemed to know an awful lot about local politics and he hadn't mentioned any history of harassment between the Crusaders and the Amos family. Come to think of it, neither had Mr. and Mrs. Amos.

Acharya was still talking. "I do have it on good authority that a witness saw a dark-skinned man running from the cemetery."

"We don't know anything for sure." Jackson crossed her arms.

"Maybe whoever told you that rumor is more than a busybody," Petrosky growled, hoping he looked at least a little scary, but his fury was waning with age and with the lack of Jack Daniels.

"You think Barnes is a suspect?" Acharya shook his head. "There's no way in hell. I've already talked to the people he saw that night, his dealer—"

"We'll need that information," Jackson said. "Names, addresses, whatever notes you have."

"I never give up my sources."

You just admitted you talked to Barnes, dickwad. "So just some guy with dark skin, running from the cemetery, eh?" He glowered at Acharya. "Should I consider you a suspect?"

Acharya snorted. "Because we all look alike, right?"

"Your people seem to think so." Petrosky glanced at the gas station building—brick, with gaudy neon in every window. No movement from inside.

Acharya balked. "My people?"

Jackson rolled her eyes. "He means journalists, printing stories about unknown colored folks and letting the masses fill in the blanks."

"Glad one of us speaks Angry White Guy," Acharya said, scowling.

"Not Angry White Guy." Petrosky sniffed. "She speaks Asshole."

Acharya's eyes widened. Then his face split in a grin—straight, sharp teeth like any good scavenger. "I'll stop trying to police your language since you seem to have such a firm grasp on it."

"Yeah he does," Jackson said, and when Petrosky looked her way, her eyes remained on Acharya, not even a hint of irritation at the man. *Interesting.* She usually wanted to punch journalists in the dick even more than he did.

"Listen, there really is a reason I followed you." He straightened his shoulders and leveled a steely look at Petrosky. "Give me an exclusive. And I've got something for you—something great."

Petrosky grunted. "How about we take you to the precinct and lock you up until you give us whatever you have?"

"It's not a what. It's a who. And I know my rights." He half-smiled, half-smirked, and Petrosky had to resist slapping the look off his face. "Come on, give me something, Detectives. I promise you won't be sorry."

Hell no, motherfucker. Petrosky turned back to the Escalade and grabbed the door handle.

"We think the killer speaks Arabic," Jackson blurted. "Or that he was speaking Arabic the night he murdered Amos."

Petrosky dropped the handle and gaped. "Fucking hell, Jackson!"

Acharya's jaw dropped. "Arabic? Really?"

"We think so, but we aren't positive," Jackson said. "And

you obviously understand why this information would be sensitive…why we need to keep it close to the vest for now."

"So, I can't print it." The hollows beneath Acharya's eyes were suddenly deeper in the growing dusk.

Jackson shook her head. "No, you can't, not yet. And you can't name us as your source. But if you have sources who can help us…"

Petrosky's jaw clenched. *Enemy, enemy, enemy*—the word rang in his ears and rattled his brain. The dead kid with the twisted neck. Julie, throat slit, lips blue. Jackson's own son, about the same age, dead on the sidewalk. She wanted to do everything she could to find this guy, and Petrosky did, too, but he'd rather beat it out of Acharya than play nice. *So much for settling those demons, old man.*

"I've got a source, a good one. But I want an exclusive. As soon as you're ready to break it—"

"Done," Jackson said.

And before Petrosky could say *I'll give you an exclusive, fucker*, Acharya had stepped to the back of his Taurus. He opened the door.

Jackson's breath caught.

A body lay sprawled on the back seat.

8

————

"THE FUCK DID YOU DO, ACHARYA?" Petrosky reached for his gun and this time he didn't stop at fingering the butt—he pulled it from its holster and held it against his thigh.

"What?" Acharya peered inside. "Hey, Simmons!"

The man stirred. Not dead.

"Who the fuck is he?" Petrosky demanded, re-holstering his weapon.

"Your dark-skinned running-away-from-the-cemetery witness."

The one Barnes had seen? Petrosky squinted over Acharya's shoulder at the lump on the backseat. Curly black hair, green T-shirt, tight-legged jeans, too tight for any self-respecting man; definitely the kind of fellow who'd own a Dachshund. "What'd you do to him?" *Slap him for wearing those stupid fucking pants?*

"*I* didn't do anything. I found him at the bar up the way from the cemetery—only guy drinking at four in the afternoon. And, of course, they had the news coverage of the Amos case on the television...lots of pictures of your scowling mug." He grinned again. "One thing led to another. He had an awful lot to get off his chest."

"How'd you know he'd be there? How'd you even know who he was?" Jackson had put out word and a general description to the patrols yesterday, but that had yielded no results.

"I have my sources. No one else saw anything at the cemetery, but a few folks know this guy—walks his dog twice a day, every day, hits the bar occasionally when he gets off work."

"So you found him, and then...kidnapped him?"

"I didn't kidnap anyone." He bent into the backseat and shook the man's shoulder. "Simmons! Come on!"

Simmons groaned and rolled onto his side.

"Rise and shine!"

The sun had already dipped below the horizon, fading the sky to a hazy purple.

Simmons finally opened his eyes. "What the fuck, man?" His jaw dropped, and he shot to seated, wincing, hand on his head, his slurred words falling from his lips like marbles. *Shit, is that how I used to sound?* "I thought we were getting Denny's."

Acharya shook his head. "I said we could go get Denny's after we visited my friends."

"I thought he was your buddy, man, I didn't think we were going to see..." He met Petrosky's eyes and apparently didn't like what he saw there. He slammed his lips closed and dropped his bleary gaze to his lap.

"The detective *is* my buddy," Acharya said, though Petrosky was no such thing. Simmons raised his head again and frowned.

Petrosky nodded to the man in the backseat. "Why don't we take a ride, Simmons?"

"Fine." He licked his lips and slowly blinked his eyes. "But one of you owes me some pancakes."

"You're awfully entitled for a guy who's impeding a police investigation."

Simmons's eyes widened, but Petrosky shook his head. "Relax, we'll pick some up on the way to the station." He deserved a few pancakes since Jackson had stolen his weekly donut, and he wanted some real coffee anyway. Mostly, they needed to sober this guy up.

SIMMONS'S EYES were still bloodshot, but after their pancake dinner, the man was walking in a straight line and didn't seem quite as belligerent as he had in the backseat of Acharya's Taurus. The food, or maybe the coffee, had greatly improved Petrosky's mood as well, yet he managed to plaster a scowl on his face as they led Simmons to interrogation. Not that it was hard; a scowl was closer to the natural state of his face than a shit-eating grin, and he was annoyed that he'd wasted an hour at the diner pouring coffee down this guy's gullet. *No more playing nice, dickhead.*

Jackson slid into the metal chair beside Petrosky and turned on the recorder. And nodded.

"You clearly knew you were a witness to a homicide yesterday morning. Why wouldn't you come into the station?" Petrosky laced his fingers on the stainless steel tabletop, the metal dull in the dim lights; one of the overheads was burned out. Probably good for Simmons, who had his index fingers pressed against his temples, elbows resting on the tabletop. "Not even a phone call to help catch a killer, Simmons?"

Johnathan Simmons. American born and raised, mixed race, with the exhausted gaze of a man who was so tired of today's bullshit that he'd rather stick a fork in his eyeball than answer one more goddamn question. Petrosky could relate.

Simmons raised his head, releasing his temples. "I didn't know anyone was hurt until I got off work, I swear."

"Then why would you run away from the cemetery? You clearly saw something you didn't like."

"I thought it was just some random crazy. I didn't want any trouble."

Didn't want any trouble. Same thing Barnes had said, almost word-for-word. Had Acharya coached him? "Let me make sure I understand, Simmons: You saw a man, a man creepy enough for you to pick up your dog and run from the cemetery like a bat out of hell, and you didn't even mention it to a co-worker? You didn't laugh about it, didn't mutter 'what is this world coming to?' You just kept it to yourself?"

"This world has been falling apart for a long time." He ran a hand through his thick, black hair. "And I sure wasn't going to call the cops about someone talking to themselves on the street. Do you have any idea what it's like out there? My mother is white, and everyone still hates me, what with the talking heads on television, the folks chanting about building a wall—hell, half of them think *I'm* Mexican."

"You aren't Mexican?" Petrosky leaned closer over the table.

Jackson muttered something that sounded like "goddammit," but he couldn't be sure.

"Maybe I should get a lawyer," the man said, face hard.

Petrosky narrowed his eyes and leaned back in his chair. Innocent men didn't need lawyers, but this guy didn't match Eden's description of the attacker in the slightest, and he'd already denied speaking any language besides English. Petrosky glanced beneath the table—sneakers size thirteen on the inside, and shiny as fuck. No way he'd been wearing the worn size-eleven boots from the impressions outside the mausoleum.

"He's kidding," Jackson said to Simmons. "And if you want a lawyer, you can call one. But this isn't an interrogation—you aren't a suspect, you're a witness to a horrific crime. We just want to catch the person who did this."

Simmons sniffed and turned his gaze back to Petrosky. Petrosky nodded. "Can you walk us through yesterday morning, Mr. Simmons? Tell us why you were out by the cemetery?"

He blinked his bleary eyes, too slow, but he sighed, resigned. "I was walking my dog."

"At one o'clock in the morning?"

"I go in to work at three-thirty—the bagel shop up on Everston. I get up, walk Jeffie, hit the gym, all before you're probably out of bed."

Damn straight.

Simmons crossed his arms.

"We need to know about the man you saw," Jackson said. "You were out walking your dog and then what? Where was he?"

"I didn't actually see anyone."

Jackson balked. "You just said—"

"I said that someone was there. I was out walking behind the cemetery. You know where the willow trees are?"

"Pretty dark out past the streetlights," Petrosky said, leaning forward to rest his hands on the steel once more.

"Jeffie's shy, likes to do his business back where it's dark, and it's secluded so I don't have to clean it up, okay?"

"Your dog could take a shit in broad daylight in the middle of the street down there. It's not the Ritz."

"Still feels wrong," Simmons said.

Petrosky shrugged. "Still is wrong."

The silence stretched. Finally, Simmons cleared his

throat. "I heard his footsteps first. Somewhere inside the cemetery."

"Did he stop? Like he was waiting for something?" *Or someone?* Maybe the killer had been stalking Johansson or Amos—or knew they were coming.

"No, he was...almost marching? Steady pace, just moving forward. I think, in hindsight, he was moving closer to the mausoleum, but at the time, I just thought he was cutting through the cemetery. Jeffie barked and the guy didn't slow. Didn't even seem to notice us."

"How do you know it was a guy?"

"I didn't, until he started muttering."

Petrosky narrowed his eyes. Their guy had walked into the mausoleum and killed Samuel Amos, but he'd let Eden Johansson go free. Was McCallum right? Had he wanted to kill her too, but managed to convince himself to stop? Maybe he'd talked himself out of going after Simmons and his little shit dog.

"What did he say?"

"Well, that was the weird part, why I took off." Simmons swallowed hard. "He kept saying, 'Don't move, be quiet, bitch,' over and over again. And then..." His forehead wrinkled. "I dunno. Some other language, but that voice was totally different. At first, I thought maybe he was talking to someone else, but I only heard one set of footsteps...I think. I guess Jeffie was barking by then, and he just kept babbling, you know?" He put his hands palm down on the table, like Petrosky's. A few inches and their fingers would be touching.

Petrosky slid his hands into his lap. "Did you hear anyone else either before or after that incident? See another person besides this 'random crazy' as you put it?"

The man shook his head. "No, like I said: I didn't see anyone at all. Not even the guy who was talking."

"What about Samuel Amos? Eden Johansson? Maybe you saw them coming in when you were running off?"

Simmons put his hands up in a *stop* gesture. "I swear, the guy I heard, he was back by the willows. No way he was talking to them."

"That's not what I asked you."

"No, okay? No, I didn't see them."

Petrosky ran a hand over his face, bristly skin catching the calloused pads of his fingers. The mausoleum was smack in the middle of the cemetery, well away from the trees, and the kids hadn't ventured to the back side of the property at all from the statement Eden had given to Bug-eyes and Captain Shock—they'd come in through the front gate and made their way straight to the building. If the killer had been hiding back behind the trees, they'd never have known he was there.

Still, if he'd been planning to kill a man, why not go after Simmons? Why let him walk away? *It's not his Modus Operandi*, Morrison's voice whispered in his ear, and Petrosky blinked hard and tried to swallow past the lump in his throat. *I need to get some sleep.*

"What language do you think he was speaking?" Jackson said. "When he was babbling?"

"I have no idea."

Petrosky raised an eyebrow. "Come on now, you'd at least know if he was speaking Mexican."

"Mexican isn't a language," Simmons snapped.

Jackson glared. "Stop fucking with him, Petrosky."

He sniffed. She always got to play good cop.

"You said his voice changed," Jackson continued, turning back to Simmons. "That it was different when he was speaking this other language. Are you sure it was him speaking? That it wasn't another person?"

"I…" Simmons looked down at the table. "Looking back,

it was probably two men, yeah. It's the only thing that makes sense. The voices definitely sounded different—way different —and Jeffie was barking so much that…well, I wouldn't have been able to hear any other footsteps once Jeffie got going."

Eden…what had she said? *It was so weird, almost like the voice was coming from somewhere else. Like it wasn't even him.* And it was awfully dark in that mausoleum. Had a second man been speaking in another language from outside the door? Or was this a split-personality thing? They'd gotten called away from Dr. McCallum to the clusterfuck at the Amos house before Petrosky could bring it up.

Simmons pursed his lips and brought his fingertips to his temples again, rubbing in little circles as if trying to massage his headache away. "Do you think that kid was still alive? When I was there?" He dropped his hands.

If Simmons had gotten there after the killing, he'd have heard Eden screaming and tearing out of the cemetery—he would have heard the cops. Simmons had heard the last words spoken before the killer had made up his mind to snap Samuel Amos's neck. Petrosky nodded. "Yeah, the victim was still alive."

Simmons's eyes filled. "I'm really sorry."

Aren't we all? Hindsight was a bitch. Petrosky knew that better than anyone.

9

THE STREET HAD a heady feel this time of night, thick and
ominous like there were eyes on you even when there
weren't. But it was better to be cautious, Jane had always
thought, whether you were at a bar, or walking home, or just
trying to avoid your uncle when he'd had a few too many. Or
when he hadn't.

She hurried up the abandoned alley behind what used to
be the Ragdoll club, straining her ears, but she heard only the
faint scuttling of claws on plywood and what might have
been a tiny squeak. She'd tried to sleep inside the old club
once, but the mold was awful, like trying to breathe through
felt—except maybe in the dead of winter, but that's when the
rats were at their worst. Not that they weren't awful now.
One step over the threshold and you risked leptospirosis,
rat-bite fever, salmonella, rabies. To think she'd once been
pre-med. What a joke.

The doorway came and went, her heart throbbing in time
to her footsteps. No sound but the thin *whoosh* of summer
breeze that occasionally hissed up the alleyway from the
road to the cemetery like breath from the dead. She walked

faster. Too dark for her liking. Only meager traffic ever wound up on the street near Whispering Willows—there were more lights on the blocks outside the cemetery, and she intended to make it to the overpass before midnight.

Hssssssh.

Jane paused, the hairs on her neck prickling...was that a human breath she'd heard? But she relaxed once more when she felt the breeze on her shoulders. She shouldn't have come out this way—she'd just wanted to be alone for a few minutes. And to wait out the cops who'd caught her panhandling. Now, police presence didn't seem so terrible, even if they were likely to accuse her of selling drugs or her body. Jane had never done either.

Crick.

Not the wind.

Surely the rats, though, or perhaps a wayward leaf against the brick. Even a moth beating itself against the glass of the streetlamp at the far end of the alley.

Crick.

Jane's insides clenched. She did not freeze—did not have the luxury of freezing, you never did out here—and walked faster, brushing the hair from her face, listening so hard her head ached from ear to temple to jaw. The skin between her shoulder blades itched violently, and the ice in her veins spread over her flesh, leaving trails of sticky goosebumps. Someone was watching her. She'd felt it enough times to know; felt it when she panhandled around the football stadium on game night, men wondering how much money for her to come back to the hotel; felt it when she was in college walking to the dorm, hordes of fraternity brothers wondering how far they could get—out loud. Felt it every time she passed the couch her uncle had always lain on; felt it before his hand clamped around her wrist.

Step one: avoid confrontation where you can. Her footsteps were a staccato vibration against her eardrums, ricocheting against the bricks, against the defunct dumpsters, a frenzy of rubber on asphalt. The mouth of the alley loomed ahead—pitch dark beyond, hazy black, but there were lights the next block up, she knew that. And people. She just had to make it.

Blam!

White light flashed behind her eyes. The world spun in a haze of pain. She fell to her knees, the back of her head singing—*agony*—hands grating against the asphalt. She scampered back, tried to push herself up, tried to get to her feet, but the dizziness dragged her back down. Jane blinked, vision blurry, dark, but she could make out...someone. A wiry man stepped from the shadows beyond the alley. Something in his hand, long, slender. A pipe? She couldn't focus her eyes well enough, she—

"Whatcha doing out this way, girl?" Low and oddly slurred. His footsteps were obscene, horrifying, the nighttime creeping of the monster beneath the bed. But she'd seen her share of monsters, and she'd be damned if she'd let this one win.

Jane reached for her boot and gripped the handle of her switchblade. *One inch closer, asshole, and you'll be crawling away without testicles.* Step one: avoid. Step two: fight.

She heaved herself backward, behind a dumpster, against the wall where the shadows were deepest, well outside the glow of the streetlamp. The reek of rat feces and old urine burned in her nostrils. She wrapped her fingers tightly around the handle of the blade, eyes on the approaching man.

"Come on over here, I've got something for you." An accent, some kind of accent. He laughed. Horribly. But there was another sound beneath it, more a feeling than a noise: a vibration. *Footsteps?* But the man in front of her wasn't walking—he had stilled, head cocked, like he could hear it too.

"Be quiet, bitch. Be quiet, be quiet." Another voice. Behind her, beyond the dumpster where she couldn't see.

Oh shit. There were two of them. The world spun, spun, spun.

Jane whipped the blade from her boot, hand trembling. If she could just focus her eyes... She got her feet beneath her, but stayed down, crouching, the knife at her side, aimed, ready.

The man behind the dumpster stepped forward, into the light, blurry still, but he was a hulking beast of a man silhouetted by the hazy yellow glare. The man in front of her hit the pipe against his opposite palm, *thunk, thunk, thunk.* The larger man moved closer.

"Okay, okay!" The man with the pipe raised his hands. "Okay, you go first."

Jane put a hand against the wall, trying to stand, but the world upended, violently. The blade clattered to the pavement.

"Be quiet, bitch, be quiet."

It was the last thing she heard before her vision went black.

10

THE CELL WOKE Petrosky the next morning, screaming, not singing—*that definitely isn't singing*—about ass mastering, the bass line vibrating the phone so hard he fumbled it from the nightstand, knocking his water glass in the process. *Goddamn phone.* He had half a mind to smash it and replace it with the old-fashioned flip kind so Jackson couldn't fuck with it again. More screaming from the cell. Petrosky's Great Dane raised his massive head...from the bed beside him. "You're not allowed up here," Petrosky muttered, and slapped the phone to his ear. The dog wagged his tail.

"Good news!" Scott's voice was deeper than it had been when they'd first met, but he'd retained that lilt of boyish excitement.

"It better be good news," Petrosky grumbled. "You're disrupting my beauty sleep." He eased himself to seated, kicking the quilt off his legs. Julie's night-light glowed pink from the corner, turning the blue blankets a hazy purple through his bleary eyes. On the floor, water puddled on the carpet from the cup he'd knocked over.

Better water than Jack Daniel's.

"Oh man, I'm sorry. If anyone needs beauty sleep, it's you." Scott laughed.

Petrosky glanced at the clock on the nightstand: seven a.m. Duke *gar-umph*ed from Petrosky's pillow. Fucker wasn't happy until he rubbed his ass on everything. Petrosky reached back and scratched behind Duke's ears, and the dog beat a steady *thump, thump, thump* on the bed with his tail. "You have something to tell me, kid, or are you just calling to piss me off?"

"So here's the deal," Scott went on like he hadn't noticed Petrosky's crabbiness. "The photos from Amos's bedroom were definitely police property—they were never released online or used by the press, and some of the ones Amos had were from older cases, before the age of social media. Those images were used during trial, but no one outside of the detectives and those in the courtroom ever saw them."

"They came from inside," Petrosky said, waving the dog off the pillow, but Duke snuffled again and nudged Petrosky's hand.

"Sounds like it."

"So we'll start looking at evidence room logs. See who checked those boxes out."

"I wish it were so easy."

Yeah, me too, kid. No person planning to steal photos from the evidence lock-up would sign in—or sign for the correct box—unless they were a complete fucking moron. Which they might be. Maybe they'd get lucky. Petrosky scratched his cheek, stubble grating against his fingertips.

"We don't know when the photos were removed from evidence," Scott said. "But they were definitely from our files; some had case numbers still written on the back."

Petrosky frowned at Duke, who had lain his giant slobbery face on the bed. The dog's tail beat the covers. *Thump, thump, thump.*

"How many of the cases Amos was studying resulted in convictions?" If any were still open, and cold, Amos might have spent extra time researching them, hoping for a clue. Petrosky would.

"They were all closed cases...I think." Scott sniffed, the *thip-thip* of paper rustling in the background. "Yeah, they had DNA, witnesses...all of them look like clean convictions."

Unless they'd convicted the wrong person, their "Amos caught a killer" theory was looking unlikely. But they still had a man on the inside involved, someone who worked at the precinct. Maybe someone who had information they shouldn't about the cases Amos was obsessed with. And it was still possible they were looking for two suspects. Johnathan Simmons and Eden Johansson both seemed to think there was a pair of killers at work.

"About the Amos murder though," Scott said. "I'm still working on getting the rest of the paperwork together, but I found a note in one of the earlier related cases, the murder in the alley across from the cemetery, that was interesting." The hiss of rustling papers came through the cell again, louder than before and somehow agitated, like whispered accusations. "Witness said he was mumbling, but that he kept repeating a specific phrase over and over."

"We know that already, Scott." Eden Johansson had said the same.

"Well, this witness said he corrected himself a few times. Like he said one word, then said it again slower and slightly differently, almost like he was in a trance or like he was practicing the language."

"Practicing the language?"

"That's what it says."

Huh. Maybe their suspect had been new to Arabic five years ago. But he'd be fluent by now, probably why Eden Johansson hadn't mentioned him stumbling over his lines, why she'd been able to pick out an actual word—a word he'd repeated numerous times. But...did that mean they only had one bilingual killer? *What the fuck is going on?* He sighed, and Duke sighed louder.

Enemy. Enemy. Enemy.

"LET'S REBOOT," Jackson said the next morning. The smell of gas station coffee and exhaust leaked into the open car window, soothing Petrosky's shattered nerves. Tossing and turning all night had not helped his mood. Nor had the lack of breakfast, but he wasn't about to stop at a restaurant—the fewer people he had to deal with today, the better.

After Scott's call yesterday morning, he'd searched old case files and older evidence bags, scoured check-out logs, and re-examined the cases Amos had been interested in—or at least where the photos in his bedroom had originated. Nothing. Scott had been right about the convictions being clean; he should have trusted the kid, like Dr. McCallum always told him.

Samuel Amos's laptop was still with the techs, along with his phone, but so far those looked clean too. However Amos had gotten the pictures, it hadn't been through email or through his cell. They'd also scoured the neighborhood around the cemetery again, this time looking for any sign of a pair of men, a big white killer with an Arabic-speaking buddy walking around downtown at the time of the murder. No dice. And Scott hadn't found any more cases that matched the killer's MO. The closest he got were a few long-ago single-killer mob hits, but no one involved had been mumbling or speaking Arabic.

"Eden said the killer was repeating 'Enemy.' Or that someone was." Jackson tapped the steering wheel—anxious.

Like him. Maybe they'd both be on edge until they had their guy in cuffs. "So, Amos was the enemy, but we have no idea why. He might have stumbled upon a clue because of his homicide infatuation, but we can't find any evidence that he was even aware of those other related cases, aware of *this* killer—and you can't solve what you've never seen. Which means he represents something else for our suspect." *But what?* They both knew a crime of opportunity was far more likely than a planned attack.

The red Tercel behind them switched lanes, and Petrosky glanced in the side-view mirror as if expecting to see Acharya's blue Taurus following them again, that smug look on his stupid face.

He turned back to Jackson. A crime of opportunity made sense, but Amos was still "the enemy." Did the killer just hate Amos's family? "I know this case has the earmarks of a random crime, but those picketer motherfuckers—"

She snorted. "Too obvious."

"Criminals aren't always smart, and those guys have it in for the councilman."

Jackson stopped tapping. "That would mean someone from the group murdered two other people five years back. What possible reason would they have to go after the first two victims if the hits are political?"

"I didn't say *all* the hits were political." But councilmen didn't wield much power anyway—an angry blog rant, sure, but murder? It didn't fit.

She shook her head. "I hate them as much as you do, but being bigots doesn't make them killers."

"Fine." He sniffed. "We'll get a group list together anyway; copycats happen. For now, we'll explore other options."

So why else would Amos be the killer's enemy? Maybe Amos did something that night in the mausoleum, something abhorrent in the eyes of the man who'd murdered him.

Petrosky considered the rosary in Amos's desk drawer—the cross. "The cemetery, the streets surrounding...that place is rife with debauchery. Prostitution, drugs, you name it. And Samuel Amos was going at it with his girlfriend inside a mausoleum. Desecration of the dead, or at least disrespect, might make him the enemy to someone devout enough."

"A moral hit? So Amos was an enemy of...what? Religion? And the killer was just wandering around out there looking for someone behaving indecently?"

Wouldn't have to look too hard down there. Petrosky shrugged. If he'd learned anything in his decades on the force, it was that the motive only had to make sense to the murderer themselves. "Zealots believe their actions are justified."

"I'm not as worried about the killer's sensibilities—anything could be a motive. Let's focus on what we know."

Which is jack shit. "I just wish our leg work yesterday had turned something up," he said. Still, the two-killers theory was worth looking into. An accomplice standing in the shadows outside the door muttering in Arabic sounded thin, but the other man could have been a lookout. Or he was telling the killer what to do, telling him Amos was the enemy.

He squinted into the harsh yellow glare of the morning sun—too bright. "Maybe we should scope out the university after this, look at students in the last few years who match the description of our killer. Those on a foreign language track." Provided Eden's account, her one translated word, was correct—which they couldn't prove. Yet.

Jackson finally released her grip on the steering wheel and reached for her coffee. "Yeah, if we want to create a panic, let's ratchet up the xenophobia. The bigger the place you start poking around, the faster the news gets out." She sipped her coffee, winced, and put it back in the cupholder.

"Those Republic Jackoffs are already creating extra press. Our investigation isn't going to do worse than that." He grabbed his own coffee—bitter as fuck, like the last dregs in a three-day-old pot, but still better than that overpriced coffeehouse shit.

"The Crusaders of the Republic just want to harass the Amoses," Jackson said. "The father said he didn't bother reporting it in the past because he didn't want to give them more power—more attention for their cause."

"And they were more than happy to escalate their efforts the second they saw an opening, even if that opening was the brutal murder of the councilman's son." He replaced his cup and sighed. "But you're right, we don't want to give them more ammunition. And there's no racial commonality between the victims."

"But they are all American. That's what the group is leaning hard on, trying to force the terrorism angle. It's like they've never bothered to research what terrorists actually do."

"We'll just rely on your little friend Acharya to get that point across to the population at large." Though they both knew that one asshole on the internet with a click-bait head-line was worth more than hard facts.

"I hate that this feels like a witch hunt."

"We're still looking for a burly white guy who knows the area." Just one who spoke Arabic, and from the state of his worn-to-the-ground boots, one who probably didn't have the funds to attend the university. He wasn't likely to have an Arabic-speaking parent if he was still stumbling over his words five years back, and if the killer had learned overseas, say, during a stint in the military, it wasn't likely he'd be wandering around practicing. Their killer should stick out like a giant pale thumb. So why couldn't they find him?

Jackson wheeled into the community center and braked hard enough to lock Petrosky's seat belt.

The community center downtown offered drop-in Arabic classes twice a week, so there was a decent possibility someone learning to speak might have shown up here. Petrosky tucked the folder with the sketch beneath his arm and followed Jackson across the broiling lot, wiping sweat from the back of his neck. Arabic met every Tuesday and Thursday evening at six o'clock, but the same teacher presided over an English as a second language course at ten o'clock—as luck would have it—today.

A slight woman in a blue dress stood at the blackboard at the far side of the room scribbling English verbs in chalk: run, walk, speak. Her black hair shone, glossy in the overhead fluorescents.

Petrosky approached up the center aisle, clearing his throat. "Ami Satou?"

She turned. "Yes?" Her voice was low and thick, no trace of any accent that he could hear. The main office said she'd been teaching on and off for the last six years, but she looked so...young. Thin, with a bird-like bone structure and dark wide-set eyes. When they shook, her tiny fingers were cool but firm and gritty with chalk.

Jackson flashed her badge. Satou's face did not change, lip still curled, her gaze steady if not dull. Perfectly composed. She remained still when Petrosky pulled the sketch of Amos's killer from the folder, the one Eden had helped with. "Do you recognize this man? Maybe from your Arabic classes?"

She glanced at the image. "No, I can't say I do. But it's a bit generic, isn't it?"

"I agree, all white guys look alike."

Jackson shot an elbow into his ribs, earning raised eyebrows from Satou.

"Why are you looking for this man? Should I be worried?"

Petrosky slid the sketch back into the folder, his ribs smarting. "We just need to talk to him. If he should show up here, call us, but don't approach him. He could be dangerous."

Satou's composure shifted—for a moment, the corners of her lips turned down, and fear glinted in her eyes, but her anxiety vanished just as quickly. "Why do you think he'd come here? Is it...a domestic violence thing? Is he after someone from the class?"

"Nothing like that. We think he may have been a student, especially in years past—we were hoping a big white guy learning Arabic might stick out."

She crossed her arms, smudging one dark sleeve with chalk. "I don't think so. I've had quite a few white men in that class, just none who look like...your picture. Most of them are older teenagers going into the military, and I have an elderly student too—wants to be able to communicate with his daughter-in-law's family. It's very sweet."

Petrosky tucked the folder under his arm. "We'll need a list of your students, ideally going back five or six years." When their killer would have been speaking more hesitantly.

"I don't take attendance. It's a free class, not for college credit or anything." She looked off into the distance, thinking. "I do know first names for half the current class, probably. Last names for a few more. I can write those down, or you could always come back later this week, visit the class itself. Although..." Satou sucked her lower lip between her teeth. "I'm not sure what city he works out of, but do you know a Larry Babcock? I think he's a cop—came to my Arabic class in uniform a few times, had his name on his pocket. They have a study group, so he might know some more people if you don't want to wait."

Babcock...Babcock. Why did that sound so famil—

Oh shit.

Captain Shock. The officer who was first on the Amos crime scene. And his partner, Khoury...was he Indian? Or Middle Eastern? Petrosky and Jackson exchanged a look. Babcock was definitely a big guy—not the hulking beast Eden Johansson had described, but anyone would look bigger lurking in the dark, especially when they had just twisted your boyfriend's head half off. And all Babcock and Khoury would have had to do was run out the opposite way Eden was headed, get into the patrol car, and drive around to the front of the cemetery.

Cops helping a lady in distress. What a perfect cover.

11

"WELL, THAT WAS EASY," Petrosky muttered, climbing back into Jackson's SUV.

"Too easy. If it was Babcock who killed Amos, Johansson would have recognized him when they pulled up in front of Whispering Willows."

"It was dark. She barely got a backward glance as she ran away." And if she met Babcock three minutes later on the street out in front, in full uniform, what were the odds she'd connect the two? She'd been in shock. Even if she suspected for a moment, she could have talked herself out of it— because it was insane.

"You think he'll show?" Jackson asked, flying up Main toward the precinct, the whizzing of the tires a low drone against Petrosky's spine.

"Oh, he'll show. I told him we needed him at the station within the hour because we had a lead."

She whirled on him. "That's what you said? If he's the killer, he'll leave town, not show up to the precinct."

"He won't leave." Petrosky sniffed. "I told him we had a

suspect in custody and that he forgot to sign his paperwork. If he did it, he'll be thrilled he managed to pull this shit off."

Jackson turned back to the road, her fingers tapping on the wheel—faster than earlier.

A convenience store approached on the right, neon signs promising "Beer" and "Liquor" from the plate glass. Petrosky dragged his gaze away—tried to ignore the way his mouth watered, just a little. Up ahead, someone had tossed a pair of tennis shoes over the electrical lines, usually representing a past gang hit or a willing nearby drug dealer, but he wasn't sure which applied here. Maybe both. Probably both.

He closed his eyes and listened to the steady hiss of the Escalade's tires against the heat-scorched asphalt, punctuated with far too many *thunk-thuds*. Amos had gotten those crime scene photos from someone in the Ash Park precinct. Babcock had been taking Arabic classes, the language spoken by the killer. Assuming Babcock was their guy... What possible reason did he have to kill Amos? Maybe Babcock had refused to get more photos, and Amos had threatened him with exposure, but that wasn't a motive for murder; Babcock wouldn't even get jail time for stealing pictures.

Unless Amos had come across some other wrongdoing worth talking about—and worth killing over. But no, a cop would know better than to leave a witness. A cop would know better than to attack when there was someone else around at all. If Babcock was providing Amos with photos, he could have gotten the kid to meet him anywhere. Why wait until Amos was in a cemetery with his girlfriend and ambush them? And those two other murders in the past—had he tried to copycat them to cover his tracks, or was he responsible for all three?

"Ass Master" blared from Petrosky's cell, and he swore under his breath, squinting at the screen: Scott.

"Better news!"

This fucking kid. Sounded like he had just taken three shots of that espresso Jackson liked.

"Out with it, Scott."

"I found calls from Amos's landline to Babcock's cell. Really sorry, Detective."

"Kid, you have nothing to be sorry—"

"Stupid. I didn't think to check the landline—high school and college kids usually use their cells for everything. I won't make that mistake again."

"I'm sure you won't." Petrosky smiled into the phone. "You got dates on the calls for me?"

"I sure do. And each time, the same week the calls took place, Amos pulled money from an ATM right up the road from the precinct, three hundred dollars a pop, a total of twelve times."

Petrosky sighed. "Rich kids."

Jackson raised an eyebrow as she wheeled into the precinct lot in a spray of pebbled concrete.

"Right? And in those ATM weeks, each and every time, Babcock was in the file room—once I knew who and when I was looking for, it was a piece of cake. He's almost never in the file room otherwise. Now, he never signed out the boxes the photos came from but…"

All Babcock had to do was sign in with a legitimate sounding request, make sure no one else was around, and pull the wrong files or boxes. They weren't as vigilant as they should be—no, they didn't have as much personnel as they should have. Petrosky had taken advantage of that himself on more than one occasion, but it was a huge pain in the ass when someone else did it.

At least they knew where Amos had gotten the pictures. Though now it was looking more like Babcock was just playing shocked when he saw Amos's lifeless body—maybe he wasn't surprised in the least.

Jackson was watching him, hand on the door handle, obviously waiting for an update. He pointed out the windshield toward the precinct. Babcock was already here, heading for the doors with that too-many-dumbbell-curls swagger.

Jackson shook her head. "Pompous bastard."

"Him, or me?"

"Both."

Petrosky stuck the phone back in his pocket. "Take me up the road for some more coffee. I want to let him sweat a minute."

"Afternoon, Officer Babcock." Petrosky grinned and eased himself into the seat across the stainless table, the same one where he'd interrogated Simmons the day before last. He set his bitter Rita's coffee in front of him. He'd had a donut on the way back, too, and dammit, he'd earned it, especially if he managed to leave tonight with Babcock in a cell.

Babcock crossed his arms over his chest—broad chest, arms and wrists thick like his neck, hands that might be strong enough to crack a kid's spine. "You said you needed me here right away. I dropped everything." He was practically pouting.

"You got a hot date?" Petrosky leaned closer, watching Babcock's face morph into a half-grin. "Or maybe you're worried you'll be late to your Arabic lessons over at the community center."

The man's brow furrowed. He leaned back in his seat.

"Why don't you tell me about that, Officer? You fascinated by world languages or what?" He could feel Jackson's eyes on him from behind the mirrored glass that connected them to the adjoining room.

"I...I guess." Babcock frowned. "I thought you had a suspect in custody. Is there something I need to sign?"

"And this sketch..." Petrosky slid the drawing of their suspect from his file. "It does kinda look like you."

Babcock smiled like it was a joke, either unworried or without feelings altogether. "Looks like a million other people too. You guys really could have done better with that one."

Petrosky tapped his index against the composite sketch, right between the eyes, silence stretching until Babcock raised an eyebrow. "You're being...weird, Detective."

"You ain't seen nothing yet." Petrosky sipped his coffee, his gaze never leaving Babcock's face. The hairs between his shoulders bristled.

Babcock broke the staring contest first and shook his head. "People warned me about you, Petrosky. I know you like to fuck around." He smiled again, but it was strained. "Just level with me, cop to cop—what's this all about?"

I'll give you cop to cop, fucker. "Tell me about Samuel Amos."

"What about him?" But his eyes had narrowed. "I didn't know him, what are you—"

"Oh, but you did know him." In a hissing rustle of papers, Petrosky replaced the composite sketch with the information Scott had printed for him and pointed to the third line. "This is a cash withdrawal using Amos's ATM card. Right up the road from the precinct."

Babcock glanced at the page and back up at Petrosky. He shrugged. "And?"

Petrosky smiled in a way he hoped looked predatory, because he sure felt like a fox on the hunt. A chubby, easily irritated fox...no, maybe a raccoon. He even had the under-eye circles.

"You met Amos on each of these days. Gave him some photos."

Babcock's jaw tensed. "I don't know what you're talking about." But his knuckles were white.

"Did you know there are traffic cams on the east corner of Main?"

"What's that—"

Petrosky lifted the coffee cup to his lips, making sure the "Rita's" logo was facing Babcock, and watched realization dawn in the man's blue eyes. If Amos had come toward the station from the ATM, and Babcock had headed toward Amos from the precinct, they would have crossed paths somewhere in the middle—the restaurant would have been a convenient meeting place. There were traffic cams that pointed right at that intersection, practically right at Rita's front door. The cameras had been broken for months, but Petrosky was betting Babcock didn't know that.

"I also have the records from the evidence lockers," Petrosky said.

"I didn't sign—"

"You and I both know that no matter what you signed out, you gave Samuel Amos those pictures. Made a nice little chunk of change for it too: thirty-six hundred bucks."

Babcock stared for a moment, nostrils flaring, then sighed so heavily Petrosky felt the breeze clear across the table. "I didn't think…it mattered. All those old cases, they were already closed, I didn't see the harm. I made sure not to give him anything active."

"I'm not especially worried about you stealing the photos. I'm much more worried about why Samuel Amos deserved to die."

Babcock's head reared back—well, as far as it could with that bull neck of his. "What?"

"Did he ask for something you couldn't provide? Threaten to tell on you? Or did he find something you didn't want him to in his personal investigations?"

"What the…" Babcock was barely breathing. "You can't be serious, I didn't—"

Switch lines. Keep him off balance. "How did you manage to change back into your uniform before you drove around to pick up Eden Johansson?"

Babcock's hands shook so hard his fingertips vibrated against the tabletop. "Back into my uniform? We were on patrol. I didn't change my clothes."

"Then why didn't Eden notice your badge when you were busy killing her boyfriend?"

And there was that shocked face again—wide eyes, gaping jaw, nostrils flaring as if he were trying in vain to suck in more air. "What are you—I told you, we were out on patrol, and we heard her screaming."

"And you drove over right away. Khoury stayed with the girl, and you ran as fast as you could out to the mausoleum and still managed not to see a damn thing."

The man's face reddened. His fists clenched. Looked like Officer Babcock had a temper. "That wasn't my fault! The killer had to be running off while the girl was running to the street! He was probably gone before we even saw her."

"Fascinating that you managed to get there so quick, too. Right place, right time?" Petrosky leaned back in his chair.

"For the last time, we were on patro—"

"How many white guys out there you think speak Arabic?" He could almost hear Jackson in his head: *You're going to give him whiplash.*

"I…no idea. What—"

"Here's the thing, Babcock; it turns out that our killer was speaking Arabic just before he twisted little Sammy's head around." It was also possible that Khoury was in the shadows outside the mausoleum—the second voice. That whole two-voice thing was still bothering Petrosky, sending little needles into the base of his brain.

Babcock shot upright and raised both palms. "Wait...the gibberish she was talking about was a real language?"

"You tell me, dickhead."

"I didn't know the killer was speaking Arabic, I swear! She said he was just mumbling nonsense!"

Petrosky wanted to jump on that, wanted to jump right down Babcock's throat, but it was probably true. Eden Johansson had told Petrosky and Jackson the same in the ambulance.

"Oh god, I can't believe..." Babcock's jaw was working overtime. "I didn't do this, my god, Detective. I know how it looks, but I swear to you, I—"

"Explain something to me, Babcock. I get why you stole the pictures. You won't get off the hook for it, but I get it—it's a lot of cash. But why were you taking language lessons? Khoury speaks English; it isn't like you two have any trouble communicating." He wasn't even sure Khoury spoke Arabic, but it seemed like a good guess, and on this point, Petrosky was lost. Sure, Amos might have been the enemy if he'd discovered some secret of Babcock's, but why mutter it in Arabic while you were murdering the kid? Just so the witness wouldn't know what you were saying? Easier to keep your fucking mouth closed altogether, and Babcock didn't seem to have issues doing that. He might be a dick, but he wasn't insane.

Babcock's face paled, eggshell to ash. "Okay, it was a little bit of a goof."

Petrosky stared at him, then said slowly, "You were learning an entire language as a goof?"

Babcock looked at his shoes. His decidedly not-size-eleven shoes—twelves, maybe. Petrosky eyed his coffee. Maybe he should have held off on that celebratory donut.

"No, I mean...okay, so sometimes Khoury talks to his wife in Arabic when we're out on patrol. On his cell. And I know they're saying dirty things, but he kept on because I couldn't speak it. So I started with this class, and now I can harass him about it and..." He was practically hyperventilating.

"What?"

"His sister's real pretty."

Khoury's...sister? "You're learning Arabic to impress a woman?"

Babcock looked at his shoes again. Which was answer enough.

12

"That fucking dipshit." Petrosky dropped into his chair, the bullpen buzzing around him. He set his Rita's cup beside yesterday's coffee that was still sitting on the desktop, pulled out his cell, and texted Scott. Hopefully, the kid was finished putting together the case files for the earlier crimes.

"He'll get his for screwing with evidence," Jackson said, plopping down beside him.

"He'll get a slap on the goddamn wrist." Petrosky knocked his stale coffee into the trash and rested his heavy head in his palms. He'd barely closed his eyes when Decantor laughed from the other side of the bullpen. Did that man ever go out on the beat? How was his solve rate so high when he spent all his time jabbering with his buddies in the bullpen? "I just can't believe it."

"You wanted it to be him."

"Yeah, I did." Not necessarily Babcock, but...someone. Someone they could take off the street and lock away, a face they could point to and say to the Amoses: "This is the man who killed your son, and we will make him pay."

Thud, thud, thud. Petrosky raised his head. Decantor, big

guy, bigger mouth. He smiled at Petrosky with a million gleaming white teeth.

"You got the latest gossip on the Kardashians or what?"

"The chief's looking for you."

Petrosky glanced at the clock on the wall, the kind with hands that kids today didn't even know how to read—three-fifteen. "Why didn't Carroll call me?"

"Same reason I'm fielding calls from your witness. Eden Johansson called once yesterday and twice today to ask if you caught the guy, but she didn't have any new information for you. I asked." Decantor reached down and touched the phone cradle—knocked it back onto the hook.

Oh yeah. Petrosky shrugged. "Just avoiding the journalists. It's been a long week already." They'd touch base with Johansson later, though. See how she was holding up.

"Thanks, Decantor," Jackson said, and the big man nodded to her, but there was a softness in his gaze that Petrosky had never seen before. Oh god…were Decantor and Jackson a thing? He opened his mouth to ask, but Jackson was already pushing herself to standing. "Let's get this over with."

Right. Probably better not to know…unless Decantor's Kardashian-loving ass hurt his partner, in which case—

Later.

"Fucking Babcock," Petrosky muttered.

"We should have called Internal Affairs."

"Fuck that. We're neck deep in a murder investigation, we can't deal with those stupid shits." The hall seemed longer than usual, and Petrosky's body heavier than it had been when he'd awoken as if every ounce of irritation had suctioned itself to his flesh. Probably the donut. Or Decantor. Or knowing he was about to get an ass reaming.

The door to the chief's office was open.

"Well, well, well, look who it is." Chief Carroll crossed her arms, her normally unlined forehead creased with agitation.

"You keep that up, your face will stay like that." Petrosky closed the door behind them and plopped into the chair across from the chief's desk. Jackson slid into the seat beside him.

Carroll's nostrils flared. "Did you see the news today?"

The news? He glanced at Jackson, who was pulling out her cell, face drawn. *Babcock already get a spot on primetime?*

He shook his head. "Nah, I like my news the way I like my journalists. Nonexistent."

Carroll's jaw flexed like she wanted to rip out his throat. "What the hell did you guys do?"

He shrugged. "Lots of shit. But I have no idea what I'm in trouble for right now."

"Stop being cute. There have been two attacks on the Muslim community in the last eight hours. One mosque tagged up with Nazi symbols, one Muslim grocery owner beaten outside his apartment."

"Welcome to my world," Jackson muttered, eyes still on her phone, probably scrolling for the stories Carroll was referring to. "My kids…kid…can't even wear a hoodie."

Was her voice shaking, just a little? Petrosky turned back to the chief, swallowing over the lump in his throat. "Are the attacks connected to the Jackoff Republic?"

"They're not taking credit, but my money's on the Crusaders of the Republic, yes—or their followers."

"We have any in custody?"

"Not yet. But we've got people looking into it. Good people." She suddenly looked exhausted.

Petrosky frowned. "I'm still not sure how we're getting blamed for this, Chief."

"These acts of violence appear to be related to a news article that came out online this morning. The piece claims that the murder at the Whispering Willows mausoleum was an act of terrorism."

She leveled a hard gaze at him, but Petrosky shook his head and said, "We have absolutely no reason to think that this is connected to extremist activity, and we haven't told anyone otherwise."

"Did you tell anyone that the killer was speaking Arabic?"

Fucking Acharya, that lying journalist piece of shit. Fire bloomed in his guts and spread to his chest.

"There's no reason to think that our sources would have printed that information," Jackson said, but her voice was too high, too tight, and her fingers were talons around her cell. "The story appears to be originating through the far right-wing channels. Maybe one of the protesters overheard something."

Which was bullshit. No one, including Petrosky and Jackson, had even known the killer was speaking a real language until they'd talked to Eden Johansson at the Amoses's, and afterward, they'd gone straight to the car. They hadn't said a word to anyone, let alone the guys waving picket signs, though Petrosky had let his middle finger do a little talking.

"Overheard it?" Carroll's face was nearly purple—he could feel the tension radiating from her seated form. Prickly. "How the fuck would any of those protestors—"

"Listen, I told Jackson we should shoot them, but she wouldn't let me." Petrosky sniffed. "You ask me, she's soft on crime, but I can—"

Carroll shot to her feet. "Shut the fuck up, Petrosky." She turned a cold eye on Jackson and leaned over the desk. "You find out how this happened. And you say one more goddamn word to the press, I will have your badge, because I know it wasn't Petrosky's suspicious ass."

"You don't know that for sure. I could surprise you," Petrosky said.

She turned his way. "And don't think for one moment that you're off the hook for Babcock. As soon as Khoury realized what was happening, he was in my office complaining about you. Expect a call from IA."

"I'm looking forward to it." Petrosky stood. "But just so we're clear, if I don't shoot the Jackoffs, can I shoot Babcock instead?"

"Get out of my office."

"Soft on crime, all of you." But for once, he did as he was told.

13

OUT IN THE HALLWAY, Jackson let out a breath as if she'd been holding it the entire time she was in the chief's office.

"Want me to go punch Acharya in the dick?" Petrosky said. Their footsteps echoed down the hall.

"If dick punching was the way to solve this, I'd do it myself. Your old ass isn't going to scare anyone." But her jaw looked hard enough to crack granite. "This isn't Acharya. I just…it doesn't seem right, does it?"

"It's fucked up, but I wouldn't put it past the man. He's a dirty rotten journalist, and he followed us for ten miles with a dude locked in his trunk."

"Simmons was passed out in Acharya's backseat. By choice."

"Whatever. Acharya's a fucking tool."

The air in the bullpen felt lighter than that in the hall, and oddly silent, as if the whole room had been waiting for them to come back from getting reamed. But only Decantor was at his desk, nose in his files, writing furiously.

"A tool, sure, but he had an exclusive if he kept his mouth shut for a few days," Jackson said.

She had Petrosky there. Why would Acharya give that up just to print that the killer spoke a few words in Arabic? It'd lose him any clout he had with the department—and he cared about clout. *I never give up my sources.*

"I'll be back in an hour," Jackson said. "Need anything?"

A cheeseburger? The metabolism of a twenty-year-old? A stick to beat Babcock with? "No thanks."

She left him at his desk, and he booted up the computer, an old bullshit PC that didn't hold a candle to the Mac Scott had helped him pick out for his house. He took the last cold slug from his Rita's coffee cup and turned his attention to the case file on his desktop. Huh. It looked heavier, thicker than it had before they'd gone to the chief's office, and...it was. Scott must have been here. He flipped open the file.

As Jackson had said, there were two earlier killings that matched the MO on the Amos murder: one near the cemetery, back behind the willow trees, and the other a few blocks up, in the alley behind a rave-style nightclub. The nightclub was abandoned now, the owners tired of fighting warrants, but dealers and working girls still walked the alley behind the Ragdoll.

He flipped the page. The first crime scene photo showed a broad-shouldered man on his belly, head facing the wrong way—Gerald Polluck, a thirty-two year old domestic abuser and former Marine. He had kidnapped his wife and taken her down behind the cemetery to show her where she'd end up if she went through with their divorce. Then he'd raped her for good measure. In the statement Mrs. Polluck had given to police:

I wish I could watch him kill that motherfucker a second time.

Touching. He read on.

Mrs. Polluck had been out in the open, back when there

were streetlamps in that section of the cemetery—she should have been able to see the man who'd pulled her husband off her. But she'd given a vague description, nothing outside of stocky, strong, and blond. And the second victim, the one from the alley...she'd refused to give a description at all.

Listed as Nicki Vasquez, the woman had been walking behind the Ragdoll club when a man she did not recognize attacked her from behind, threw her into the garbage beside the dumpster, and attempted to rape her. He slammed her head against the concrete, ripped her underwear, and was prying her legs open when he was torn off her by another man she "did not see," though she'd been able to describe her attempted rapist in explicit detail. A working girl had found Vasquez's would-be attacker dead in the alley with his head turned halfway around, and called police without realizing Vasquez was unconscious behind the dumpster. The ID in her shoe was used to admit her to the hospital, and they'd managed to get a few questions in before she vanished from the ICU. Her driver's license was a fake, of course. The real Nicki Vasquez had answered the phone when they'd tried to track the woman down.

He swept his empty Rita's cup into the trash. No obvious connections between the murder victims—different races and ages, which they already knew. But the attacks took place in the same general area, and now, with the more complete case files Scott had provided, it seemed clear all the victims were on top of a woman at the time of the murder. The suspect could be a vigilante, patrolling the neighborhood, saving women from attack. But with Samuel Amos, he'd made a mistake.

Petrosky drummed his fingers on the case files, frowning at his blank computer screen. Eden Johansson hadn't been in danger, but the first two victims *had* been saved by the man in question—by the killer. Those women had a debt to him.

Maybe they'd protected him by not revealing his identity. He couldn't talk to Mrs. Polluck, who had died in a car wreck three years ago, but the woman formerly known as Nicki Vasquez…fake name, but back then, would she have worried whether her savior was caught, if he was okay? And if so, might she have called the station? Eden Johansson had called here three times in as many days, and she hated the guy—he thought. Decantor had even noted each call in the file, that perfectionist bastard.

He flipped to the section on the second killing. Much thinner than the first. The detectives hadn't pushed the investigation too far—without cooperative witnesses, they'd have been unlikely to get a conviction. Then again, without Amos, without the death of an innocent kid, maybe Petrosky would have let it slide too.

At least the last detectives had kept phone logs. Around a dozen calls noted, though most appeared to be random tips, with numbers that matched the area code downtown—probably the woman who had found the body behind the Ragdoll, or other working girls anxious about a killer in their midst. None looked to have panned out. But two calls piqued his interest: *Anonymous female caller, asked if killer had been apprehended.* One number seemed to match that of an earlier tip where the caller reported seeing the suspect hitchhiking, but a witness trying to hide wouldn't call that often, and definitely not with tips to find the killer unless she was trying to throw them off—which seemed far-fetched. But the other… He had a date and a time, and half a penciled phone number where it hadn't been rubbed off in the paper's crease. Would that be enough? Not for him, but maybe enough for Scott.

He snatched the desk phone from the cradle. "Hey, kid, got a job for you." Out of the corner of his eye, he saw Jackson re-enter the bullpen—coffees, thank god. But why did she have three?

"Tell me," Scott said, and Petrosky did and listened to the kid's fingers clicking over the keyboard. "Give me three minutes..." *Clack-clackity-clack.* "Dad's asking about you, by the way."

Jackson stopped by Decantor's desk, and the big man put his pen aside, looked up at her, and said something that made her laugh. Fucking Decantor. Probably some shit about Britney Spears. Was Britney still a thing?

"I'll be over this week, okay?" Petrosky said, watching Jackson set the extra coffee on Decantor's desk. "Tell your dad I'll bring some of those pork rinds he likes."

The typing stopped, then started again. "Neither of you needs to be eating pork rinds."

Maybe not, but cancer had been trying to kill Scott's father, George, for a long time, and he was finally in remission as of six weeks ago. What better way to celebrate than pork rinds? It was how Petrosky had celebrated surviving his heart attack. Well, that and watching a sadistic murderer's brains explode into red mist. "If I bring tofu, he'll kick my ass."

"True enough." Scott laughed. "Want to hold one more minute?"

"Nah, call me back."

Petrosky dropped the phone back in the cradle as Jackson set his coffee beside him and practically fell into the chair.

"Don't you have a desk, Jackson?" What was it with his partners and space issues? He not only had to share a car, but he practically had to share his fucking seat.

She propped her feet on the desktop, narrowly missing the file folder...and his steaming coffee. "It wasn't Acharya. It was Barnes."

Petrosky felt eyes on him; he glanced over at Decantor who promptly looked away. "Barnes didn't tell us anything about someone speaking Arabic," Petrosky said. "He didn't even know."

"Nope, he just said they were brown. And when he was talking to Loni Trumbull, that's what he told her. Brown with a little wiener dog."

"Loni...the redhead who's always on basic cable blabbering about Mexicans?"

"That's the one. She visited the group home after us, got Barnes to go on some social media live-stream bullshit. Probably paid him well, or well enough; hell, he might have done it for a meatball sub. But the only one who said anything about the language was Loni herself."

"Who told her? That information had to come from somewhere."

"She says no. That it wasn't a stretch to assume the brown-skinned man was a foreigner and that Mexican or Muslim were the most obvious choices."

"She just pulled it out of her ass?" But she hadn't, not exactly. She'd told her audience what they wanted to hear.

"Yeah. Then she asked me why the police weren't taking it more seriously. Why we'd rather let terrorists walk than actually do our jobs." Jackson shrugged. "I told her we'd be down to pick her up. Suspicion of being an accomplice because of the inside information."

"She lawyer up already?"

"I'm sure. She gets sued twice a week." Jackson sipped her coffee and winced. "Shit. Hot."

"I kinda want to punch Acharya anyway." He glanced over when his partner didn't respond. Jackson was chewing on her lip. "Maybe if you buy Decantor more coffee, he'll pick Loni up for us. He definitely will if you buy him dinner." Though she might have done that already.

She blinked. Gaze steady. Jaw relaxed.

Hmm.

The desk phone jangled—shrill—and Petrosky jumped. Jackson laughed. "Not used to answering that, eh?"

"Better than that 'Ass Master' bullshit." He pulled the bulky receiver to his ear.

"Best news!" Scott said. "I've got you a cell. And a name."

Petrosky smiled. "I'll bring you some pork rinds too, kid. You've earned them."

14

TRINA LAYTON, formerly known as Nicki Vasquez, had veins like roadmaps on her pale arms and the gaunt cheekbones of a horror movie ghost. But the cheekbones looked purposeful; her face was heavily painted in shades of beige, her eyelids done in blacks and purples that you wouldn't find on even the most sleep-deprived beat cop. Tarantula lashes.

Layton narrowed her eyes at Jackson through the crack in the door. Nice building, a block of new condos in Ann Arbor. She hadn't disengaged the sliding lock yet, which in her line of work, was probably wise. "Can I help you?"

"Ash Park PD, ma'am," Jackson said. "May we come in?"

Layton's face hardened into a million painted lines of pastel stone.

"This is not about you." Petrosky stepped up behind Jackson, hand on the door, and met Layton's gaze. "We don't care about what you do, or more specifically, who you do." Jackson's arm tensed like she wanted to punch him, but he kept his eyes on Layton. "We need your help. The guy who stopped your attacker five years ago…he might be in trouble."

"What attacker? I don't know anything about—"

"Alley behind the Ragdoll." The folder Petrosky'd tucked beneath his arm felt heavy. "You watched a man get his neck snapped."

Layton's eyes cleared, but her brow remained furrowed—suspicious. "You really think he might be…" She sighed.

"We know he saved your life," Jackson said. "Let us return the favor. We need to find him before anyone else gets hurt."

The door swung shut.

Jackson rolled her eyes. "So much for tha—"

The sliding lock clanked. Then the door opened, and Layton stepped back and waved them in.

Every surface in Trina Layton's home was as meticulous as her face. They followed her through the foyer into an ultra-modern living room done up in light gray leather, with gray walls, gray cabinets, even gray throw pillows. Weirdly reminiscent of Mr. Johansson's persona, except these had style. Hopefully she didn't touch anything with her face, or there'd be splotches of beige and purple everywhere.

They sat across from one another in the open kitchen. Layton's eyes stayed tight on the other side of the table, maybe trying not to look at the folder he'd laid on the gray wood. "So what's going on? Did you find the man who…the guy who saved me?"

"Not yet. And for the record, we understand why you ran," Jackson said. "I wouldn't have stayed either, in your place."

Layton frowned and drew her eyes to Petrosky. "I thought you said he was in troub—"

"He's a hero, I get it," Petrosky said. "If he just took out rapists, I probably wouldn't even bother looking for him. He's doing our job for us, really."

Jackson glanced his way—she probably knew he wasn't kidding.

"But this time, he killed an innocent kid, Ms. Layton. College student at the park with his girlfriend."

Layton's lips tightened—disgust? At Petrosky or the murder?

"We think he might have been coerced," Petrosky continued. "That someone else might be urging him to harm people."

Jackson raised an eyebrow—*Use your poker face, Jackson, Jesus Christ*—but there weren't any laws against lying, and he'd tell Layton anything if it helped lead them to their killer. Then again...maybe the coercion theory wasn't totally unreasonable. Though they had no leads on a single killer, let alone a pair.

Petrosky turned back to Layton, whose pinky finger was vibrating against the gray wood. *What do you know?* "Do you remember anyone else there with him?" he asked. "Someone in the background behind him, maybe?"

She looked at her watch—gold, tiny diamonds glittering around the face—and blinked. "No. There was no one else."

"Maybe someone muttering in the background? Farther down the alley, telling him what to do? Maybe saying something you didn't understand?"

"I...no, there was just him. One man. But he was talking in two languages."

There went their two-killer theory.

"You're sure?" Jackson said.

"Of course I'm sure, why wouldn't I be—"

"Because when you gave your statement, you said you didn't see anything or hear anything other than him stumbling over his words." Jackson leaned over the table so far that Layton sat back in her chair, sliding her hands into her lap. "It's weird that you remember so much more now."

Her eyes glittered, defiance, but also...intelligence. "They would have arrested me if I'd stayed around to chat. Now the statute of limitations for both prostitution and solicitation is up."

"Maybe you just didn't want him to get in trouble," Petrosky said softly.

"He saved me." Her lip trembled ever so slightly.

Petrosky put his hand on Jackson's arm, and nodded to her. His partner relaxed back in her gray chair as he turned to Layton. "I understand why you'd want to protect him. But we have to protect the innocent people out there. And while he might be doing a lot of good, he made a mistake." He opened the folder and pulled a photo from it, the only thing he'd brought: Samuel Amos, high school graduation, grinning for eternity. "He didn't deserve to die, Ms. Layton. Please help us before anyone else gets killed."

Layton stared at Amos, his smiling face, eyes bright with hope, with life. She sniffed and paused so long he thought she might refuse to answer, but then she cleared her throat. "It was dark, so I didn't see him well. Light hair, cut real short. And he was...big. Muscular." She shook her head. "He saved me, you know? He really did."

That much was true, but he sure hadn't saved Samuel Amos. "What about what he said? You told the officers he was speaking in two languages, stumbling over the words." The other witnesses had identified it as gibberish.

"Yes, two languages. And I know exactly what he said." She blinked. "He said he wasn't the enemy."

He wasn't *the enemy?* His heart quickened. That enemy thing hadn't been released to the public. But why say that? If Petrosky were trying to calm someone down, he'd say, "it's okay," or "I won't hurt you," but never "I am not the enemy." Petrosky watched Layton's face for a twitch of the brow, a tremble in the lips, anything to indicate uncertainty, but she stared back, unblinking. Resolved. "What were his exact words?"

"That's it. He said, 'I am not the enemy.'"

I am not the enemy.

"He said it over and over," Layton said, "even if he did kinda…stumble sometimes. Like he was confused. Dazed, you know?"

Jackson cocked her head. "So you speak Arabic?"

"I speak lots of languages." Layton crossed her arms, eyes locked on Petrosky's.

"Where'd you learn?" Jackson asked.

Layton finally drew her gaze to Jackson, a hooded sultry kind of look, the kind you'd give…a john. "I know all kinds of men, Detective. You think I can't be smart enough to understand them all?"

"You're fluent in Arabic from the streets?"

The sultry look vanished—replaced with venom. "Okay, you're right. Okay? I'm not fluent. But I can tell what language it is, and I know swear words, the…dirty stuff too." Her nostrils flared. "In this industry, it pays to know if they're calling you a pretty little bitch or an ugly cunt. It's the nasty ones that hurt you on purpose—better to be prepared." Her jaw had hardened. Angry. And it sounded like she had a damn good reason. "So, yeah, I recognized the language, like I'd recognize French or German. And after…I kept hearing him—his voice, you know? On repeat, even in my dreams. I finally looked it up."

Sounded like a traumatic reaction, replaying certain moments over and over. "Did he say anything else?" Petrosky asked.

Her gaze dropped to her lap, her shoulders tight. "He was…I guess he was muttering a little too." She bit her lip. "But in English."

Petrosky waited. Layton was definitely keeping something back.

"He…he might have said to be quiet." She raised her head

once more and put her hands back on the table, palms down. Short, neat nails; understated, unlike the rest of her. "But I'm sure it was just because he was freaked out over what happened, didn't want anyone to hear."

She was talking like she was defending him—what had he said that needed defending? Then again, their perp had been muttering in the willows too...which Simmons had heard. Maybe Layton had heard the same thing.

"Did he call you a name?"

She averted her gaze.

"Trina?"

"Be quiet, bitch. Okay? He said, 'Be quiet, bitch.'"

This isn't right. "Be quiet, bitch" *and* "I am not the enemy"? Those phrases felt at odds, though whether he called them names or not, he clearly didn't see the female witnesses as enemies. He had saved Layton. And Mrs. Polluck. He'd probably thought he was saving Eden Johansson too.

But he'd been wrong.

15

DOCTOR WOOLVERTON WAS a thin little twerp with thick, green-framed glasses and a permanent prissy sneer as if he were trying like hell to get his ass kicked. When Petrosky entered the morgue, Woolverton shoved his glasses up the bridge of his nose.

"What do you have for me, Doc?"

Woolverton eyed him suspiciously—nothing new there— then dropped his gaze to the dead kid. Samuel Amos, laid out on the stainless steel table on his belly, head turned to the side in almost the same position as it'd been when Petrosky first saw him in the mausoleum, though Woolverton had closed his eyes with a tiny stitch beneath each eyelid.

And his neck...shit. At the mausoleum, Petrosky had noted the bulging bones beneath the skin, but in the brilliant glare of Woolverton's examination lights, the rearrangement of the bones was a horror show, like gnarled arthritic knuckles. The now-stitched incision Woolverton had made down the spine didn't help. Black. Angry.

"Fracture of the C-1 vertebrae," Woolverton said. "Would

have affected his ability to breathe and speak right away, and caused loss of bowel and bladder control."

"The witness said he was still moaning when she ran out." Petrosky bent to peer at the bruising around the kid's ears. Fingertips. Palm. "Were there two injuries?"

"Two inju—"

"Well, he was still alive and moaning when she left. Did the killer wrench him around a second time, or did he die from the initial injury?" He wasn't sure why it mattered; either way they were dealing with a man who clearly wanted Amos dead, but maybe the suspect had some fun watching the kid struggle to breathe. Or maybe he put him out of his misery right away.

Woolverton shook his head so hard his glasses slipped down his sharp nose once more. "One injury. If your witness heard him moaning, it would have stopped shortly. A fracture this severe…the suffering didn't go on for more than a few minutes." Woolverton sniffed. "Small miracle, I suppose, that he didn't suffer long—even if he'd lived, he would have been a vegetable."

Petrosky's gaze dropped to the bulging disks in Amos's neck. He closed his eyes a beat longer than a blink and refocused on the ME.

Woolverton pursed his lips, but they relaxed as he said, "The girlfriend called the office here earlier today. If you talk to her, let her know he was gone fast. And that there wasn't anything she could have done to save him."

What the hell? "You didn't tell her that when she called?" *Thought you'd extend her suffering for fun, asshole?*

"I didn't know. I hadn't completed my exam yet. Busy week, unfortunately."

Petrosky narrowed his eyes at Woolverton, but the man's steady gaze softened the tightness in Petrosky's shoulders.

The Medical Examiner might be a bit of an asshole, but he was honest to a fault, which Petrosky appreciated...usually. Besides, they all had a bit of asshole in them. Some of them more than others.

Woolverton cleared his throat—too high, and raspy, like a cat hacking up a hairball. "She did the right thing, running away. If she'd tried to fight this guy...no way in hell."

"Why do you say that?" Not that he disagreed—any resistance and they'd be looking at two bodies—but Woolverton didn't usually make blanket statements about living people. He was only an expert once they stopped breathing.

"To do this kind of damage is damn near impossible if you don't know what you're doing, and sometimes even if you do—you're looking for someone with specialized training and massive strength." He frowned, face tight. "Very hard to do," he repeated. "The only other time I've seen this was in school in New York. Had a rash of killings related to one of the crime families there."

Petrosky straightened and raised an eyebrow. "Hitmen?" Scott had found mob hits when he was searching for related crimes.

"I'm not saying this guy was part of a professional hit, but your killer was strong, fast, and highly efficient. Other than that mob case, I've never seen anything remotely like it."

Petrosky ran his palm over his face, already bristly with five-o'clock shadow. What possible reason would anyone have to send a hitman? The councilman, Amos's father, popped into his mind, but there was nothing so dire at that level of government. Nothing worth killing the man's child over. They'd looked. And if Samuel Amos himself had information worth killing for, worth calling for a hit...

No, that was nonsense. The other victims weren't defined targets beforehand, they were crimes of opportunity. If

Amos was chosen ahead of time, it meant Amos knew the identity of this killer in particular, but they had no reason to believe that was true. Amos didn't have photos from the Polluck crime scene, or Layton's scene. Nothing indicated he was aware of those crimes at all.

But Amos was at the cemetery. Because Meredith Lawrence had been killed there. Coincidence? Petrosky let his focus drift over the kid's face, Amos's now-closed eyes, his graying flesh, the discoloration around his spine.

Their killer wasn't worried about some punk kid from uptown. This killer stayed in his zone, like a cop on the beat. Or…a military man on patrol.

And he only attacked those he saw as enemies. Not the women, he'd made that plain—the men. But if he thought he was doing the right thing, why stop for five years? But he knew: jail, getting married, having a kid, moving away, old-fashioned guilt…any of a million life circumstances could lead to a pause in criminal activity, even criminal activity done with the best of intentions.

Woolverton was staring at him, but the doctor knew better than to ask if he was okay. Petrosky nodded his good-byes and headed for the car, the killer's words on repeat—*I am not the enemy*—inside his head. In fucking Arabic. Their perp could be fighting impulses, like Dr. McCallum said, feeling guilty even as he was doing it. Maybe the words were for him and not for the women at all, trying to convince himself that he wasn't that bad.

Yeah, whenever I want to feel better about myself, I'll just whisper, 'I am not a dick' until I believe it. Like that would help.

Jackson was still in the driver's seat where he'd left her, cell at her ear, her voice a low buzz in the background. She did not look up when he closed the door.

The neck break…so efficient. Like Woolverton said, it

could be a hitman, but a hitman would have a specific target, not engage in blitz attacks. So what were they left with? A special forces guy who'd snapped? Decided to go vigilante and hurt those who were hurting others? But if rapists were the enemy, then why kill Amos? *Because the killer fucked up.* Or maybe he'd escalated beyond the point of caring.

If only there was a way to narrow a list of soldiers, but they couldn't just request the names of everyone deployed more than five years back—there were two hundred thousand soldiers deployed in any given year, far too many to sift through. Without a name, a social security number, or even the specific service, they were screwed.

Jackson pocketed her cell, her face tight. "So?"

He squinted at the sharp downward turn of her mouth, the subtle twitch in her lip...she was worried. Maybe her son —her youngest had special needs and sometimes had episodes at school. The boy liked to hang out with Petrosky, though; kid wasn't into idle chitchat, but he was a great listener if you weren't boring. Old cop stories were pretty interesting, even if he left out the scary parts for the kid. "Do we need to go get Lance?"

"No. Everything's fine." She started the SUV. "Want to fill me in?"

He didn't press it. "Woolverton said it was a clean break, considerable strength, which we knew. But with all that and what Layton said...I'm thinking military, maybe special forces. Enemy is war zone talk." Though why would he say it in another language? It was only by chance that Layton figured it out, and the killer had no reason to believe she would be able to understand.

Jackson eyeballed him, then nodded. "We can poke around at the veteran's hospital in the morning. See if they know any special ops folks who talk to themselves. In Arabic."

"Right." It didn't explain why their suspect had been practicing the language here, stammering over his words or why he'd say "be quiet, bitch" to women he was supposedly saving. But if they had a soldier on a mission, even just a mission within his own mind, he wasn't going to stop.

Soldiers never did.

16

THE STREETS WEREN'T FULLY dark, not yet, but even in the
dead of night, he didn't need his eyes; he could feel her
approaching, could taste her on the breeze. He inhaled,
deeply, slowly...salt—meat. And *flowers*. Perfume, from the
east.

Click-clack, click-clack.

The gloaming thickened. He pricked his ears, listening
hard to the steady tapping of shoes on asphalt, one set now;
would there be more? His belly ached—sour. But he had no
time for that, not today. He had his orders. He always had his
orders.

Click-clack, click-clack.

Closer.

The sound bounced off the walls around him, off the
dumpsters, off the brick. They'd hear. Someone would hear
her. His chest was rigid, lungs frozen.

Click-clack, click-clack, click-clack.

Closer.

Click-clack, click-clack.

There.

Long dark hair. Short skirt. High shoes. *Click-clack-click-clack*. She did not look his way, and why would she? He was hidden in the deep shadows beyond the doorway, hidden in a place no one would think twice about. No man's land. And if you were still enough, quiet enough...

Click-clack.

She passed.

Click-clack.

Farther.

Click-clack.

And then he heard it, a low syrupy drawl that made the flesh bristle between his shoulders: "Where you goin', girl?"

He crept out of the shadows and followed.

17

THE VETERAN'S hospital was a colossal structure of brown brick right out of the 1930s. More windows, though, and bars on every single one above the first floor to keep people from leaping to their deaths. Which, unfortunately, was all too common. Petrosky had been close himself—more than once—and entering this building was a reminder of those dark times. Well, that and of pulling himself back out of the hole after his heart attack.

Dr. McCallum had helped. So had forgiveness, not for the bastard who had killed his daughter, or the fucker who'd brutally murdered his partner—he'd never have that in him —but for himself. For not being able to stop any of it. For letting it happen like a fucking asshole.

Okay, so he wasn't perfect, but at least he wasn't a drunk. Anymore.

He and Jackson took the elevator to the fourth floor, and she followed him through the maze of hallways to the cardiac wing. He knocked twice on an already open door near the end.

"Edward!" Dr. Rosenberg smiled at him from behind her

stack of files—one of the only people who could get away with calling him that. She came around the desk and embraced him. Her head only came to his shoulder, but he'd always thought she seemed much taller—she was downright imposing if you had the balls to cross her. He'd missed a follow-up cardiac appointment once, and she'd chewed his ear clean off when he'd called to reschedule. But she'd still given him some insight into the case behind the missed appointment, more than he ever needed to know about the blood thinners they'd discovered in the victim's purse.

Now she poked him in the chest through the thin file folder he carried, her intelligent brown eyes crinkling at the corners. "How's the ticker?" Her whole face brightened when she smiled.

He couldn't help but smile back. "Still ticking."

"You still doing that once a week donut thing?" She glanced over at Jackson, his current emergency contact since Shannon had moved to Georgia.

Jackson nodded, and Rosenberg turned back to Petrosky, eyebrows raised. "You know you're better off with *no* donuts, right?"

"Yeah, but what kind of life is that?"

Rosenberg sighed and returned to her seat behind the desk, waving them into the rickety wooden chairs across from her. The dark circles under her eyes, barely concealed with makeup, made his chest ache—not from the stent. Great doctors like Rosenberg, the docs who took on the workload of three doctors in any normal hospital, deserved leather, at least, but government funding wasn't exactly pouring in to fully staff the place, let alone dress it up. The powers that be spent a lot more cash to send people to war than they did to take care of them once they returned.

"I'm assuming you're not here on a social call," Rosenberg

said now, closing the open file on her desktop and pushing it aside.

"No, we're not." He eased into the chair. "We're looking for a killer."

"Surprise, surprise." She folded her hands on top of the desk. "Lots of people with blood on their bayonets around here, not that I'd call them murderers. But what makes you think I'd know the one you're after?"

"Oh, I don't think you know him, not exactly."

Rosenberg stilled. She narrowed her eyes. "If you have a general question about symptoms or cardiac drugs, I can help, but—"

"That's not really what I'm after either." Their guy was speaking a second language the people around him didn't understand. Jackson was right: the words weren't for them. He was talking to himself. "I'm really hoping someone from the psych ward would recognize his face."

Rosenberg crossed her arms. "You want me to call Dr. Idowu."

"Come on, Doc, is that any way to talk about your wife?"

"Saying she's a doctor? She earned that title, and you know it." She met his gaze—cold steel.

Petrosky put his hands on his knees and leaned forward in his seat. "Listen, I'm not asking you to do anything illegal. But maybe she'd just...come chat with us. And if your wife happens to recognize our sketch, or maybe knows a giant, blond, Arabic-speaking special forces fellow who likes to talk to himself..."

She sighed, pulling her cell from the pocket of her white coat. "Go wait in the cafeteria, Edward. I'll see what I can do."

THE CAFETERIA BUSTLED with the weary energy of overworked doctors and harried social workers and family members desperate for good news, though it was possible that the air of malaise was entirely in his own head; he wasn't in the habit of going to hospitals unless death was imminent. Petrosky stepped aside to allow a grizzled thirty-something man on crutches to wing by, and scanned the plastic chairs, then the long metal serving bar full of sub sandwiches and macaroni salad and pudding and fountain sodas. A pocket of grinning white-haired men guffawed from the table in the front corner, one of them leaning heavily on a metal hospital-issued cane and wearing a chestful of stripes.

"Should we eat?" Jackson asked. "Might as well, instead of just wasting our time waiting for a woman who is surely too busy for your bossy ass."

"Everything's a dead end until it isn't." Petrosky shook his head and headed for a table in the back. "And she'll be here." Idowu was efficient, with a brusque no-nonsense manner, and as highly regimented as you'd expect from an ex-army doc. Besides, they'd come at the right time, the same time he'd come in months past: right after rounds when the patients' lunch trays came up to the ward. The only time the doctor might have ten minutes to spare.

"You think she'll show up based on all of your two interactions with her?" Jackson slid into one of the chairs, the metal leg squealing against the tile.

Petrosky edged around the table and eased down beside her; then smiled as Idowu breezed through the cafeteria door with a clipboard under her arm. A brilliant orange headwrap covered her hair from the nape of the neck to her forehead.

"Detectives." She had a South African accent that rounded her vowels and hardened her *T*s into staccato bursts that hit your ear like a rap on a high hat. She slid into the plastic seat across from Petrosky and tossed her ledger onto the table with a clatter. "I hear you want to pick my brain. But you have to understand that I'm not at liberty to name any patient no matter how much you beg." She raised her eyebrows at Petrosky—*get on with it*. The sharp gleam in the doc's eyes hadn't changed.

He slid the sketch from his folder. She barely glanced at it. "You'll have to do better than that. Muscular, I assume? Lots of the men who come through here hit the gym same as they did when they were active duty. Old habits."

Petrosky nodded. "How's this: We're looking for a white guy who speaks Arabic. He may have some kind of mental illness, something that makes him talk to himself. Probably lives near here—he seems to know the area." His gaze slid past Idowu as another man entered. Blocky from jaw to calves, black hair, hammer fists balled at his sides. He wore jeans and a T-shirt, but he had the slitted eyes of a man who was still in the combat zone, gaze darting this way, that way, seeking prey—or looking for whomever was hunting him.

The man turned away, but his fists stayed clenched: the meaty fists of someone willing and well-able to wrap them around your throat for looking at him wrong.

"The killings appear to be motivated by perceived wrong-doing," Jackson said, barely glancing at the hammer-fisted man. "Stopping rapes in progress. Two of the witnesses would have dropped to their knees and thanked him if he hadn't run off."

Idowu drummed one finger on her ledger, looking past Petrosky—thoughtful. "Have you considered the group homes?"

"Been there, done that." But homeless people were harder to find, and the fact that the boots had been so chewed up made homelessness all the more likely. Petrosky put his fore-arms on the table. Idowu wouldn't release names, and he had to admit that a soldier speaking Arabic wasn't unusual, not these days. But maybe she'd recognize what their killer had been saying. "Our guy kept repeating the same thing—'I am not the enemy.'"

Idowu pursed her lips. "If I was dropped into a war zone, that's the first thing I'd learn."

Shit. She was right. He'd been so wrapped up with finding the killer that he'd misinterpreted the situation. Wouldn't be the first time. So where did that leave them?

"So, Detectives, you're down to a bulky, blond veteran?"

Petrosky sat back in his chair. "Yeah, but someone strong enough to break a man's neck with his bare—

They all stopped as the clatter of dishes rang out, then the low guttural scream of a man being attacked. The beefy man Petrosky had seen enter stood at the table just behind them, pieces of ham and cheese sandwich and French fries littering the floor around his feet. His nostrils flared, not in an aggressive way—ashamed. His hands clenched and unclenched. He stared.

The scream rang out again. Petrosky looked past him toward the front corner. The old man with the stripes had abandoned his cane, and lay beneath the table on his belly, hands over his head. Screaming, screaming, screaming like he was dying. And that screaming, Petrosky knew that—

Petrosky's lungs slammed shut, and for a moment, he saw his best friend's head vanishing beside him, blood and bone splattering his cheek, but when he blinked again, the room was back, and his heart was throbbing painfully in his throat.

"Excuse me, Detectives." Idowu stood, peering at the man now crawling beneath the table—his screaming was a knife in Petrosky's guts. "Our work is never done."

To that, Petrosky could relate.

18

"YOU SURE YOU want to waste more time on this? Just because you have a gut feeling that this guy is a homeless vet doesn't make it so."

They'd already tried three shelters, each one more point-less than the last. "It can't hurt," Petrosky said, "even if he probably hightailed it out of Ash Park once the press started sniffing around."

"You either think he's here or you don't."

But Petrosky didn't know which—neither of them did, not for sure. Either way, their killer wasn't likely to be out hunting for more victims, and if he was hiding, they might have a little time to find him before he killed again.

Jackson sipped her coffee. "Better than going back to the Ragdoll, I guess."

They'd taken a side-trip down the same alley where Trina Layton had been attacked. The Ragdoll had long since been boarded over—the only window on the back end, a chest-high, four-by-four square, probably used to belong to the kitchen, but it had devolved into a walk-up drug delivery window and more recently into a place for the vermin to enter and exit. One peek inside the empty building had told them all they needed to know: no way their guy was hiding there. Even if there had been room for a sleeping bag amidst the piles of busted boards and broken glass and rat piss–soaked newspaper, anyone staying longer than a few minutes would be eaten alive.

Jackson drove, evening light catching her forehead through the windshield, her fingers tapping on the steering wheel. Every once in a while, she squinted at her phone. Waiting for a call? But if she wanted him to know what it was about, she'd have said.

He frowned at his window. Scott couldn't hack into the hospital records...or wouldn't. And while Dr. Idowu did agree to watch for people meeting the description—"Can't hurt to call if I see someone down in the lobby"—the home-less veterans in Michigan totaled over five thousand. Even if they narrowed their list of suspects by hair color and build, they'd still have a thousand men who might match the description, and no good way to track them on the streets except old-fashioned pound-the-pavement police work.

One more. One more stop and they'd move on. Petrosky watched the eerie glare of dying sun against the graffitied buildings, the light casting one particularly well-done portrait of a woman's face in a deep reddish haze that made her appear demonic.

THE SOUP KITCHEN was located two blocks up from where Trina Layton was attacked, and saved; currently empty except for twenty cafeteria-style tables, and a middle-aged man behind the long metal serving area at the front of the common room. The worker glanced up, plate in hand, and pushed his hairnet up on his forehead as Petrosky and Jackson approached. He smiled so hard his cheeks were like golf balls high on his pasty face. Why was he so fucking jolly?

"Hey there. You here to volunteer?" His bright blue eyes crinkled as he grinned wider, presumably at the prospect of not having to put out all the food himself. "I wasn't expecting you, but we can—"

His face fell when Jackson flashed her badge; he gripped the dish harder. His jaw tightened.

"Usually, I have to speak to make people that irritated," Petrosky said.

The man glanced his way and set the dish on the stack. "You looking for someone?"

Jackson nodded as Petrosky pulled the sketch from the folder. "Very good, Mister…"

"Dubicki. Justin Dubicki."

"You seen this guy?"

Dubicki narrowed his eyes at the sketch and shrugged. "I don't think so. But it's hard to say."

"We'll make it easier. He's big, real stocky. Hands that look like they could snap a man's neck…because they absolutely can."

Dubicki's brows furrowed. "Wait, this guy…killed someone?"

"We just have some questions about an open investigation." Where had this guy been? The case was all over the news; they'd even run the sketch this morning, hoping to calm some of the terrorist rumors.

Dubicki looked past them at the front windows, at the orange-red light leaking onto the floor.

"You expecting someone?" Jackson asked.

"Oh, I…no." His gaze dropped to the counter. To his

hands, planted against the top. White knuckles. On his forearm, a badly pixelated outline of a hula girl swayed her hips as the muscles tensed and relaxed.

"Maybe you should come with us, Mr. Dubicki. Hang out at the precinct for a bit? Maybe that'd help you remember?"

"I…you can't take me anywhere, I didn't do—"

"Then why are you so nervous, Mr. Dubicki?"

"I just…I might know a guy like that. He's not super tall, but he's extra…wide? Muscular, like you said. Neck like this." Dubicki raised his hands and demonstrated—like a goddamn basketball. "But I don't know where he is, and I don't know how to get in touch with him."

Fucking asshat. "Why hold that back?"

Dubicki dropped his gaze to his hands again—cagey as fuck. Suspicious. "He…he seemed like a good guy. And I know he's done his time, military guy, you know?"

A good guy? That wasn't enough reason to hide information from the police. And from the way Dubicki was scanning every inch of the room except where Petrosky and Jackson were standing, he was hiding something much more personal.

"Listen, Dubicki. You and I both know that's not the whole story, and with one call I can get whatever I need on you." He slipped his cell from his front pocket, and Dubicki put up a hand.

"Okay, okay." The man sighed. "I'm on probation."

"Ah, so this gig's your community service, eh?"

He nodded slowly.

"And the guy here is your buddy? Maybe someone you aren't supposed to be associating with?"

Dubicki bit his bottom lip. "No, I…I didn't think so, anyway. He just comes in here every once in a while, gets a tray. Bums a smoke, too—sometimes I go smoke with him.

We only talk about the weather and stuff, though, nothing like...what you're talking about."

Jackson whipped out her little notepad, and the man's eyes widened. "So how about you tell us everything you know about him," Jackson said, "and we'll consider not calling your PO. I'm sure they'd love to hear that you refused to cooperate with law enforcement in a murder investigation."

Dubicki balked, and raised one finger as if shaming them. "You can't do that, I know my rights."

"Your rights don't extend to what I do or don't say to the person who controls your fate, hoss." Petrosky sneered as the man lowered his hand—shaky. "What're you on probation for anyway?"

"I...nothing really. They just thought I did something."

"No shit," Petrosky snapped. "What was it?"

"I...this girl was passed out and...we had sex."

"So you're a rapist." And he'd called her a girl, not a woman. Did he like them younger? Petrosky leaned closer, so close he could smell the guy's rank sweat. "How old was she Dubicki?"

He kept his gaze on his hands. Then whispered, "Fifteen."

Petrosky straightened, fists clenched. *Fucking piece of shit, no wonder the killer likes him.* But...that didn't fit. The only reason their killer would be friends with an asshole like this was if he was...stalking him.

Were they wrong? Was the killer actively choosing his victims and following them instead of committing crimes of opportunity? But Amos was the glitch; he wasn't a rapist, and nothing in his background suggested wrongdoing except procuring the creepy photos that wallpapered his bedroom. And even that was better than half the shit teenagers were into these days. Probably more productive than video games too.

"When was the last time you talked to this man?" Jackson asked.

"It's been…" Dubicki looked at the ceiling. "Maybe two weeks? He only comes in occasionally, twice a month or so."

Two weeks—so he hadn't been in since Amos's murder. Where'd he been eating since then? They had already checked for panhandlers near the local restaurants, and no one had seen their guy.

"What's his name?"

"I never got his name. He never said it."

Petrosky sighed, knuckles aching. He forced his fists to relax. "You got anything useful for us so we can pass along a good word to your PO?"

"Well…I called him Jarhead once." He met Petrosky's eyes —hopeful, like a lapdog with a tug toy. "He didn't like that. Got up and left before he finished eating."

Sounded like the man had some issues with his time in the service—or he'd never been a Marine. SEALS might not take kindly to "Jarhead" either. Maybe their guy had been dishonorably discharged, but again, that information would be impossible to procure without a name. "What time does your friend usually show up here?"

"Dinner. Always dinner."

"What days?"

His golf-ball cheeks twitched like he was trying and failing to keep his face neutral. "Now that you mention it… maybe the weekends. I don't think I've ever seen him here during the week."

"And you've been here how long?"

"Almost three years."

"He's been coming here all that time?"

Dubicki nodded, mute. Their perp hadn't gone anywhere. Whatever had stopped him from killing for those five years hadn't been a matter of being pulled from the streets—it was internal. A choice. And he'd chosen to go back to killing.

Jackson gave Dubicki a card. "If you see this man again, call us right away. And I'll pass your cooperation along to your PO."

Petrosky would pass nothing along but a swift punch to the dick at the earliest possible opportunity. If he'd driven himself, maybe he'd have waited outside this place until Dubicki came out—and run him over. Maybe not, but the thought made him feel better. "Who the fuck gave him community service for rape?" Petrosky muttered when they'd gotten into Jackson's SUV.

She shrugged and turned right out of the lot. The dusk was thicker now, the sky easing into an ashy purple. "He served some time too. You saw those shitty tattoos."

"Not enough time," Petrosky grumbled. "And with the whole murdering rapists thing...does Dubicki seem like the kind of guy our killer would pal around with?" Maybe Dubicki had just told them what they wanted to hear.

"I can't imagine Dubicki would let the world know about his criminal history. He didn't even want to tell you when you asked directly."

"Yeah, but we're cops." She was right, though; the only way their killer would know that fucker's history was if Dubicki was chatty with people he believed wouldn't judge him. Petrosky kinda hoped Dubicki had let it slip. Though if he had...he'd probably be dead already.

"If he's coming here a couple times a month, we should see about a detail," Jackson said. "Might get lucky."

Petrosky grunted agreement. But if their killer was stalking Dubicki, maybe they should wait a little, catch the man in the act of snapping Dubicki's neck. Two birds.

Jackson maneuvered the SUV around a nasty pothole and

glanced his way. "Want to grab dinner? Hopefully, Scott will have something for us by the time we finish."

Petrosky eyed the dashboard clock. "I have to head out. Emergency meeting."

"Emergency meeting?" Jackson raised an eyebrow. "Do you mean a hot date?"

Petrosky glowered at her—*Let it go.*

She smiled more broadly. "Tell Linda I said hi."

19

THEY MET AT RITA'S. Again.

He probably should have made a reservation at some fancy restaurant, but it had been so long since he'd taken anyone out that he wasn't sure which places were worth the trouble. Besides, this wasn't a special occasion, just dinner with a friend. A friend he used to share a life with—had once had a child with. He pushed those thoughts aside.

Linda was waiting for him in the same corner booth, a cup of coffee already in front of her on the table. She looked up and moved to the edge of the seat as he approached.

He put out a hand and slid in across from her. "Don't stand up on my account."

She shifted back to the middle of her bench and picked up her coffee, appraising him from beneath…mascaraed lashes. Not tarantula lashes like Layton, subtle. But she was frowning. Disappointed?

You always were good at disappointing her.

"Sorry I'm late," he said.

"Par for the course for a detective's wife." Her cheeks pinkened beneath her makeup—makeup? That was new too.

"Sorry, I mean...you know what I mean." She broke eye contact when their server arrived with waters.

"Have you guys had a chance to look at the menu?" The waitress was a little slip of a thing with bird wrists and a sunny disposition that made her feel vaguely fairy-ish. She took their orders for grilled chicken sandwiches and salads, Petrosky grateful for the interruption. But he wished he'd ordered fries.

"So, how was your day?" he asked, turning back to Linda before he could change his order. The detective's wife. *Ex-wife*.

She smiled, but her eyes widened as if he'd just told her he was considering joining a cult.

"You okay?"

"Yeah, it's just been...a long time since you asked me that."

He sipped his water, wincing. Bitter. *Lemon, fuck.* "I know, I know, I was a shit husband, rub it in a little more."

Her face fell.

Dammit. "Hey, sorry, I was just being sarcastic."

She nodded. "I should remember that cops have these weird coping mechanisms, huh? Like social workers." She smiled, but this time it was strained. She sipped her coffee and looked at her hands. The silence stretched until the waitress returned bearing a tray.

Way to fuck it up again, old man. When the plates were settled, Petrosky stabbed a bite of lettuce and said, "So we have this case."

Linda looked up from her sandwich. Surprised? Or interested? It was disarming that he couldn't read her as well as he once had; and he'd never been able to read her as well as he could read a perp. Social workers, like cops, were good at keeping their feelings close to the vest.

"Military guy," Petrosky said around a bland mouthful of salad. "Or we think he is anyway. Running around in worn boots in the wee hours of the morning, snapping people's necks. The whole situation is just bizarre."

Linda was staring at him intently, sandwich forgotten on her plate.

Petrosky shrugged. "He has this complex...I think. But you're the professional." Linda had been a social worker in Ash Park for over thirty years; she knew the reality of this city as well as he did. "In two of the cases, our perp came upon a crime in progress and murdered the perpetrator. A rapist, both times." He took another bite of salad for good measure, then went on: "So he finds these college kids in the cemetery, right? But this time, it isn't a rape. I'm thinking he has some issue with sex? Maybe he can't tell the difference between an attack and a consensual act." He let that sink in while he tried the chicken burger. Needed salt...or a deep fryer. And his water...what was with people and the fucking lemons?

"Rape isn't usually a difficult thing to discern," Linda said. "Not if the victim is conscious."

"Even if someone's unconscious, just that fact alone makes it an attack."

"You know what I mean, Ed. In the dark, it might not be obvious unless there's a struggle, and rapists aren't fans of streetlights." Her eyes narrowed. "I suppose if your killer just walked up and heard the normal sounds of passion, he could get confused. Some types of moaning can sound like pain when they're really pleasure."

But Eden had said they weren't making noise, not yet, and the killer wouldn't have been able to see inside the mausoleum.

Linda stabbed a tomato and met his gaze. "Let's assume he got confused; you're probably right about the complex thing. Maybe the killer saw a loved one raped in the past, or heard about the attack, dealt with the fallout. A parent, a sister, a wife with PTSD...it can be a rough road for both the victim and the people who care about them."

Petrosky nodded and washed another bite of salad down with the lemon water. He grimaced.

"So his goal...he's killing rapists," Linda said.

Petrosky set the glass aside and nodded.

Linda was still staring at him. "You don't want him to stop."

He gazed into her eyes—no judgment. Just knowing. Because if their killer hadn't fucked up, if he hadn't killed an innocent kid, she wouldn't want the guy to stop either. Could this perp have saved their daughter's life? *But hers wasn't a blitz attack, old man. That killer chose Julie because he wanted to hurt you.*

Petrosky swallowed hard, ignoring the sharp pain dead center in his chest, and ran a hand over his face again—he should have shaved before he came. Freshened up, at least. The gray button-down and blue jeans he was wearing were the same ones he'd beat the streets in. Linda had gone through the trouble of drawing on her face with tiny little tools, and she was wearing a dress too; green. When was the last time he'd seen her in a dress?

"You look really nice," he said.

She smiled. "Thank you, Ed." But she didn't return the compliment. She had no reason to.

What am I doing? Shannon had been kidnapped because her husband, his partner, was getting too close to the truth in a murder investigation. His daughter, Julie, had been brutally attacked and murdered because he was a cop. If something happened to Linda...

He looked over Linda's head, out the window of the diner, and the blackness seemed deeper than it had been earlier—forbidding. He should be staking out that soup kitchen, waiting for their suspect to return. What if this was the day the killer unexpectedly showed up?

"I think your take on the killer is a good one, Ed."

He smiled at her though it hurt his cheeks. Just hashing it out with Linda had clarified his thoughts, things he hadn't even known he was considering. Maybe they needed to expand their search radius, go back even further than Scott had already—perhaps they'd find other attacks in the years before the first murder, victims with close relatives that matched the description of the killer. It was worth a shot. It'd be a hell of a lot easier than stalking the soup kitchen for weeks until the guy came back—if he came back at all. And if he was smart, a seasoned military fellow...he wasn't going back there, not when he knew they were looking for him.

"Thanks, Linda. I appreciate your input."

"I'm glad I could help," Linda said and smiled—genuine. Same way she'd smiled on their first date. On the first night they'd worked a case together. And later...she'd smiled at him later too. They'd had good years together. How easy it was to forget that.

He wiped his mouth on his napkin and set it beside his plate. "This is just like old times, isn't it?" But there was something missing, lurking behind the smiles they were offering like consolation prizes. And they both knew what it was.

His chest ached. His lungs weren't working right. He tossed a twenty on the table. "I've got to get back to work."

She looked away, but as he climbed from the booth, he thought he saw her lower lip tremble. His chest spasmed harder, painfully, but it released just as quickly.

He paused beside the table and met her eyes. "I'm sorry, okay?"

For everything.

20

HOW HIS CAPRICE still stank like old French fries, Petrosky had no idea, but it was comforting—a reminder that some things didn't change, at least. The streets, too, felt ripe with memory; some good, some bad, all familiar. Even the fast-food places. He didn't go there much anymore, but damn if they didn't trigger a little burst of nostalgia.

Petrosky inhaled rancid fat, old salt, and the deeply embedded musk of nicotine, and squinted through the wind-shield into the dark. He was probably just thinking about fast-food so he didn't have to think about Linda. And the other things he'd lost. His attention lingered a little too long on the liquor store fifteen minutes from his house. The building passed. But there was another liquor store five minutes away—even closer to home.

He pulled out his cell.

Scott answered on the third ring. "Hey." His voice was strained.

"You all right, Scott?"

"Yeah. What's up?"

Petrosky filled him in on the relative-of-a-rape-victim

idea and maneuvered his car closer to home and pajamas and television and Duke. The old boy probably missed him. Duke stayed with the neighbors while Petrosky was at work, but that big oaf never left his side once he got home. To think he'd once belonged to a killer. Two of them, in fact.

"You there, Scott?" Silence. The call had probably dropped. Petrosky listened to the blinker—*tick, tick, tick*. A few more miles and he'd be home, and he could call back from the landline. Fucking cells. That's how they got you, made you pay for all the minutes and then they—

"I can get started tonight," Scott said. In the background, something crashed, the bright clang of breaking glass.

Petrosky frowned. "What's happening, Scott? Your girlfriend throwing stuff at you?"

"Sorry, I'm at home. Dropped a dish." He sighed. "Dad's not doing so well."

Petrosky turned his blinker off. And hooked a U-turn.

GEORGE SCOTT SMILED from his seat on the leather couch when Petrosky walked in, but his mahogany face was unusually sallow, dull as Trina Layton's living room—as Mr. Johansson's lame suit. As Samuel Amos's dead flesh. *Uh oh.*

Petrosky nodded to him. "What's happening, George?"

When Scott had decided to make the move down from Vermont, his father's illness had been a major factor. But the Vietnam veteran had been functioning well here, taking in the occasional ball game with Petrosky—though Petrosky wasn't a huge sports fan—and sitting with Petrosky in the park while Duke chased balls or rested his bull head on George's knee. The man had even kicked bowel cancer.

Now George sat wrapped in a hand-stitched quilt, next to a pile of tissues on the glass end table. Had the cancer come back? But no, that had never given him the sniffles before. Petrosky set the bag of pork rinds on the table, and George smiled at him. "You know Evan's going to have your ass for that."

"I think I can take him."

"Not anymore—he's a giant now." George laughed, thick and mucusy, but his chuckles soon degenerated into hacking.

"What's the doc say about that cough, George?"

"Eh, I ain't been to the doc. Had a cancer check a week ago, and it was clear—this is just a cold. Has to be."

"In the middle of summer? Aren't you the lucky one." If it got worse, Petrosky would dose him with cough syrup and take the man in himself. Pneumonia could be a bitch.

George laughed again and snatched the pork rinds off the table just as Scott—the younger Scott—strode in from the back hallway, laptop balanced on one spread palm, his other hand still on the keyboard.

"I thought I heard you come in," Evan said, eyes glued to the laptop. His voice was low; tired. When Petrosky first met Evan Scott, he'd been a tall, skinny, Urkel-looking kid, but though he'd kept his trademark enormous glasses and his gangly walk, the kid was starting to fill out—his yellow T-shirt now stretched tight across his broad shoulders.

Petrosky nodded to him and eased into the chair next to where George had set up camp. "You sounded pretty busy when I called. Figured you wouldn't mind if I made myself at home."

"I told you to just walk in, Ed, don't pay this boy no mind." George's voice was gruff, but he tipped a wink at his son, who was now staring at the pork rinds on his father's lap. The kid frowned at the snacks and gestured to the laptop.

"Got a few hits on rapes just before the time the first killing happened," the younger Scott said, eyes narrowed at his screen. "I kept the radius small, five miles around the cemetery: one husband, one brother, one boyfriend, all military or ex-military, all present when the victim filed the rape report." He shook his head. "The husband threatened in open court to kill the man who attacked his wife, but never did anything even when the rapist walked, and the brother is in prison now—insurance fraud." He tapped more keys. "The boyfriend...lives in Virginia, according to his social media profile. He could have traveled up here, maybe, but..." He shrugged. "I'm not sure this will help, but I'll expand the search radius, look back further, see what we get."

The bag rustled, then a harsh crinkle as George tore the pork rinds open.

Petrosky ran a hand over his grizzled jowls. This was going to be fucking impossible. Even if Linda was right and their man was avenging a specific incident, there was no way to tell when that attack might have occurred. Or where. Hell, he could have seen his father rape his mother as a child in fucking Egypt. And even if it had happened right here in Ash Park, there was no way to tell if it had been reported; most rapes weren't. They needed to narrow down their suspect list.

So much for luck. Petrosky reached for a pork rind.

"You're gonna catch the plague," George muttered.

"I'll take my chances," Petrosky said around a mouthful of grease and salt. George's immune system was trashed, even with the cancer in remission. Chemo hit hard. And the damage stuck around. *As do heart issues.*

Scott closed the computer and fumbled the laptop to his chest. "I'll keep on it, Detective."

"You don't have to call me that."

"Well, you're kinda the boss though."

That much was true. But Evan Scott was the child of a friend, and having the kid address him as "Detective" was like having people call him "Sir" in the grocery store. Lately, that made him feel old...well, older.

George shoved another pork rind into his mouth. "Yeah, you should call the man who's poisoning your father something more appropriate. Like putz."

Petrosky grinned. "I prefer asshole if we're being choosy."

"How about old rotten sonofabitch?" George tossed back another pork rind—*crunch, crunch, crunch.* "I can barely taste these, but they sure go down easy." He reached for the remote and pulled up the game. Men in ball caps running around in tight pants—what was the point? "You up for the Tigers? I taped it on that..." George turned to his son. "What do you call it?"

But Scott had already retreated down the hallway.

"Yeah, I can stay a bit," Petrosky said, settling back in the chair. "Have to get Duke in about an hour though." The big fellow would be sleeping in his bed tonight, always did when Petrosky was away all day long as if the dog had a snuggle quotient he couldn't let ride even for one evening.

"Babysitter for your dog." George grunted. "Imagine that."

"Not a babysitter. Duke has a job there."

George raised one bushy eyebrow. "Those girls didn't give him a job, they just owe you."

Petrosky ignored him. "Security detail. Pays better than a detective's salary." He grabbed another pork rind and let the salt tingle the roof of his mouth before riding the oil down his throat.

George snorted laughter, coughed, recovered. "Sounds like a sweet gig. Maybe that dog can get you a real job."

"I should be so lucky." Petrosky let his mind wander as umpires called strikes and fouls and balls and home runs, the incessant hollow *pop* of the bat against the ball reminding him of a cork. If he closed his eyes, he wouldn't be able to tell the difference. So easy for noises to get confused.

Like what had happened today in the hospital cafeteria.

Pop.

That clattering tray, the man with the stripes, screaming, covering his ears…and Petrosky, watching his best friend's head explode all over again as he had thousands of times since the day it had happened.

Over and over and over. Those images had vanished for a long time—when he was so distracted by Julie's murder that every flashback was of her slit throat—but now, with this case, his time in the military seemed closer than ever. He could almost taste the sand in the back of his throat, smell the iron of Joey's blood—feel brain matter, wet and sticky on his face.

Simmons's voice came back to him, their witness who had been hiding out behind the willows: *He kept saying, "Don't move, be quiet, bitch" over and over again.*

Petrosky put his feet on the floor and straightened in his chair. When you were in the throes of flashback, time went wonky on you—he knew that for a fact. His flashbacks were generally short-lived, at least they were now, but for a few seconds, he still lost track of where he was in space. What year it was. And what the appropriate response to the situation might be. His chest always responded with panic, as if he were right back there in combat.

Pop. A man in dirt-stained pants ran for first base.

Petrosky stared until the television went blurry. There was also the incongruity in the killer's words: "Be quiet, bitch," and "I am not the enemy." They had thought he was speaking to himself, trying to talk himself out of it, or maybe trying to make himself feel better about being a monster. But… *He told me to run.* What if he wasn't talking to himself or to the women, at least not the ones who were there with him in that moment? What if he was talking to someone who had been there in the past?

That's why they hadn't gotten anywhere with the hospitals or the group homes. They'd been looking for someone who was delusional, schizophrenic—hallucinating. But they hadn't examined trauma, and in a war zone, the risk of trauma was exorbitant.

Their killer wasn't delusional. He wasn't seeing things that weren't there.

He was reliving them.

21

THE DARK WAS thick like grease, and caustic—like the stench from the burning oil fields. It was the newspapers, perhaps, the hot wretched mass of shredded cardboard and plastic and discarded cloth. The feral rat pups hidden beneath. And their shit, always their shit, sour and musty and steeped in ammonia.

"Nice night, isn't it?" The voice came out of the dark at the far end of the building, a low husky drawl—danger in that voice, malice under the sugary-sweet. *How did I get here?* His heart squeezed in his chest. But he remained silent—*don't think*. When the time came, he'd know. No need to ponder—to plan.

He blinked. His eyes had long since adjusted, but there was no amount of adjusting that would allow him to see far past the bottoms of his feet; the streetlight that glowed from the end of the alleyway cast a hazy yellow through the hole where a window used to be, the sill inexplicably littered with jagged pieces of glass even after all these years. Gooseflesh rose like nails on his back. Perhaps even the rats felt it, the hollowness that wafted from the cemetery, not only old death but imminent pain. It was the energy always present in war, in places of torment—the energy of those cut down, and those soon to be.

It was a killing zone.

He could smell it—the tang of iron, cloying in his throat, the deeper, almost sweet musk of bodies putrefying beneath a too-thin layer of earth. Shallow graves where your boots sank too far in the freshly tilled sand. He could smell it now under the thick ammonia stench of the rats—the blood.

"This way." That voice again, syrupy with sincerity, but there was only one reason to talk like that—to reduce resistance.

"You comin'?"

The hairs on his neck prickled, and his jaw clenched with hatred, though he knew the voice was in his head. *Not real. Ignore it. Not real.*

He inhaled, careful not to move his lower belly, and let his breath out slowly and just as cautiously. Sweat dripped down his spine. The muscles in his thighs sang with the urge to leap to his feet, to run. He had always wanted to run, to escape, to find a way *out* and *home*, but there was no way, not alone—you stayed with your men, or you died. Even if you hated them. Even if they made you sick. And they were here, he could feel their presence.

And they never slept.

Whiskers, a squeak. A female, pregnant by the girth of her, lumbered past the bottom of his worn right boot. The rat did not look his way, but the one that followed, a pup, glanced up briefly before running over his leg, its skittish nails pricking his shin through his jeans.

He watched.

He waited.

Silence.

Outside, someone shuffled past, a man from the sound of

the heavy footfalls—drunk, the antiseptic tang of liquor barely identifiable in the already sour air. He could not see him from his position beneath the window, but nor could passersby happen upon him there unless they entered the building, and no one would. Even the streetwalkers knew better. The rats were known to bite.

A huskier specimen slunk from the pitch beyond his toes, eyes gleaming yellow in the barely-there glow. A bull. Dominant. Aggressive. And beneath the ammonia, below the harsh reek of their shit, another scent rose, salty, fatty like…good corned beef.

In the darkness behind it, other creatures were slinking nearer to his boots.

They watched.

He watched.

The rat sniffed his heel, whiskers vibrating. It sniffed his calf.

He waited. Silent. And though his eyes did not move, did not so much as blink, though his hands remained still at his sides, he could feel the blood pulsing down through his shoulders into his fingertips. His hands were his weapon. The only one he needed.

"Where you goin', girl?"

Ignore it. Ignore it.

"Ever been with a man in uniform?"

He inhaled once more, shallow. A mission, he had a mission. That was the only thing that made the nightmares stop. But never the voices—they were always there.

The rat put its front paws against his knee, tentative, then jumped back—and watched too. It was testing, perhaps to see if he might be dead, but though the rat surely knew better, still it crept up once more. Near his thigh. It sniffed his thick fingers, whiskers brushing the pads like wire. The fur on its back rippled, barely, the tiniest of vibrations as it readied its head, its jaws, its teeth.

It lunged for his kneecap.

His hand snapped around the rat's shoulders, too high for the thing to twist around and bite him, too late for the back legs scratching at his wrist.

His other hand wrapped around the animal's hind quarters. The rats beyond his boots scattered in a rustling, panicked hiss.

He twisted. The pop of gristle and bone.

It squeaked once and was still.

He wrapped it in the paper sack he'd laid beside him. And sat back. And watched.

Silent.

Waiting.

22

THEY'D BEEN LOOKING for related crimes here in Ash Park, but they really needed to expand their search area to include the entire world.

Fucking convenient.

Petrosky spent the night with the laptop open on top of the covers, Duke snoring like a lawnmower beside him, one enormous paw thrown across Petrosky's knees. He didn't want to waste precious killer-finding daytime hours researching hunches, especially when he wasn't sure this line of logic would lead to finding their perp even if he was correct.

But nor could he settle his mind enough to rest. What horrific event might their killer be reliving? What had this man witnessed that could trigger him to kill over it for years? From the victim profiles, Petrosky thought he knew.

Rape during wartime was as old as war itself. From the Crusades to the factional wars in the Congo, the rape of women and young girls was as brutal as it was commonplace. His jaw clenched tighter with each line he read. Invading soldiers generally killed the men and raped the women, sometimes staking women and girls to the ground for passing soldiers to brutalize as they wished—including rape with sticks, knives, or guns. Victims often required extensive surgery to survive. Many didn't make it out alive.

If he'd been stationed near a place like this, if he'd seen the aftermath of these horrific attacks, had been one of the soldiers to cut the girls' bindings and carry their bloody bodies away from the corpses of their mothers and sisters...

Yeah, he'd kill a motherfucker if he saw it happen again— if he saw another rape firsthand. Hell, if they could put all rapists on an island, Petrosky would be first in line to punch in the nuclear codes. Fuck those guys.

Duke snuffled and buried his face deeper beneath Petrosky's leg, avoiding the blue glow of the screen. He was getting the sheets all wet, that drooly bastard. Petrosky scratched the dog behind the ears anyway, and dropped his gaze back to the screen, but scrolled away from the pictures, stomach sour. If he was right, if their killer had seen such an attack overseas, it would explain the "I am not the enemy" thing. Those women, traumatized, bleeding, maybe even staked to the earth, baking in the sun, surely would have fought anyone who tried to touch them, even if they were there to help. A few words of comfort, a promise in their language—Petrosky could see it.

But... *Be quiet, bitch.* Rescuers were unlikely to use that phrase, and the killer had said the line in English. Had he heard other men saying it to...their victims? And if they were speaking English, and Amos's killer lived here in the United States...

It didn't narrow it down too much further than what they'd had before, but it could help once they had a suspect. Maybe they'd get lucky.

Lucky, there was that word again. Who was he kidding? He hadn't been lucky about anything in his whole damn life.

If he was lucky, he'd still have a child. Still have a wife. If he was lucky, his partner would be alive, and Shannon would be here in Ash Park with Evie and—

He scratched behind Duke's ears again. "You're the lucky one. Did you know your first owner was a homicidal maniac, old boy?" The dog garumphed and nuzzled Petrosky's hand.

Petrosky blinked his sandpapery eyelids, thinking. English-speaking soldiers. Arabic-speaking victims. *What now?* Even if he knew the trigger, did it help? Actually... He sat straighter. If their guy had been triggered overseas, maybe he'd attacked other perpetrators there too. A rash of soldiers with broken necks, or even one or two, would stick out more than landmine injuries. But there were too many years to go over, too many soldiers, too many locations, and those injury files were property of the US government—they couldn't even get access to local hospital records. Unless he happened to run into a veteran who specifically recalled some guy running around in the sand, snapping necks like twigs, he was shit out of luck.

He sighed. Maybe he should call Acharya.

Fuck that. This case would have to be on life support before he leaned on a goddamn journalist. Maybe he'd find a blog post. An old newspaper article. Something about soldiers with cervical spine fractures. *Anything.*

He scrolled, scratching Duke's ears, squinting at the screen. One hour. Two. He was ready to throw the damn thing at the wall and pass out beside Duke's disgusting puddle of drool when an image caught his eye: a soldier in a wheelchair—cracked spine? He clicked on the headline.

"Injured Soldier Gets Warm Welcome Home."

The governor, or the nondescript man who had been governor seven years back, stood behind a dark oak podium, a thick-armed man in military garb at his side, a bird pinned to his chest. The article identified the man in the wheelchair as Jeffery Dunne, his mother a renowned professor, father part of...ah, the governor's task force on crime. No wonder he'd gotten his face on the internet. Petrosky read, looking for information about Dunne's injuries—nothing. *Weird.*

Was it possible that Dunne had been injured in a jeep rolling over, or some other accident? Of course. But there was almost always a snippet of text describing the accident— if it bleeds it leads, and the lookie-loos loved details. This one just said "injured overseas," but the incident was bad enough to leave him quadriplegic. Petrosky zoomed in on the photo and squinted at the man's face—no sign of injuries on the skin, no burns or shrapnel scars, not on his face or arms or hands. Petrosky couldn't see behind the tubes that snaked into the man's throat, but he suspected he'd not find evidence of additional injury outside of a broken neck. And Dunne had been hurt in Iraq, where they most definitely spoke Arabic.

Jeffery Dunne. Patient zero?

Duke grumbled, his floppy jowls wetting Petrosky's leg.

23

Jackson met him the next morning out in front of his house, coffee in hand. From Rita's, not from a coffee shop. Sucking up for something? Had she called Acharya again?

He took the cup and whistled. Duke barreled through the open front door and leapt toward his partner as he locked the house.

Jackson knelt and buried her face in the dog's neck, Duke panting happily. "Hey, boy!"

Jackson had spent an awfully long time telling him she hated dogs, but when he'd had to go in for surgery—just a little issue with his pacemaker—she'd offered to take Duke, with the option to drop him back at the neighbor's if she couldn't handle it. Her son had always wanted a dog, she said, but she'd been afraid he wouldn't take to an animal. She'd wanted a trial run.

She had almost refused to give Duke back.

Laughter drew his attention from the lawn next door, and Petrosky glanced over. The neighbor was already halfway across her drive; Billie, short for Belinda, but he'd never tell her he knew that. Twenty-two, gray hair, because that was a thing now, with a thirty-year-old's hard-lived gait. Her face was bright and clean—no hint of the ashen pallor she'd had when he first met her. No track marks either, not anymore. She'd been living next door for almost ten months with her...well, she called the other three women her "sisters," but he'd picked them up off the same street where he'd found Billie.

Billie smiled at Duke, and the big dog pulled his face from Jackson's neck and looked up. "Ready, boy? Got us a playdate at the dog park!" She pulled the Caprice's keys from her pocket. The girls had his car most days, for school, work, whatever. That was the main reason he usually let Jackson drive.

Jackson straightened, calling after them, "You're fickle, Duke! That's what you are!" Billie smiled her goodbyes and headed for the garage where she kept the leash, Duke trotting obediently at her heels.

"That dick," Jackson muttered.

Petrosky watched them go, and nodded to the other girl —*woman*, Jackson chastised him in his head—who'd just emerged from the house. Candace waved at them as they headed for the Escalade, her dark face glowing above her red button-down blouse. Professional, her makeup neutral for the secretarial job he'd helped her find; he'd told her new employer that she'd spent time with him in the department. He'd just conveniently forgotten to specify why.

Jackson nodded to Candace and put the Escalade in gear. "You get a new one?"

Petrosky buckled up and waved to the girls—women. Whatever. His *friends*. "Sometimes people just need a chance, Jackson."

"Yeah, and I'm sure I'd feel better if someone bought me a house and let me live there rent-free while I got on my feet." She maneuvered out of his neighborhood onto the main drag. "You just want someone to keep your dog and mow your grass."

Petrosky watched the last oak tree vanish in the rearview, replaced with brick and mortar buildings and concrete curbs and glass-blocked convenience stores. "I cut my own grass, Jackson."

She snorted. "Nice comeback."

"I thought so."

She stopped at an intersection and turned his way. "So where are we off to?"

"To see a general." He sipped the coffee. Bitter. Just the way he liked it.

GENERAL DELANEY, formally Colonel DeLaney, the man from the article Petrosky had found the night before, had since retired from active duty. He currently worked as a protective intelligence analyst for one of the automotive companies—whatever the fuck that meant. And he had an open appointment this morning.

The inside of the building was as white and sterile as a hospital. They followed DeLaney's Ryan-Reynolds-looking assistant up a long marble hallway to a door bearing the general's name. The man himself sat behind a glass desk that Petrosky wanted to cover with fingerprint smears. The general stood when they entered.

DeLaney looked different without his fancy colonel get-up. The man wore a starched white shirt and a light suit that matched the steel of his eyes. Red and blue striped tie. Almost an American flag on his own.

"So, Detectives," he said when they were seated. "You had a few questions for me about a speech I gave?" His voice was low and as smooth as shit after taco night.

Jackson raised an eyebrow at Petrosky: *it's on you, that speech thing was your idea.* She was always judging him for something. Lying to witnesses. Buying a house for hookers—ex-hookers. The usual.

Petrosky cleared his throat and leveled his gaze at DeLaney. "You were on active duty with Jeffery Dunne, is that correct?"

DeLaney's face remained impassive. "Yes. We were stationed in Iraq. I was his commanding officer." He narrowed his eyes. "What's this all about?"

"Nothing to worry about; he's not in trouble." Unless he was a rapist who only escaped with his life because their killer hadn't perfected his neck-snapping yet. And if he was, Petrosky was an equal opportunity face puncher; hopefully Dunne still had feeling in his jaw. "We came across an article about that press conference you did when Dunne returned home. The injuries he sustained might be similar to those in a case we're working now."

"You think a neck injury sustained during wartime is similar to a recent...assault case?" DeLaney sniffed. "I'm not sure what you're after here."

"Just humor me, Mr. DeLaney."

"General," he snapped, and now his eyes flashed fire. "General DeLaney."

"My apologies." Petrosky leaned back in his chair, feeling the heat of Jackson's arm beside his, the muscles in her forearm twitching as she pulled out her notepad. "Let's start over, shall we? Pretend we're reporters looking to do a story on the heroes of our time."

DeLaney's mouth puckered like he'd just eaten something sour.

"You gave Dunne high praise during your press conference," Petrosky tried again.

"Dunne was a good soldier. One of the best."

"But despite his injury, he wasn't awarded the Purple Heart, which leads me to believe that his injury wasn't sustained as the result of his service."

The general's jaw clenched. "Just what are you getting at, Petrosky?"

No more Detective, eh? "I'm just wondering how he got injured. Why one of the best soldiers out there didn't come back with a Purple Heart."

DeLaney's face was hard as stone. "I don't recall."

Petrosky leaned over his knees, watching the rigid set of the man's shoulders; had he been so tense when they'd arrived? "You know everything else about the guy. Enough to give a press conference and offer glowing—"

"He did his job," DeLaney said sharply. "And I offered appropriate accolades based on his tour of duty. Are you implying that his injuries, sustained during his deployment in service of the United States, are somehow null and void?"

"I'm just curious about how he got hurt." He glanced at Jackson, whose face was as tight as the general's. Something was definitely wrong here. DeLaney knew how Dunne got injured, but if Dunne was a model soldier, there'd be no reason to fudge the facts. Or pretend to have fucking amnesia.

The general's eyes darkened into tiny chips of slate. Savage. Maybe the general had a penchant for rape as well as politics. He was probably a lot of fun at parties. "I think we're done here," DeLaney said.

But we haven't even gotten to the raping and pillaging. Petrosky cleared his throat. "Listen, I did my time overseas, too, so I'll level with you, General: We have a murder investigation going on. We think our suspect could be the same guy who attacked Dunne all those years ago."

A stretch, but possible. And even if he was wrong, it

wasn't like he was going to get anything else out of DeLaney without that kind of kick to the gut.

The statement seemed to have the desired effect; DeLaney's jaw dropped, though he recovered quickly and rearranged his face into a mask of incredulity. "You think a soldier attacked Dunne? One of my men, under my command?"

"Now, now, we didn't say anything about a soldier." But that was precisely what he'd meant, and from the way the man's face reddened, DeLaney knew it.

"How about a list of the men who served under you?"

"I don't have that information."

Jackson straightened, pen at the ready. "No problem, we'll take what you can remember. First and last names, general appearance, anything."

Slowly, carefully, DeLaney regained control of his features, but that twitch at the corner of his eye...he was nervous. DeLaney thought a soldier was possible, Petrosky was certain. And the general didn't want them to know about it.

"I don't recall the men who served under me. I suggest you contact the Department of Defense for a list." The corners of his mouth twitched up—smug. He knew they weren't going to get anything from the DOD. Shit, even if they had a name and a social security number, which they didn't, the process of procuring military records took months.

"You remembered Dunne."

DeLaney shrugged. "He's the only one I gave a speech about. But all this was years ago. And war isn't pretty, as I expect you know—I've tried to forget."

Petrosky had tried to forget, too, had done pretty well until this case hit too close to home. But you didn't forget entirely in the face of direct questions—couldn't. "What happened over there, General?" *What are you hiding?*

"It's time for you to leave." DeLaney pushed himself to standing—big guy. With strong hands. Petrosky couldn't imagine him running around in shitty worn-down boots, but stranger things had happened. And what better cover for a big-shot retired officer than a down-on-his-luck vet?

"When did you come back, General?"

"What's that got to do with—"

"Let's try an easier one." Petrosky let his lip curl in mock disgust. "Where were you Saturday night?"

Now DeLaney eased himself back into his seat and crossed his arms, smiling wolfishly. "Not that it's any of your concern, but I was out to dinner. With my wife."

"And after?" But if DeLaney was the killer, if this man hated rapists enough to kill, he wouldn't have given a press conference praising one of them.

If I'm even right about this. He examined DeLaney's face. An amused glitter had emerged in his irises.

"I was at home all night. Watched television. Fucked my wife." DeLaney sniffed and pushed a button on his desk phone. "This is about Whispering Willows." Not a question. "I heard that was terrorists; no idea why you'd be asking me."

"You know better than that, General." Petrosky said, voice low, sharp. DeLaney had known what they were after the moment they'd stepped into his office. "Do you watch all local crime so closely?"

"Just when it's plastered all over the news." He glowered. "And I don't like your tone."

"I don't like your face, General, yet here we are."

The office door banged open. More men in suits. These ones with guns. DeLaney's Ryan-Reynolds-y assistant was nowhere to be seen.

Jackson and Petrosky stood and showed the men their badges. The men gestured to the door.

No other words were necessary—they were done with DeLaney for now. Hopefully, next time they saw the man, they'd be there to arrest his sorry ass.

24

JEFFERY DUNNE HAD a face like a weasel, the bleary eyes of a drunk, and a body like...well, a skeleton. His leg muscles had long since wasted away, turning Dunne's immobile frame into a mere ripple of bone beneath the thin sheet. Someone had pulled the covers to the lower part of his ribs and laid his hands on the top—had those thin fingers been responsible for torture? Had he been their killer's first victim because he'd been brutalizing someone else? Petrosky wasn't sure. He could feel the wrongness of the general in his fillings, like the itch you get just looking at a nest of roaches, but he didn't know about Dunne. Innocent until proven, and all that shit, but right now, he'd rather err on the side of saving innocents like Samuel Amos. The killer wouldn't stay hidden forever, even if he'd probably be out of commission until the publicity died down. And even then, everyone had a motive to protect their killer. The victims, all but Eden Johansson, didn't want him to get into trouble. The general clearly had some reason to keep his answers guarded—but he knew why Dunne was attacked, Petrosky was certain. But there was at least one guy who still had a bone to pick with their killer: the guy who'd had his neck snapped like a twig. The man lying immobile in a hospital bed.

Petrosky entered the room, and Dunne followed his movements with watery brown eyes—his sockets deeper than they should be. Jackson was out in the hall of the Sandusky long-term care facility, distracting the nurses. If this guy was a rapist, Petrosky might have more luck on his own; not like Dunne would see Jackson as an authority figure. And these infantry guys...they bowed to authority.

Well, some of them anyway. Himself notwithstanding.

Petrosky grabbed an upholstered wooden chair from the far wall and hauled it up beside the hospital bed where beeping monitors and hissing tubes played in harmony, a song of slow but persistent decay. "Mr. Dunne, I have some questions for you about your attack." He flashed his badge.

Dunne raised an eyebrow. At least that muscle worked. "My attack, sir?" His voice was grating, harsh and raspy. "You mean...this?"

"Your broken neck, yes." The hospital staff hadn't been forthcoming about his condition, but Petrosky had gleaned enough from the orderly. Fracture in the cervical spine, medical assistance for everything below the throat. Mother visited rarely. Father never.

"Is this about my disability payments again?"

Why not? "Yes. Yes it is."

The respirator hissed from its stand beside Dunne's bed: *shhhhh-clunk, shhhhh-clunk, shhhhh-clunk.* "What do you want to know?"

"Just walk me through how it happened."

Dunne looked past Petrosky at the wall. Then the ceiling. Inventing the right answer instead of telling the truth, though he'd surely told the story dozens of times in the past. The hairs on Petrosky's neck prickled.

Shhhhh-clunk. "I was out on recon duty," Dunne said finally.

"What were you looking for?"

"Anyone. Invaders. We'd taken one of the eastern villages, but we weren't sure if the enemy might come back."

Because you had their women? Their children? Why else would they bother returning to a military-occupied village?

"Anyone walking with you?"

"No, sir. There weren't enough of us."

That might narrow their list of suspects. "How many were in your squad?"

Now his gaze darkened. "I can't recall, sir."

"Ballpark."

"Maybe a dozen."

Dunne couldn't recall a dozen people? Sounded like DeLaney. Everyone had amnesia. But that wasn't his main problem with the story. Even for recon in a tiny village, they should have at least split into pairs. "So you had no one out there to watch your back?"

"No, sir. It was supposed to be...Miller? I can't remember his name for certain. But he ate something bad and he...well, sir, he had the shits."

"And DeLaney didn't assign someone else to go out with you?"

Now Dunne frowned. Eyes tight.

"I mean, it wasn't really recon, I guess." Looked to the ceiling again, then the window. "More just keeping an eye out."

Liar, liar, liar. And that didn't answer his question about DeLaney—Dunne hadn't even verified the general was there. "What happened next?" Petrosky said instead of pressing. He'd circle back later, put the guy off-balance.

"I was just walking, sir, and someone came up behind me,

and that's the last thing I remember." He said it matter-of-factly, like a robot, no feeling whatsoever—rehearsed.

"Strange that someone would just wander up behind you and try to kill you."

"The enemy's sneaky, sir."

"But it wasn't the enemy that attacked you, was it?"

Dunne blinked, steadfastly refusing to meet Petrosky's eyes. *Shhhhh-clunk. Shhhhh-clunk.*

"You falling in love with the wall, Dunne?"

The man finally dragged his gaze to Petrosky's. "They didn't know who did it, sir. No one else was around."

"Just the enemy." *Who would have been far more likely to shoot you in the back.*

"Yes, sir."

"What about the women from the village? The children? Were they your enemies?"

Dunne's eyes had gone cold. "They were harboring terrorists, sir. We did what we had to." *Shhhhh-clunk.* "And no one there was innocent; it was a small place, less than fifty people living there in these little huts, far outside the city so they could plan their attacks in secret."

Fifty people? Plan their attacks in secret? *Please.* But now they were getting somewhere.

"How many of them did you kill, Dunne?"

The respirator hissed. *Shhhhh-clunk.* "What does this have to do with—"

"You say you were attacked by one of them—the enemy. I think you were attacked by one of your own."

"What? Why would…" Petrosky watched Dunne's mouth, the twitch at the corner—defiant. "It was the enemy."

"Right, because if it was combat, you'll get more compensation. Is that it?"

Dunne's nostrils flared.

"Truth is, I don't care about your disability payments."

"But you said—"

"I lied, like you've been lying to me this entire time." He glared at Dunne. "I'm here because I'm chasing a killer. English and Arabic speaker. Military training. And he's out there murdering people the same way he tried to kill you." *Probably.* Petrosky pulled the chair closer to the edge of the bed, knees pressing against the frame. "But the people he's killing here...they're bad guys, Dunne."

Dunne's cheek twitched. "You think he's some kind of... revenge killer?"

"Now what would he need revenge for? I thought you were just out wandering around. Unless..." Petrosky leaned over the bed toward the man, so close he could smell the antiseptic tinge of the alcohol they used to clean Dunne's trach tube. "Maybe you were doing something you weren't supposed to. Maybe seeing it bothered him so much that he wasn't able to forget it."

"That's ridiculous, I—"

"How's security here?"

"What?"

Petrosky straightened. "I mean, if I were to tell the press that you're alive. A fact this guy surely doesn't know since you're still breathing." The killer might have missed that press conference, a tiny snippet on the news and a back page article, but he wouldn't miss the barrage of publicity Petrosky could bring in the light of the killings. And their perp was certainly watching more closely now that his freedom was at stake.

Dunne's face reddened. "You...you can't do that!"

He could. And he would no matter what this guy said now. He'd use him as bait if he had to. "Why do you care?" Petrosky said, the chair squealing as he shoved it back. "You have nothing to hide, right? And the 'enemy' you're so sure attacked you is overseas." He stood and started for the door.

"Wait!"

Petrosky turned back. "You want to amend your statement?"

"Listen, I didn't see him. I don't know who did this. If I did, I'd tell you, I swear."

On this, Petrosky believed him. Their killer was stealthy, efficient, but he had clearly blended in until he got home. Otherwise they'd have shot him for his trouble. The tube wiggled again as Dunne said, "But there were others. Before me."

Spill it, fucker. Petrosky returned to his seat. The respirator hissed.

"About a month before my attack, there was another guy, a soldier, died down in the valley just outside the village and..." *Shhhhh-clunk. Shhhhh-clunk. Shhhhh-clunk.*

"And what? Something weird about the scene?"

Dunne's neck moved, the trach tube rising and falling— *like he's trying to swallow a goddamn tennis ball.* Then he resumed watching the wall.

"They find this guy with a woman down there?"

Dunne's eyes went glassy. His mouth vibrated. Rage? Or fear?

Petrosky leaned back in his seat, hand on the bed beside Dunne's wasted knee. "This woman he was with...even if this incident had happened on American soil, the statute of limitations for rape is up. Though I suspect you know that."

Dunne's brow furrowed. Thinking. Considering. Did he know there was no statute of limitations on war crimes?

"I'm trying to find a killer, Dunne. The man who snapped your spine in half damn near twisted a kid's head clean off. And if he finds out you're alive, he'll come out here. I think you know that as well as I do."

Dunne closed his eyes. "They were the enemy."

Keep telling yourself that, fuckhead.

Shhhhh-clunk. Shhhhh-clunk. Shhhhh-clunk.

When Dunne's eyes opened once more, he looked ten years older, and...haunted. "We found her in the clearing. With his body."

"Name?"

"His name was...Ortiz. Almost sure, but—"

"First name?"

"Charles? I think. I can't really remember, it was a long time ago."

"He die of a broken neck?"

Dunne's chin moved in a way that made it seem like he might have been nodding had he full control of his muscles. "Yeah."

"What were the names of the other soldiers in your unit?"

"I swear, I have no idea." He closed his eyes a beat longer than a blink, lower lip trembling, then a hissed whisper: "They say my memory is screwed up now. Brain inflammation from the spinal injury. That's why I thought you were here." Petrosky studied his face, his wide, scared eyes. He believed the guy.

"What about the woman in the clearing with Ortiz? Who was she?" If the other soldiers had found her and hurt her—or worse—after the killer murdered Ortiz, maybe the perp regretted not telling her to run off. Maybe that's why their suspect had said it to every witness since. *He told me to run...he said I was going to live, but only for now.*

"I don't know who she was. Some woman from the village. There were..." He sighed, closer to a wheeze—the sound of regret at how it had turned out, but not horror at what he'd done. Petrosky's fists clenched.

"We didn't kill all the women. They cooked for us sometimes."

"No wonder your buddy Miller had the shits." *I'd have*

tried to poison him too. "What about the children. Did you kill them?"

Dunne closed his eyes. Which was answer enough.

Jesus.

"So, you killed their children, forced them to cook for you, and then what? Raped them when you felt like it?"

"We thought they might have information."

Bullshit you did. "And rape was the right way to go about getting it?" But he knew as well as the man in the bed that this tactic was more common than anyone wanted to admit.

Throw him off. Catch him off guard. "So you found Ortiz in the clearing. What did the girl look like?"

He blinked, rapid-fire. "What?"

"Long hair? Pretty? Young?"

"I…young, I guess. Long hair."

"What'd you do to her?"

His throat bobbed, bobbed, bobbed around that tube. "No, you've got it…" His voice was thinner, higher—*Can you see how much I'd love to strangle you, fucker?* "She was dead, sir. The guy who hurt me and killed Ortiz…I think he…I think he…fucked that girl to death." His words trailed off, but his eyes had brightened. Excited? *Because she was the enemy.*

"What the hell is wrong with you?"

"I'm just saying, there was blood everywhere, all over her legs, and there was a stick up inside her, and she wasn't moving, and…" *Shhhhh-clunk.* "Ortiz was kinda beside her there. I forgot a lot, sir, but I'll never forget that."

Petrosky stared. Their killer…he had gotten there too late. And watching a girl get stabbed to death with a branch would trigger anyone to attack. Anyone with a soul.

Dunne licked his lips. "I always thought the guy broke Ortiz's neck, and then murdered her so she couldn't say who did it."

Except that their killer didn't hurt his female witnesses.

Petrosky stared at Dunne, whose eyes were on the wall again —*Look at me, you fucker.* "If Ortiz was an innocent bystander, why did he take that pretty girl down into the valley?"

Dunne blinked at the wall, silent. *Shhhhh-clunk. Shhhhh-clunk. Shhhhh-clunk.*

Enough bullshit. Petrosky rose from his seat and bent over the bed, his nose inches from Dunne's face. "Did the man who attacked you kill the girl you raped?" He reached out and grabbed the trach. And pinched.

The tube jerked. "Hey!" Dunne croaked. "You—" He tried desperately to inhale, his Adam's apple putting up more of a fight than the man himself ever could.

"You think the same man who crippled you killed that girl?"

He released the tube long enough for Dunne to hiss: "Yes."

Petrosky squeezed again. "Did he kill the girl you were raping?"

"I…" Dunne's eyes rolled back in his head. A monitor shrieked.

"Did he? Did he hurt the girl you were brutalizing, you fucking piece of shit?"

"No!" It was a wheeze. "He…he let her go."

Petrosky dropped the tube and stepped back.

Dunne's eyes were furious, burning. "You motherfucker, you goddamn mother—"

"What are you going to do? Chase me down and fuck me to death with whatever object you find lying around? Kill me the way your friends did those innocent women?"

Dunne wheezed. Coughed. *Shhhhh-clunk.*

"Some way to talk to a disabled veteran." Jackson's voice.

Petrosky whirled around to see his partner leaning in the doorway. "I'm an equal opportunity asshole, Jackson; he might be disabled, but he's not fucking special." But she was glaring at Dunne, not at him. How much had she heard?

Petrosky headed for the door as the nurses rushed in to the musical shrieking of the monitors.

THAT NIGHT, Petrosky ran frantically through a world scorched by yellow sun, sand in his nostrils, assailed by the stink of dust and metal. And though his face was wet with his best friend's blood—Joey's blood—though his lungs burned, he couldn't stop. Because *she* was screaming. He could hear her screaming.

Julie.

His baby girl. Someone was hurting her, raping her, they were going to kill her, he could feel it—

I can't let her die, it's all my fault, hang on, baby! But no matter how fast or how far he ran, he couldn't see her—only sand. Only the burning yellow sand. Panic choked the air from his lungs.

Then the screaming stopped. Petrosky blinked, and someone else was there, Dunne, right in front of him like a mirage: broad-shouldered and stocky and walking toward him over the blazing yellow, blood on his shirt, crimson streaking his face, his hands dark with gore.

Julie, Julie, where's my daughter?

Dunne's eyes were the same as they'd been in the hospital room—glazed with horrible excitement. He noticed Petrosky. And smiled.

Petrosky rushed him, leaped for him, watched his hands grab Dunne's head, palms just below his ears, the stink of iron cloying in the back of his throat, the bristle of Dunne's hair pricking the pads of his fingers. Twist. *Crack.* Those horrible eyes went dull.

He wasn't even a little sorry.

25

"You got rats chewing on your lines?" Decantor was halfway to his desk, heading closer with those long loping strides of his, giant shoulders square like a fashion model. Eyes way too goddamn bright for nine o'clock in the morning.

Petrosky closed the file he was working on and leaned back in his chair, bleary-eyed even after two cups of coffee. The ride back from Sandusky had been hard. He'd taken Julie to Cedar Point when she was ten, and twice yesterday, he'd sworn he'd heard her voice coming from the backseat. *Are we almost home?* Then the nightmares: Julie screaming. Petrosky had given up on rest around four and taken a stroll with his dog, but the nagging unease in his spine had not relented.

"Rats wouldn't shock me," Petrosky said.

Decantor sighed. *Decantor, like the thing you put mimosas in for brunch,* Morrison whispered. *But he spells it differently.*

Decantor reached around Petrosky's computer and grabbed the phone receiver with his beefy fingers. And slammed it into the cradle. "There you go. Go see the chief.

Next time, you're on your own, I'm not your secretary." He turned on his heel and stalked away.

Whoa. Decantor was agitated. Decantor was never agitated—Petrosky'd always assumed that obsessing over the Kardashians kept him calm by distracting the man from his demons.

Petrosky pushed himself from his chair.

In his peripheral vision, Petrosky saw Jackson stand too, at her own desk for once—Morrison's old desk. "What the hell did you do?" she asked.

Petrosky watched Decantor plop down in his seat and followed Jackson from the bullpen. "He's just pissed because his make-believe girlfriend married that rapper guy."

"No, what did you do to the *chief.*"

"Plausible deniability."

"You have to trust someone, old man."

"I trust you."

Her face had hardened. She dragged her gaze away and pushed past him into Carroll's office.

Petrosky sniffed. *Here we go.* He'd barely taken a step inside the room when Carroll snapped: "Did one of you inform a journalist that the first victim of your active, unidentified killer is still alive?"

Petrosky slid into the chair, though he suspected he'd be kicked out sooner rather than later. "I might have."

"Goddammit, Petrosky, you can't put civilians' lives in danger."

"He's not a civilian. He's a fucking criminal."

Carroll spread her palms on the desk, the tips of her dark fingers going pale. "Let's say you're right about all of it. Let's say that the guy who's killing people here in Ash Park is the same man who attacked a few of his fellow soldiers overseas. Let's say this Dunne guy is a rapist—maybe a murderer." Her gaze was sharp, an arrow straight to his forehead. "That means the man who put him in that bed now knows he failed in his mission to kill him the first time."

"He might have known that before."

"And thanks to the story that ran first thing this morning, the killer also knows exactly where to find him."

"We have no reason to think the killer's wandering around here now—he's probably holed up in Canada if he knows what's good for him," Jackson said. "What exactly was the story about?"

Carroll frowned. "Your journalist friend printed Dunne's full name and photos of him, both from the war and more current. The piece also states that he was injured during active duty in Iraq and that he is now a person of interest in the *Exorcist* case."

Jackson raised her eyebrows. "I—what?"

"The *Exorcist* case. That's what your journalist dubbed it. On account of the...neck thing." Carroll tapped her own neck behind her earring—gold hoops? She must have a parent-teacher conference later or something. "Any internet search is going to pull this article up. And one of the photos that ran with the story is a picture of Dunne in his hospital bed, the logo of the long-term care facility in plain sight on the blanket."

Petrosky tried not to smile. He might buy Acharya a donut. Or a burger. What did journalists like? Pickles? No, lemons. If anyone could take the worst shit in the world and turn it into something lucrative, it was a journalist.

"I meant the person-of-interest thing," Jackson said. "Why is he a person of interest? He's not a suspect for obvious reasons, and I checked with the facility for phone calls, even hang-ups to his room in case the killer sought him out in the past. Obviously, this journalist got the wrong information or simply made it up for the sake of the story."

Jackson's voice was clear, but Petrosky heard the accusation beneath the words, the defensiveness that he hoped would slip by Carroll. But he doubted it. Carroll examined Jackson's face, then Petrosky's. The wall clock *tick*, *tick*, *tick*ed.

Finally, Carroll sighed and pulled a pen from her desk drawer. Maybe she'd try to stab him with it. "I'm going to pull the detail off Eden Johansson later today."

Ah. The pen was for self-defense. He straightened. "You can't—"

"You just said you don't think the killer's around. And I can't spare the manpower, especially since I had to yank Babcock off the street while Internal Affairs completes their investigation. And if you're right, the man at the hospital is in more danger than Eden Johansson."

"So what? That's not on us, that's the Sandusky precinct's problem." And Petrosky wanted someone watching Eden, even if she was probably safe—it'd been a week, with not a single sighting of their suspect, but having her protected just felt...better. He cleared his throat. "She's still got Nazis all over her front lawn."

"They aren't even picketing now that the press has stopped showing up. Now they've all gone back to...whatever those assholes do."

"Dating their own right hands," Jackson said, glancing briefly at Petrosky. He nodded when her mouth twitched.

Carroll cut her eyes at Jackson then leveled her gaze at Petrosky once more. "You should have alerted the locals in Sandusky. If you want to use someone as bait, you have to have officers there to catch the suspect when he shows. What'd you think, they'd let the perp walk in and kill Dunne, and you'd get the killer from the video surveillance? Parking lot cameras?"

Yes. "Don't be absurd." But if Dunne was to be believed, their killer had attacked two soldiers overseas, out in the open, and managed not to come under suspicion. Stateside, he had stayed deep in the shadows, too—maybe they wouldn't have ended up with video footage at all. It was a risk he would have been willing to take.

Now Carroll turned to Jackson. "Did you know your partner called the press?"

Jackson sighed. And shook her head—bright, furious eyes, but there was hurt there too. But if he'd told her, she'd have said they needed to protect Dunne. Just like the chief was doing now. And god help him, he'd really wanted their suspect to take Dunne out—that rapist fuck didn't deserve to live.

"You've got the week, Petrosky," Carroll said. "Find this guy before he hurts someone else—before he kills Dunne. Now get out of here and do your job."

"Sure thing, Chief." He'd already stayed longer than he'd expected to.

26

THE SLAMMING office door reverberated down the hall in time to their footsteps.

They were almost to the common room when Jackson said, "He's not going to that hospital in Sandusky. He's not about to blow his cover now, and he's too damn...*good*. Stealthy. The attacks didn't happen every night, so he had to be out routinely, spending who knows how long casing the same six-block radius. And not a single person knows who he is."

"Or the people who do know are willing to look the other way." Amos's face—the only innocent victim of the bunch—flashed in Petrosky's mind. Could he take the burden of another dead innocent if it meant five more rapists dead? Ten? He shook the thought off.

No donuts in the common room today—not that he deserved them. The table along the far wall was empty save for a haphazard stack of napkins and three Styrofoam cups. And the coffee pot, bottomed with thick, bitter-smelling sludge. He made a beeline for the coffee. "Maybe we should set up a sting—go wait for him in the cemetery." But the manpower Carroll'd require would scare the guy off, and Petrosky wasn't going alone, not this time. Might be old age. Or the fact that Shannon had promised to slap him if he wasn't careful—and she wasn't above slapping his corpse.

"A sting. Good call…if you want to get your neck broken." Jackson frowned at the pot. "Look, we've gone over this. If he was still out there hunting, we'd have more bodies—he's gone, or in hiding. If I were him…"

"Yeah, I'd have run too." And any time they spent sitting in the dark waiting for him to show up was time they weren't actively figuring out who he was. Besides, Petrosky'd rather be the one hunting than the one being watched.

He switched on his cell while Jackson poured their coffee, the aroma bitter when it hit the Styrofoam—acrid, like char. Could you literally char coffee? If anyone could, it was the Ash Park PD.

"You know, you really should give Carroll your new cell number," Jackson said, eyeballing his screen. He tipped it away from her.

"I have you to tell me what to do, Jackson. Why do I need Carroll?"

"You have Decantor too. One day he'll punch you for his trouble."

"I could use an all-expenses paid hospital vacation." He narrowed his eyes as Scott's name flashed on the screen: missed call. "You talk to Scott lately?"

Jackson shook her head. "I hit his office before I came up to the pen, but it was locked. I think he's working from home today."

Again? That wasn't good. He'd have to go check on George before he went home tonight, and—he scanned the list of missed numbers—maybe he should call Linda too.

No, it was in her best interests to stay away from him. He

and Linda…they'd tried it before, a friendship, a marriage. None of it had worked. And yet…

And yet.

He hit the button to return Scott's call.

The kid sounded even more tired than he had the other night as he filled Petrosky in on his findings. The late night text Petrosky'd sent had apparently found Scott awake and looking frantically for something to keep his mind off his father's condition. It was just a cold, George was certain, but cancer was an illness that stalked you and the people who loved you. Going through treatment, then remission, those long nights in hospital rooms… Scott wouldn't get a good night's rest until his father was well, but even then, he'd be sleeping lightly.

Petrosky clicked off the cell and stuck it back in his pocket. Stressed out or no, Scott was a miracle worker. "Scott found our other dead soldier in an old social media post put up by some member of his family. Dunne was wrong about the first name, but not the last. The family called Chandler Ortiz's death accidental."

Jackson raised an eyebrow, handing him the coffee cup—hot. "The guy found with a snapped spine and a bloody rape-stick in his hand was an accident? Sounds like a cover-up."

Or the Ortiz family just hadn't wanted to share the gory details on Facebitch, or whatever that thing was called. "Scott also got the names of a couple more people who served with Dunne—scoured online interactions. One was arrested on domestic violence and sexual assault charges in Florida the year after he returned home and died in jail. Another is currently inpatient at the veteran's hospital here, but his physical profile doesn't look like our killer." Guy was probably under Idowu's care, actually. The general's little band of raping murdering fucks hadn't fared well—except for

DeLaney himself. "Hopefully we can get a list of names from the guy," Petrosky said. "See who else served with Dunne."

"And if we can't, maybe that's an area Acharya can help with. Especially now that he's your new best friend."

"He's not my—"

"I'm just saying, the press gets ahold of an incident like this, a cover-up? That's front page stuff, and it will spur investigation. Without that…it'll be harder. Military records get sealed or lost, and they'll probably insist they have to take care of it in-house. Who knows if justice will ever happen?"

"We won't need Acharya. We'll just find our perp, and the rest of the chips will fall." He'd give his left nut to see that rat bastard DeLaney—*oh, sorry, General DeLaney*—rot in a cell. Maybe he was okay with Dunne living too. Lying in that room all day, no visitors, no family—seemed like a shit life.

Call Linda.

No.

Petrosky frowned.

"Don't give me that look," Jackson said. "You called Acharya so our killer would go after Dunne. You don't get to judge me for trying to access military files."

Wait, what were they talking about? "I wasn't judging. Just thinking." He swallowed a mouthful of coffee—oily sludge, horrible stuff. Still better than the coffeehouse.

Jackson abandoned her cup on the table. "I'm thinking, too, Petrosky. But I'm thinking about our killer, a renegade soldier with no regard for human life."

But that wasn't true. "He has plenty of regard for human life, just no regard for rapists." And…he shouldn't care about the lives of those fuckers.

She brought her own cup to her lips. "You sound like you admire the guy."

"I don't—I mean, I don't hate him, or I wouldn't hate him—"

"Except for Amos," Jackson finished.

That was the anomaly. The one innocent victim. "You talk to Eden Johansson again?"

"I've called her a few times." Jackson leaned against the table and eyeballed his coffee, and he sipped it again for good measure. "Everything was consensual, like she said. She didn't resist. Didn't say no. The killer just made an error."

"Because he can't tell the difference between an attack and a little nookie."

"What the fuck kind of language is that?"

"Old white guy word, Jackson. Get with the times."

She rolled her eyes as they made their way from the common area—one final glance at the film on the bottom of the pot—and back to the bullpen. Past Decantor's desk, where the man was squinting at his computer screen. Four or five other cops sat in their zones, scribbling frantically in worn case files, probably trying to get done for the day to go home to their wives, their children. Jackson was already on her cell.

Petrosky plopped into his chair and almost dropped his cup at a crash from the other side of the bullpen. Decantor was standing up, his chair on its back. Glaring at...him.

Petrosky's hackles rose. "The fuck's wrong with you?" Petrosky called across the pen, earning raised eyebrows from some of the other officers.

Decantor sniffed, but did not break eye contact. "You should know."

All the other cops in the pen were looking their way now, unmoving. Even Jackson had turned, phone held away from her head.

Petrosky came around his desk with Jackson's voice in his ears—*he's going to punch you for his trouble.* He lowered his voice: "You can't be that upset about a few phone calls."

Decantor righted his chair and shrugged into his jacket. "I was on my way to babysit your witness."

Huh? "Dunne?"

Decantor shook his head.

Ah. Eden Johansson. Carroll must not have made the call to pull her detail yet. "I didn't assign you to that, Decantor. If it were up to me, I'd have picked someone with less of a penchant for celebrity gossip—you'll bore that poor girl to tears."

Decantor snapped his jacket lapels into place. "I'm not upset about that. I'm upset because I stopped here to grab a few files before I headed for the Johanssons's place." He snatched up a stack of manila folders from his desk as if to drive the point home, and pressed them to his side. "Khoury was supposed to stay there until I arrived, but he's been pretty pissed about his partner and…"

Petrosky's chest hurt. "And?"

"Eden Johansson was attacked."

27

OAKLAWN WAS nice as far as hospitals went. Jackson said it was dated, but Petrosky was even more dated and she seemed to like him okay—sometimes. Outside, rounded windows bulged from the sea of brown brick like lumps in gravy. Inside the hospital, the too-bright fluorescents made his eyes ache. The antiseptic stink was no easier on his nostrils, though it did remind him of the alcohol smell from Dunne's breathing tube, which brightened his spirits somewhat. But not enough.

Rage burbled in his gut. They'd fucked up, the Crusaders had gotten to her, or maybe the killer thought Johansson knew something more, that she could identify him. Petrosky wanted to go give Carroll a piece of his mind, but it wasn't really her fault. Khoury, though...that guy was going to get a crowbar to the liver. He stretched the muscles in his neck— hard, painful. What if they'd failed? Was Eden gravely injured, even dead? Decantor hadn't said, and the possibility had gnawed at Petrosky on the drive over, Julie's face flashing in his brain, blue lips, dead eyes, *my fault*.

Decantor was already at the front desk when they

arrived, talking to a curly-haired woman in pink scrubs. Not hitting on her; his broad shoulders were stiff as he gestured to something on her clipboard.

"I told you to step on it," Petrosky muttered, hurrying through the lobby.

"I wanted to get us here in one piece," Jackson fired back.

"Just because you've got kids doesn't mean you have to drive like my grandmother."

"Like they had cars back then."

Decantor noticed Jackson and Petrosky and nodded to the hall, where a red sign glowered angrily from the far end: EMERGENCY ROOM. But the morgue was also located in this direction. *Fucking hell.* Petrosky followed the others, lungs painfully tight. Jackson's lips were a thin, bloodless line.

He forced out: "So what's the skinny, Decantor?"

"The skinny?" The bigger man laughed.

"It's something new he's trying," Jackson snapped. "So what've you got?"

Decantor cut his eyes at Petrosky, mouth drawn—regret? *Grief?* "Sounds like someone ambushed her when she was on her way to her car. Grabbed her purse, smashed her face against the side window."

Head injury. *Fuck.* "What's her prognosis?"

"Huh?"

"Is she going to fucking make it?" Or had he lost another girl on his watch? So many lost. A lot saved, but never enough.

"Yeah, man, she'll be fine, relax." His eyes had gone wide, one eyebrow at his hairline. "Broken wrist, sounds like, some scrapes and bruises, but nothing serious. She'll be out in a jiffy." He cocked his head. "What do you think about that one —jiffy? Am I speaking your language?"

"Not until you stop pretending the Kardashians are

something special." But the tightness in Petrosky's chest had eased. A broken wrist? That wasn't their killer's doing—Eden Johansson wouldn't be breathing, let alone "fine." He pushed the square "Door Open" button at the end of the walk, but the glowing EMERGENCY ROOM sign did not seem quite as ominous as it had moments ago. Had he really thought she might be dead when they got here? *You're losing it, old man.*

Decantor strode purposefully past the waiting area, and gestured to the third cubicle on the right: a makeshift room marked by metal rods strung with cloth.

"I'd seen him before," Eden was saying, and she glanced over as they ducked inside the blue curtain. Detective Sloan —short like any good Irishman ought to be, dark hair, thick black eyebrows—stood on the opposite side of Eden's gurney-bed. The mattress looked uncomfortable, probably to urge patients to vacate as soon as possible, but more importantly, the gurney was specifically for people on their way home. They weren't admitting her. She really was okay.

"Go on," Sloan prodded in a low, thick vibrato that reminded Petrosky of rubber on asphalt.

Eden sniffed; there was dried blood beneath her nose, and a bruise across the bridge. Looked sore, but not broken. He winced anyway. "He was at the protests," Eden said. "One of the guys with the signs, grabbed my arm when I walked by trying to get to Sammy's house."

"This was one of those Nazi fucks?" Petrosky blurted.

Her bloodshot eyes widened, but she nodded. "Yeah."

"What did he look like?" Sloan asked.

"White guy, dark hair, kinda long. Scraggly."

Well that was most of the population these days. Half the reason he didn't like the coffee shop was his incessant fear that he'd open his coffee to find a hipster hairball.

"Big nostrils. Huge," she said. "Like…a pig."

Sloan nodded. "Upturned. Okay. Tattoos?"

"Not that I saw. But…he was wearing this hat." She bit her lip. "I think it had a picture of a car on the front of it."

"What kind of car?"

She shrugged and winced, grabbing her arm, and when she spoke again, her voice was tight. "An old one. Like one of those old muscle cars, you know? That's what my dad calls them." She turned Petrosky's way. "Are my parents here yet?"

Decantor stepped up. "I'll call again now. They were up in Ann Arbor for work, but they should arrive soon."

Eden inhaled hard, a long, whispery hiss. "Can we take a break? Real quick? I'm kinda…I'm a little dizzy." Her voice trembled.

Sloan nodded, glancing Petrosky's way, face set like he wanted to say no. "Of course."

But the longer they waited, the more distance they put between themselves and the bastard who'd done this. At least they knew one thing: he was at the protests. Petrosky pulled his phone from his back pocket.

"I see you have it on this time," Decantor said.

"Don't be silly. I always have it on." He tapped the icon for the app Scott had installed while he was "watching the game" with George the other night. He'd forgotten all about it until now.

Jackson raised an eyebrow. "You're on social media?"

"Yeah." Petrosky grimaced at the screen. "Scott showed me this trick the other day." He went to pull up the…shit what was it? Not the Jackoff Republic, the…

Crusaders of the Republic. He punched it in.

Jackson peered over his shoulder. "You're Wanta Lawmore?"

"What? Who has more law in 'em than me?" He glanced at Eden—one corner of her mouth had turned up. Sloan handed her a little plastic cup of water.

Jackson groaned. "And you're from Slammer, USA? You

should have just put in your bio that you're a trolling detective."

"Nah, it says right here in my About section: 'definitely not a cop.'"

Eden's laughter was the sweetest thing he'd heard all day.

The Crusaders' group was public, which was their first mistake. Their second error was that nearly all of their members also had public profiles. Didn't these fuckheads know anything about Big Brother? If he were a criminal, he'd button that shit up.

Then again, most criminals weren't all that smart. The people in this group were case in point.

"GOT THAT LAYING BITCH."

He flashed the screen to the others. The message had been posted one hour ago, so it was still near the top of the page, all caps. You could always tell a moron by their use of excessive capitalization and the inability to spell the most basic of words. Laying instead of lying? Come on. The name would have tipped him off anyway: Bubba Halstead. If that wasn't the most redneck name he'd ever heard…

Petrosky scrolled through words of congratulations—and of anger that one of their "kind" had lied to save some Muslim. He ground his teeth and typed:

"Sounds like a real chicken."

Jackson frowned at him.

Petrosky forced his jaw to relax. "You know, with the laying?"

Decantor guffawed. "That is the worst dad joke ever." Sloan chuckled from the corner, a rumbling growl. Eden laughed, too. Only Petrosky stared at his screen, waiting with a lump in his throat.

He wasn't a dad, not really. Not anymore.

The little notification button blinked: a response.

"DAMN RITE SHE WAS"

Ohh shit, the fucker was online right now. Technology pissed him off sometimes, but not today.

"Damn right? He thinks you meant she was scared?" Jackson said.

"I'm sure he thinks lots of things that aren't true." Petrosky tapped on the man's profile and turned the phone to Eden.

"Yeah, that's him." Her eyes filled.

"You sure?"

"One hundred percent. He was even wearing that same hat he has in his profile."

Petrosky squinted. Ah, there it was, Bubba holding his hat —printed with an old Monte Carlo—over his heart. Like any good American. He put his thumbs back on the tiny keyboard.

"You going out to celebrate?"

Jackson laughed. "Are you hitting on him?"

"I don't need to. He'll invite me anywhere." Petrosky tapped his stock photo image: a redhead in heels. "Just look at this photo of me in a ladies' business suit. It's positively *arresting*."

"ALRDY PARTYNG AT REYNOLD'S!!!!!!!!"

At least the fucker had spelled the name of the bar right.

"Decantor, you want to take this?" Petrosky asked. "My business suit is at the cleaners." *And I have a killer to catch.* He turned his phone Decantor's way and watched the man's face light up. And when he looked over at Eden Johansson, she was smiling too.

"Yeah. I'll call Khoury, tell him to meet me over there—he hates these guys."

"Good." Hopefully someone would punch Khoury during the arrest—payback for leaving Eden to get hurt. If they didn't...there was always tomorrow.

Sloan said he'd wait for her parents and escort the Johansson family home. "Meet me back at her place after you lock that idiot up."

Decantor nodded to Sloan, then leveled his gaze at Petrosky. "If there's anything I can do, and I mean *anything*... you call me. I'm getting real tired of this shit." Then he slipped back outside the curtain.

Petrosky scrolled through the app, taking screenshots of the encounter in case the guy wised up and deleted shit before trial. *The internet is forever, asshole.*

"They make this way too easy," Jackson said, watching him.

He nodded and re-pocketed the cell. If only their killer would do the same.

28

THEY SHOULD HAVE BEEN high on the news of Bubba's arrest —Decantor and Khoury had pulled him from the bar without incident—but Petrosky's gut was twisted in knots. He slugged back Pepto-Bismol as Jackson hit the parking lot of the veteran's hospital. Again.

Idowu met them in the lobby this time, under a big bubble atrium that was right out of an action movie. He kept waiting for military personnel in black jackets to come through the glass ceiling, whizzing to the earth with weapons drawn.

Idowu's arms were crossed. She didn't have her legal pad. He'd called ahead and left a message that they were coming, but she sure didn't look like she appreciated it.

"Detectives, it's a busy day. What can I do for you?"

"We have some new information," Petrosky said. "We were hoping you might be able to help us. Or more specifically, that one of your patients might."

Her gaze darkened. "How would you know who my patients are?"

"We had a list of suspects—I called your patient's mother,"

Jackson said. "She was rather forthcoming."

"Who's the patient?"

"Bezon. Julius Bezon."

"Bezon's your suspect?" Idowu balked. "You're wasting your time. He hasn't been out of this hospital in months. If you're looking—"

"We don't think he did it."

"I'm sorry, I don't understand. Give me the bullet points."

Petrosky did. Meeting Dunne, and his account of the events in that long-ago Iraqi village—murder and rape. The twelve unidentified infantry members. Ortiz's death. And their theory that the killer was reliving traumatic moments from that time period, perhaps being triggered by seeing similar crimes. "We need the names of the other men who served with Ortiz," Petrosky said. "One of them is our killer."

Idowu stared for a moment, then drew her big brown eyes to the glass dome above their heads and sighed. "I can ask for his cooperation. Otherwise..." She shrugged.

"Can't you just give him some of that truth serum shit? Stick him with something?"

Her head snapped back down.

"He's kidding," Jackson said.

But he wasn't. If they failed to get those names today, they'd be stuck scrambling for clues...and hoping their guy didn't come out of hiding and kill someone else. He'd rather not risk it, if only because the guy might hurt an innocent—if he could be sure the perp would only kill rapists...

Idowu blinked at Jackson. "Did his mother tell you anything else?"

"Just that he's schizophrenic."

"What?" Idowu's eyes widened, her eyebrows creeping up her unlined forehead toward her headpiece. Turquoise today.

"He's not?" Jackson asked.

"You know...let's just say that claiming schizophrenia...

it's easier for families sometimes. Not that I'm saying that's true this time, mind you"—she looked pointedly at Petrosky —"but if someone was to walk in here with severe post-traumatic stress disorder with psychotic elements, it might be easier to just say schizophrenia."

"Psychotic elements like—"

"Breaks with reality. Hallucinations. Delusions. We see this often with PTSD here because wartime…the human brain is not well-equipped to process those events. The sympathetic nervous system gets a little wonky."

"Wonky?" Petrosky said. "That's the technical term?"

"Yes." No smile. No further explanation.

He cleared his throat. "Our killer may be dealing with something similar. He repeats a phrase that seems at odds with his actions, telling the woman 'be quiet, bitch' while also repeating that he is not the enemy."

"I see." She pursed her lips, squinting. Thinking. "Yes, with the right trigger…he may feel as if he's back in the war, in that same situation. He could even be seeing those soldiers' faces, the original attackers, on his recent victims—like a hallucination."

Ortiz's face on Amos's body? Maybe. Wartime was often difficult to reconcile with morality, and their guy had seen a woman raped to death with a sharp stick. That would fuck anyone up.

Anyone who wasn't a complete psycho.

JACKSON WAITED IN THE HALL—"HE tends to get uncomfortable around groups larger than two"—and Petrosky followed Idowu into the man's room. Bezon smiled at the doctor as they entered, the kind of goofy grin a little kid gives you when you arrive with a stuffed animal. But the man's face was all sharp planes and angles, not an ounce of filler in the hollows under his cheekbones. Bezon kept all his chub in the gut resting on his ample thighs—the thick ass planted on the edge of his bed. Eyes curious, but calm. How many people had he killed in that village?

Petrosky slid into a chair across from Bezon. Idowu remained standing behind him, her posture more relaxed than in the atrium—maybe trying to put her patient at ease. "Like we talked about, Julius, Mr. Petrosky has a few questions for you."

"Just one, actually." Petrosky gestured to the legal pad in his lap, kindly borrowed from Idowu. The doc had warned them that Bezon had a tendency to shut down unless he felt comfortable—that he'd always refused to talk about his time in the war. A list of his fellow raping-and-pillaging comrades was going to be a huge stretch for a guy who hadn't discussed it for seven years...and counting. "I need the names of those you served with in Iraq."

Bezon stiffened. "No." But his eye twitched, hard—an angry wink.

"Surely you remember a few of them, at least? Maybe you remember Jeffrey Dunne?"

Bezon looked down at his round belly. "He broke his neck."

"He did. Do you know how?"

"He fell."

Huh. "What about Chandler Ortiz?"

Bezon flinched like he had a fly in his ear, but there were no flies that Petrosky could see—no bugs at all unless the guy had lice. If he did, he probably deserved it. "He fell too," Bezon said. But his arms were trembling.

"There were a few other people with you, right? Your friends?" *Your raping, murdering friends?* Petrosky dropped his gaze to the man's hands, clenched like talons on the edge of the bed—thin, but on a trigger they'd do some damage. Or with a stick.

"No friends of mine," Bezon spat. Angry at the implication—Petrosky hadn't expected that. He was acting more like their vigilante suspect than the rapists.

Make him comfortable, Idowu's voice whispered in his mind. Of course, she was right; this guy was already angry at being connected to the group. Petrosky was one wrong word away from the silent treatment. "I can understand that," Petrosky said softly. "Sometimes we're stuck with a bunch of assholes, am I right?"

Bezon blinked at him. He nodded slowly.

Petrosky shifted in his seat, the cracked wood biting into his thighs. "I served overseas, near where you were deployed, actually. Watched a buddy of mine die right in front of me, and the bastards who did that...I'll never forgive them."

Bezon was watching him intently now, and the gleam in his eyes tugged at a place deep in Petrosky's chest because he recognized it in himself—guilt. Guilt that he'd lived. That he hadn't been able to do things differently.

Maybe this guy hadn't hurt anyone. Maybe he'd seen those atrocities and it had broken him because he wasn't a fucking psychopath like Dunne and the good general.

"I carry that around with me," Petrosky went on. "Every damn day. But if I had a chance to go after the motherfuckers who blasted a hole in Joey's head, I'd do it in a second. I'd tell the world their names and let the universe sort it out." Sand burned in his throat. His ribs were a vise, far too small for his throbbing heart.

Bezon dropped his head and stared at his knuckles, clenched and white and angry.

"In your place, I wouldn't want to protect them. I wouldn't want to carry that too. It's less of a burden if you don't have to be alone with it." But it wasn't. The pain stayed —it always stayed.

Bezon raised his head, his eyes brimming with tears.

"The men you're protecting...one of them is hurting innocent people, Julius. Here. In this city."

Tears trailed down Bezon's cheeks.

"Detective..." Idowu put her hand on Petrosky's shoulder, but he lowered his voice further still. "Just tell me who was there with you. Help me before someone else dies. Help me save a life."

With tears streaming down his cheeks, Julius Bezon did just that.

29

JACKSON FLIPPED the last of the folders closed and made a note on her pad. Bezon had remembered the names of six soldiers, which brought their grand total to ten men, including the general. The odds of finding a few of these guys were in their favor, even if it would take a little luck. And at the moment, it seemed luck was on their side; the bullpen was gloriously empty save the two of them.

Jackson slugged back her police department coffee and winced. She set the cup back on the desktop—his desktop.

"Don't you have your own workspace, Jackson?" He rubbed at a sore spot just above his heart. Maybe he should go back and see Dr. Rosenberg...if she wasn't pissed at him for trying to wrangle information. Yeah, maybe next week.

Jackson gestured to the folder in his hand. "We can ignore the ones who live out of state—"

"Ignore them?" Petrosky snapped. "They're still rapists. Murderers. Someone should pick their sorry asses up and—"

"Focus, you old bastard." She stared daggers at him.

Petrosky rubbed harder at his achy chest and pushed aside the file he'd been looking at, one of the soldiers from

Dunne's and Bezon's group. Some Utah finance manager with twerpy little eyes and a twerpier mouth. Stupid hair plastered to his head in a bowl cut like the ones Petrosky's own mother used to give him when he was five. Jackson was still looking at him, lips tight.

Fine. He slapped the folder shut. They could come back to these bastards, but none of them were going to walk, not if he had anything to say about it.

Petrosky inhaled slowly, forcing his heart rate to slow before he blew his pacemaker clear into his rib cage. "So, who do we have left in state? Who had opportunity for these killings?"

Jackson tipped her pad. Four names circled in blue ink: Vernon Collins, Todd Rose, Aldrich Cook, and Rye Turner. More than he'd expected. "Four out of twelve? With Bezon and the general, that's a full half of the squad that ended up in Michigan."

"Yeah, they came back from overseas at the right time. Remember that study like ten years back about how Detroit was the worst city for veterans?"

He did. And the initiative right after, Project Foundation or something. They'd set up a few apartment buildings for returning veterans, let them live there free, gave them money for college if they stayed local, even had some funds for schoolbooks and shit. Turned out, these guys had taken advantage of the program—except for General DeLaney and Rye Turner. Not that this helped them now. Jackson slid a folder from lower in the stack and opened it to the driver's license photos of their four suspects.

Different hair colors: one black, two brown, one reddish. None of them blond like Eden Johansson and Layton had described. Either the women had lied—highly unlikely—or he'd dyed it, or the single streetlight in the cemetery glared in such a way as to make him look blond. Both times. Witness statements were often a little wonky, as Dr. Idowu might say, but goddammit.

"It could be any of these guys." Petrosky stifled a yawn, running his hand over his face. He suddenly felt twenty years older—even his bones felt heavy.

"Yeah. None of them are especially huge either," Jackson said. "At least not according to their driver's licenses."

"What about employment records?"

She shuffled the files. "Collins is still military, works recruitment out in Holly. Rose is a bank manager. Cook is a psychologist, if you can believe that." She rolled her eyes —*fucking shrinks*. "No recent tax forms on Turner, so he's either unemployed, or being paid under the table—can't even be sure he's in Michigan. We just know that his family was from here."

"Rye Turner," Petrosky muttered. "Sounds like a fucking sandwich."

"You're just hungry." Jackson wrinkled her nose, maybe in distaste. *Come on, Jackson, even you have to admit sandwiches sound amazing.* "We still have a lot more research to do; not sure yet who was in the state during the earlier murders."

Right. Alibis. The driver's license images lay in the middle of the desktop—four men staring at the ceiling from beside the sketch of the killer. Petrosky searched their faces, looking for similarities to the sketch—*which of you fuckers is it?*—but came up short. "It'll be faster to talk to the ones we've already located. Ask them to clear themselves." Then they'd double down looking for Turner, the only one they didn't have an address for—put out his photo, see what came back. Maybe he wasn't in Michigan at all. Maybe they'd find him in Seattle with a man bun, growing hemp, living in one of those tiny one-room shed-turned-house things people loved to talk about but wouldn't actually live in.

"Clear themselves?" Jackson snorted. "I'm sure a bunch of murderous rapists are going to be incredibly forthcoming."

"Might be not all of them are guilty. Look at Bezon." That guy had been as traumatized as their killer by what he'd seen in the village; it was still possible that he'd participated, that his own actions had pushed his break with reality, but Petrosky didn't think so. He'd seen people break—seen monsters break after doing monstrous shit—and he could practically smell it on them, the guilt like sour vomit under whatever cologne they used to cover their secrets. Bezon didn't have that monster in him; Petrosky'd have bet money on it. And he felt in his bones that their perp was on the right side of the rapes. The overseas murders.

But here...the soldier was a killer. Samuel Amos deserved justice.

Petrosky stared at the photos. Looked again at that goddamn generic sketch. Wider set eyes, but not too wide. Middle-of-the-road jaw. Collins was the biggest—had the lightest hair too. But he couldn't see their hands in the driver's license photos. He suddenly felt certain that if he just looked at their fingers, he'd be able to tell which of them could snap a spine in one fell swoop.

"How many of these guys are married?" he asked instead.

Jackson pointed: Rose, Collins.

"I doubt our guy is married or has a girlfriend. He seems to see any sexual activity as threatening, can't tell the difference between consensual sex and rape. The moment he sees either, he flashes back to that village."

Jackson nodded. "Maybe. But there's lots of variability in sexual activity among couples. Maybe she's getting it elsewhere, or she's okay without."

"Yeah." He eyed the pictures again. Resisted the urge to put his head on his desk. *Coffee, more coffee.*

"You okay, Petrosky?"

"Huh?"

Jackson leaned closer. "How's Linda?"

"I wouldn't know." Petrosky stretched his arms above his head, trying to shake the cobwebs from his brain as he drew his gaze to the far side of the bullpen, to the wide square windows through which the darkness glowered—night already? *Shit.* Their perp might kill again at any time, and who was to say the next murder would be justified?

They'd have to visit these guys first thing in the morning. All except...

Petrosky reached for the folder, his eyes on Sandwich Man.

The shoes. The worn-flat boot print.

"This guy..." Petrosky tapped the driver's license photo of Rye Turner, the picture nine years old already. "Expired?"

"Yep. Was up for online renewal five years back, but he never bothered, and I already called his last known address in Ferndale. No go. Only family is a cousin in Long Beach, but the guy didn't even know Turner had been deployed, hadn't talked to him since they were little kids—before Turner's father died."

"Was he murdered?" Petrosky asked, heart rate increasing. The violent death of a family member could trigger someone not previously prone to aggression.

"Nope, just an older parent; he was almost sixty when Turner was born."

"Mother?"

"She was forty-eight when he was born and sent him off to war without telling him she had cancer. She died during his deployment; was living on social security, no inheritance. Not a single friend that we could find either."

If Petrosky had come home from war carrying that kind of baggage to find his last source of emotional support had vanished, maybe he'd have lost his shit too. Rye Turner was looking less like a sandwich and more like a killer. "The fuck, Jackson? He's our best bet, why didn't you lead with this?"

"Just checking to make sure your brain's still working." She winked. When he frowned, she said, "We have no address, no phone, nothing, so we need to chat up the others anyway—they might know where he is."

Petrosky nodded. "Agreed. Let's run his photo by Eden Johansson first, though, see what she says."

"I'll do that on my way home." Jackson stood, and he glanced up.

"You heading out now?"

"Lance has been having some issues lately. I think me being gone so long during the day…" She looked down, her eyes tight as they had been so many times during the last few weeks. Stressed.

Not drama with Decantor, not a new relationship—her son. Her ex-husband helped exactly none with Lance, acted like the boy didn't even exist. It chapped Petrosky's ass. He'd have given anything to bring Julie back.

"Take it easy tonight, okay? Get some sleep?" Jackson grabbed her suit jacket from her desk, her own desk—she had her own workspace after all. If only she'd move her chair back over there. "Need a ride, or is your harem picking you up?"

He stared at the photos, one, then another, a prickly feeling taking root between his shoulder blades—his instincts trying to talk to him. His gaze drifted to the sketch. *Are you still out there? Are you hunting?* "I'm good."

"You are not," she called over her shoulder. The door to the stairwell opened with a *scree* and clanged shut again.

He waited a moment, listening to the sudden silence. Then he picked up the desk phone. He had one more thing to do before going home.

"I'M glad you called instead of taking an Uber." Billie held tight to Duke's leash, but the dog wasn't tugging her along—he stayed at her heel, ears pricked, alert. He'd been like that since Billie had parked Petrosky's Caprice up the road from the cemetery; compelled to protect. The way Petrosky felt compelled to...see. To look at these streets for himself. It made no sense, he knew it didn't—the guy wasn't going to just wander out of the shadows and shake his hand, and he'd smell a sting a mile away—but Petrosky had spent enough time in the armed forces to understand habit. Routine. He couldn't shake the feeling that their guy was still there, lurking, waiting. Watching.

The buildings on their left blocked his view of the sky, but from the shadows on the ground, he knew the moon was glowing softly from somewhere beyond the walls of brick and steel. Billie's hair gleamed silvery-gold in the light from the streetlamp.

"Such a gorgeous night," she said. She inhaled deeply and sighed, a little smile gracing her full lips.

"You sure you want to be out here?" He'd told her he'd drop her at home, but Billie had insisted on accompanying him, said walking was good for the soul.

But what would he tell himself if she got hurt? No, he was being overprotective— overbearing, as Dr. McCallum would say. Their killer didn't hurt the woman; if he went after someone, it would be Petrosky himself.

Their footsteps reverberated up the empty street. The dark was thick and cozy with a humidity that made the sweat bead on the back of his neck. Better out here than behind the cemetery, that dim, lonely stretch of gravel, the fork leading to the long-forgotten pavilion...just peeking back there had made the air feel warmer, heavier—muddy. But they had nothing to worry about even there, not really; Duke would wrap his jaws around the guy's throat before he got within three feet of either of them. And he'd never be able to hurt anyone again. *If Duke's fast enough.*

"Have you been exercising?" Billie asked, and her voice reminded him of Shannon. Shannon used to ask him that every other day before she moved out of state. She still asked him, but only every three months or so. When she called.

Petrosky eyed the streetlight a few blocks up the way, the only one on this road besides the one in the center of the cemetery. To his left, shadows encroached upon the brick buildings, blotting out the doorways—more than enough room to hide a man, even a large one, in the blackness. But there was no movement there now. Not even a rat. *Of course there's not.* But the prickling between his shoulders had not relented.

"Yeah, I've been walking," he said. "Doing a lot of pacing at the office."

Billie smiled at him again, her teeth a gilded moonbeam silver, like her hair.

Their footsteps echoed against the brick—*thunk, thunk, thunk*—along with the tapping of Duke's nails. The cemetery was closer now, off to their right. The spikes of wrought iron were softened by the moon, their sharp tips glowing orange.

Duke whined and nudged his hand, and Petrosky scratched his ears. They went on, listening to the subtle breeze hissing through the cemetery grass.

The road where Layton was attacked loomed on their left a block up. The streetlamp cast just enough light to see into the mouth of the alley—lots of shadows. What were they hiding? Their suspect knew how to stay safe from prying eyes—and he only needed seconds to attack, kill, and disappear.

"You okay, Eddie?"

"Yeah. Just thinking." Petrosky eyeballed the streetlamp, the large swaths of shadow—the light at the mouth of the alley. No matter how sick their suspect was, no matter his intentions, he had the presence of mind to sneak up and attack and then vanish back into the shadows. How many attacks had he let slide because he didn't want to get caught? Maybe he wasn't as altruistic as he seemed.

Either way, their killer wasn't just slipping into flashbacks. He was watching, waiting—a soldier on a mission. Bad news for them. They'd have trouble finding him even if they staged an attack. *So why am I here?*

Petrosky stiffened as they passed the alleyway, straining his ears, waiting for the snap of a twig, the gentle thud of worn boots on the asphalt, the whispered words that preceded the attacks, but all he heard was the beat of their sneakers, Duke's panting, and the throb of his own heart. Then...a *click*.

He whirled around in time to see a cat—mangy, matted fur—skittering up a downspout, claws scratching maniacally against the metal—*scritchshcritchscritch*. Duke turned back and cocked his head; he stopped walking. Billie whistled—"Come on, big guy." Duke garumphed and followed again, reluctantly at first, but within ten steps he was panting happily once more.

"We're not just out on a walk, are we?" Billie said.

"I told you it might get you killed."

She rolled her eyes. "You say that about everything."

He balked, eyes still on the road ahead. "I told you there was a murderer out here. That I was going to take a walk and look for him."

"You say that all the time, too."

"I don't always tell you they'll snap your neck; or that they'll snap mine if they think I'm a bad guy." Sweat dripped off his neck and down between his shoulders. "We'll just stay in the light."

She smiled at him. "You always say weird shit, Eddie. But you're not the bad guy—and I'll make sure whoever we meet knows it." She elbowed him, grinning, and Duke peered up at her—*wag, wag, wag.* "And anyway, you're the one who said it isn't worth living your whole life scared. It's a lovely night for a walk."

"Well, shit, I didn't think anyone ever listened to me."

She met his eyes—determined. With all she'd seen, some maniac with a penchant for saving rape victims was hardly going to scare her.

He sighed, scanning the street once more. What had he been hoping to find? If he did see their perp, what was he going to do? Shake his fucking hand? No, bring him in, of course, bring him in but...

The killer wasn't out here. There was no logical reason to believe he was. As much as Petrosky wanted him to be watching, casing, all within easy range of handcuffs—or a bullet—sometimes his gut was wrong.

He smiled at Billie, though it hurt his face, just a little. Scratched behind Duke's ears.

"So tell me about your day," Petrosky said as she threaded her arm through his. Billie was right. It was a lovely night for a walk.

30

ALDRICH COOK WAS a cagey bitch with a little wisp of a mustache that looked like a rat's tail and a face to match. He sat behind his gleaming oak desk with his fingers steepled, the way Dr. McCallum sometimes did, but this guy was no McCallum—that would require empathy. Cook raised the little hairs on the back of Petrosky's neck in a way Bezon hadn't. A smiling monster. Cocky as fuck.

Eden Johansson hadn't identified Turner as the man who'd killed her boyfriend, nor had she recognized any of the other men—"None of them seem right." But despite this, they were still viable suspects; everything else fit. And witnesses were often wrong.

"We had an interesting conversation with one of your old comrades," Jackson said. "Julius Bezon?"

Idowu had assured them that Bezon was in the hospital for the long haul, which should protect him from a guy like Cook—should the man decide to play murder-the-witness.

"Ah." Cook nodded knowingly as if they'd just told him that their sex life wasn't perfect and that they needed a little shrink-y assistance. "Even back then, well before I finished

my doctorate, I knew there was something off about him."
Had to bring up your fancy-ass degrees, didn't you, asshole?

"How so?" Jackson asked.

"Oh, you know. Wandering around at odd hours. Talking through you instead of to you. Nightmares. Used to scream himself awake—never got any rest around him, but he fueled my interest in psychology, and well…" He gestured to the room around him, to the glass sculptures on the shelves. The modern painting on the wall behind his desk looked like someone had sneezed green-yellow mucus on a canvas; it had probably cost more than Petrosky's car. "It turned out well enough for me."

Bezon had felt everything so deeply it had driven him insane, and their perp had experienced so much grief or guilt that he was willing to kill to ensure the things he'd seen didn't happen again on his watch. Now they were talking about a man screaming himself awake, and Cook was grinning like a fool. No feelings whatsoever?

"Where were you last Saturday night?" Jackson asked.

Petrosky watched the man's face. Might as well cover all their bases, and if he was being honest, he hoped he'd get to see the little fucker squirm.

But Cook's eyes stayed exactly the same, as did his smile, his little rat-tail 'stache unmoving on his lip. "I was at home all night. With my fiancée. Why?"

"A fiancée, huh? Pretty old for a first-time groom." Petrosky scanned the shelves, the desk. No wedding photos. No pictures at all. "Any kids, Cook?"

He shook his head, not like a normal person—emaciated movements devoid of passion. "No kids. Never felt that pull." He narrowed his eyes but kept his lips the same.

"Do you speak any other languages?"

"A little Spanish. I'm not fluent, but I can get along while on vacation." He smiled—*Faker*. "Are these really the questions you came here to ask? My secretary seemed to think it was important."

"Oh, I'm so sorry," Petrosky said. He gestured to Jackson. "Really...she and I...we apologize for holding you up. We know you have important work to do here."

Cook's shoulders relaxed. He stood, smile wider. "No problem, Detectives. If you have other questions, email always works well."

Petrosky crossed his legs. "One more thing. Do you remember Oscar Dunne?"

Cook lowered himself back into his chair and laid his hands, palm-down, on the desktop. Careful, deliberate, *slow*, like he was holding something fragile between his ass cheeks. "Yes, of course. He was injured during our deployment."

"Who found him?" Petrosky watched Cook, scanning his face, his shoulders, his—*ah*, the tiniest twitch in his pinky finger. But that fake smile remained plastered on his maw.

"I'm sorry?"

"Dunne. Do you remember who found him after he got hurt? Who was first on the scene?"

When Cook remained silent, Jackson leaned forward. "We're just looking for a little information, Cook. Help us out."

"I'm sorry, Detectives, but I don't remember. I assume this is about a case, something recent, but I don't have much time to watch the news. I find most of it to be too...sensational."

"Fair enough," Jackson said, but her eyes were spitting fire.

Cook smiled like that was a compliment.

"What about the other men you were deployed with? Are you in regular contact with them?"

"Haven't been for some time. Those days are well behind us."

"True, true." Petrosky sniffed. "But did you know there's

no statute of limitations on war crimes?" He leaned back in his chair, watching Cook's face for any indications of distress, but if the good doctor was uncomfortable or nervous, he no longer showed any sign of it. "That's a useful tidbit, isn't it? And people who answer our questions…well, some might get a bit of a break." Hopefully not much of one, but that wasn't up to him—civilian law enforcement had no influence over war crimes tribunals, regardless of what he was saying to Cook.

"I have no idea what you're—"

"Do you know what guilt does to a person, Cook?"

"Well, of course." The man's mouth curved into a smug smile. "I am a psychologist, after all."

Which means jack shit. This guy was far too composed—he wasn't going to give them anything. Unless they made him sweat. "So you know what happens when all that guilt festers inside, and the person has no fancy office to distract themselves?"

Cook crossed his arms and leveled his gaze at Petrosky. "I don't have anything I need to distract myself from."

"No one said you did—why did you automatically assume I meant *you* felt guilty? Is that one of those Freudian slips people keep talking about?" *React, fucker.* Petrosky pushed himself to standing and slapped a card on Cook's desk, knocking one of the sculptures—some stupid oversized marble run through with wisps of orange and blue—off its stand. It rolled onto the floor and shattered. "Oh shit, sorry about that."

Jackson rose and headed out, nodding to Petrosky. Cook remained sitting, his face a mask. He didn't glance at the card or the shattered orb, but his arms had tensed, his knuckles white.

Petrosky turned back with his hand on the doorknob. "You're the shrink, Doc. What happens when you have nothing left to lose? When you're a prisoner in your own brain?"

Cook's smile faltered. Not much, but enough to make that rat-tail mustache tremble.

Petrosky lowered his voice. "Turns out your pal Dunne doesn't have much of a reason to hide your secrets anymore; or the secrets of the others in your little village-raiding group. Between him and Bezon, we've got a hell of a story." He pulled the door open. "Who knows when your office might be raided by uniforms. Kinda like what happened to those unfortunate villagers in Iraq...except you'll probably live." As he walked out, he glanced back once in time to see Cook's smile fall.

TODD ROSE LIVED in an adorable little Birmingham suburb that made Petrosky want to punch a kitten. How the fuck had these guys come home from Iraq and gone on with their lives after what they'd seen? After what they'd done?

But Petrosky had too. He'd joined the academy, made detective, had a family, all while working through bloody flashbacks that seemed to come out of nowhere. The only reason those flashbacks had vanished for a time was because he'd been obsessed with Julie's death. Knowing she'd been targeted because of him, knowing he hadn't been able to save his own daughter—he'd almost killed himself too many times to count. If he'd actually pulled the trigger in some Iraqi village, killed a bunch of innocents, it would have fucking destroyed him. Like it had Bezon. And their suspect. He was still considering this when Rose's wife settled them in wing-backs in a spotless blue-and-yellow living room and sat on the tufted couch beside her husband.

Jackson pulled out her notepad. They'd decided in the car

that Petrosky would take the reins; rapists responded better to other men, and they weren't sure what brand of sick-o Rose was. Yet.

In fact, Rose was the most usual looking fellow Petrosky had ever seen without being as boring and gray as Mr. Johansson—bland, pasty face, clean-shaven, dull brown eyes, dull brown hair, the exact number of wrinkles around the eyes and mouth that you'd expect from a thirty-something bank manager. Petrosky was shocked there weren't precisely two-and-a-half children coloring quietly at the dining room table. And Rose's hands…tiny. Spindly. Weak. Not enough upper body strength to jerk someone's neck around—he didn't think.

But what drew his attention most was Rose's wife, Marcy. Brilliantly blond and waifish, white blouse, long blue skirt that matched the stripes in the curtains. She kept her gaze on the coffee table between them, steadfastly refusing to look at him or Jackson. Wringing her fingers like dishrags.

"So this is about a case?" Rose asked. His voice was average too—a steady tenor.

Petrosky nodded slowly, his eyes still on the wife. "Your deployment to Iraq… Do you know where to find the men you served with? Are you still friends?"

"I…no. I mean, some of us were close briefly after we came home, living in that apartment building downtown, but as soon as we graduated college, got jobs…" He shrugged.

"And where were you last Saturday?"

"Here." Rose frowned. "We had house guests, my wife's mother in from Nebraska. Just left yesterday." Marcy nodded agreement. "What's this all about?"

"We have reason to believe that one of the men you served with is responsible for a series of murders in Ash Park."

Marcy raised her head, eyes widening—irises a deep, rich emerald, like fresh-cut grass.

Rose's jaw dropped.

"You look surprised, Mr. Rose."

Rose finally blinked. "I...I mean, I am. You think one of the people from Iraq..."

"Why would that be so shocking, Mr. Rose? Two soldiers in your division were attacked during your deployment. Chandler Ortiz was murdered, and Oscar Dunne got his fool head twisted around so far he'll never walk again. Never breathe on his own either. I'm honestly amazed you and your team managed to save him."

Rose's head jerked up, down, up, down. "We did a lot of CPR. And one of our helicopters was grounded in the next major city over."

"Do you remember the names of the men who were there with you, helping to save Dunne from certain death?" Was the killer among them, faking like he was helping when really he wanted the guy dead?

"Let's see...me. And Collins." He frowned. "I think Miller was there too."

The elusive Miller—Dunne had mentioned him also, but they hadn't found any records of the man. "Why save him?"

"Excuse me?"

"Dunne. One-in-a-million shot that he'd live. With everything else that happened in that village, I'm surprised you were able to make time to fly off into the sunset with an almost certainly dying man."

"You don't leave your own men behind." His gaze hardened.

"You left Ortiz."

"He was dead."

"Right, dead—murdered. And yet the idea that one of you is a murder suspect is a shock?"

His jaw dropped, but he recovered quickly. "Ortiz and Dunne...I mean, that wasn't one of us. We were in enemy territory, any of those Iraqis would have cut off our heads and shit down our necks just for giggles."

"Ah, yes, that little village on the outskirts, all the enemy women and children milling around, snapping people's cervical spines like assassins."

Rose sat taller, spine straightening as if in defiance of the idea that it could ever be broken. Marcy laid her hand on his arm, where the muscles had gone rigid, but yanked it back just as fast, as if she'd been shocked. Petrosky frowned. Rose may not have murdered Samuel Amos, but that didn't mean he wasn't hurting people.

"I'm not trying to bust your balls here, Rose, but one of the men from your squad is a killer." *Or all of you.* "With a renegade on the loose, a man who was once close to you, I just want to make sure that you stay safe." Petrosky drew his gaze to Marcy. "Do you feel safe?"

If Rose noticed Petrosky was watching his wife, he didn't show it. Marcy finally met Petrosky's eyes. And swallowed hard. *That's a no.*

"We're fine," Rose said. "I've never felt like I was in danger, even when I was over there."

"Even in enemy territory?"

Rose shrugged. Marcy looked away. Her demeanor alone led Petrosky to believe that there was something wrong with her husband, but Rose had a better poker face than Cook. Still, he'd wager this guy wasn't upset enough about those overseas crimes to be out killing perpetrators now. And from the state of his spic-and-span cookie-cutter house, Rose wasn't someone who'd keep a pair of old shredded boots in the back of the closet.

Rose was studying the window at Petrosky's back. "You

think whoever did that to Dunne...you think he's after all of us?"

"I thought you said it was the enemy who did that to Dunne."

Rose narrowed his eyes. "But you just said it wasn't, you just said it was one of—"

"I wasn't there, Rose." Petrosky leaned closer over the wooden coffee table, carved edges, spindly legs. "I'm just trying to get a feel for what happened. Who was there, who might be a suspect."

Rose's gaze drifted to the ceiling...remembering or manufacturing a story? "Cook's always been a little weird."

Petrosky leaned back. "Cook would surely disagree."

"Yeah." A smile. "So maybe don't tell him."

Ah, we're comrades now, eh? What else could he squeeze out of him? "What about the general who was there with you... maybe he was a colonel then. What was his name?"

"DeLaney?"

"Yeah, that's the one." Petrosky forced a smile. "So was DeLaney there when Dunne was attacked?"

Rose shook his head. "I don't think so. I can't remember who was there, really. It all happened so fast." And when he leveled his gaze at Petrosky, the dull brown in his eyes had gone even flatter. He wasn't going to tell them shit without a little encouragement. Just like Cook. And two panicked soldiers would increase the odds that one of them would slip up, maybe tell the wrong person their darkest secret—or out the others.

"Was DeLaney the one giving you and the other men orders in the village?"

"I mean, he was in charge." Rose swallowed hard, his Adam's apple bobbing—like Dunne, but without the breathing tube snaking out of his neck.

"Do you speak Arabic?"

"What? No."

"Did DeLaney tell you to murder the women and children in that village?" *Whiplash*.

Rose's neck went still, as did his chest. "Excuse me?"

"Maybe he told you to rape them too? Or did he just want you to slit their throats?"

Marcy had stopped breathing, her chalk-white face making her eyes look even darker—greener. But Rose...he was beet red from the tips of his ears to his now clenched fists. Was Rose the kind of man who took his anger out on his wife?

"How dare you!" Rose roared. His composure had slipped away as cleanly as if it had been flensed from his bones.

Petrosky stood. "You know as well as I do that the things you did in that village would never be accepted by any military court." *Or by any decent human being.* "And I'd hate to have to call witnesses as to your state of mind after you realized you gave up the general when no one else did." That was a lie, DeLaney had told them he was there, but Rose's pink face paled.

Jackson rose from her seat. "If you have a name for us, a real lead on this killer, maybe we'll look at a deal," she said.

Petrosky's fists tightened, heat slinging through his veins like molten steel. He clamped his lips shut. *A fucking deal?* She was playing Rose, he knew that—it was the same line he'd fed to Cook—but just the thought made him want to hit Rose in the face. Then throw him off a freeway overpass.

Jackson handed Rose her card. Petrosky gave his to Marcy. Hopefully she'd use it before this guy hurt her, or worse.

But he knew better.

31

VERNON COLLINS HAD GONE HOME sick according to the recruitment office where he usually spent his nine to five. *Interesting.* Despite his gainful employment, running off made Collins Petrosky's top pick for killer, just ahead of the evasive Rye Turner. And Collins was the biggest of the four men. And had the lightest hair. Plus, still being in recruitment, he'd probably have a spare pair of old boots lying around. It was possible he really had felt ill; the only other worker at the recruitment office said he'd looked pale and harried—"Probably got the runs." But nothing made you run like being a murder suspect.

"Can you imagine being in a situation like these guys, what they saw, what they did, and actively trying to recruit more young people into the service?" Jackson's knuckles were tight around the steering wheel, the tires humming against the asphalt. The engine whined.

Petrosky grunted. But he could imagine it, could see that brutal dull gaze, Collins frothing at the mouth for more action. Jealous of the new recruits, but relishing his ability to relive each horror show he was a party to as he described the far-off places each new kid was going to see in their travels.

To be fair, he could also see an innocent man in Collins's position encouraging his recruits to consider their commitment to the service long and hard—not everyone could live with what he'd seen. Maybe this was his way of giving back, overcompensating for his own trauma by making sure new soldiers were stable enough to serve...or discouraging them altogether. But from Collins's recruitment stats—better than any other recruiter in his building—and the video he'd put out on social media, smiling at the camera, telling the world what a fantastic opportunity the service was... Petrosky was betting on Collins glorifying his time overseas along with the atrocities he'd committed. A man like that deserved to be in a box.

The tires squealed as Jackson took a hard right. "I forgot to tell you: Eden Johansson's coming in tomorrow morning to talk to the DA about Bubba the Racist Head Smasher."

"Coming in? You're making her—"

"Hey, I'm not making her do anything," she said, turning onto a tree-lined street, every house set back from the road with uniform bushes and short little walkways past flowerbeds of tulips and columbine. Linda used to love tulips. Did she still?

"The DA certainly isn't going to go to her house," Jackson said, "but Eden said she'd feel more comfortable at the office next door to the station anyway. Sounds like she's still looking over her shoulder."

Jackson checked her GPS and hooked a left down another side street. Merrick Road was a carbon copy of the street they'd just turned off of, but instead of tulips, the flowerbeds boasted more ornamental grasses—unless the homeowners had just let the lawn overtake the flowers. He'd never been good at telling whether that shit was on purpose. Not that it really mattered.

"I can understand her watching her back after getting her face busted up," Petrosky said. "I hope they get ol' Bubba on a hate crime. Then he gets aggravated battery. What's the minimum on that?"

Jackson snorted. "No way the hate crime thing will stick. He attacked a white girl."

"For the made-up crime of protecting a Muslim."

"Don't worry," she muttered, squinting out the windshield at the passing houses. "Rich white girl with connected parents? They'll get him on something."

She braked so suddenly that Petrosky's seatbelt caught on his gut. "What the fuck, Jackson?"

"We're here."

Collins's house had the same damn hedges as the rest of the neighborhood, straight and creased like a newly made barracks cot. The edging around the closely shorn lawn was perfectly uniform. Perfectly green. A long, thin rectangular window glinted from the space above the front door: eight square pieces of stained glass—red, green, blue, yellow, repeat—all spotless. He didn't even have to go inside to know he could bounce a quarter off this guy's bed. But the car...

A dark green Buick LaCrosse, shiny and unblemished, sat in the driveway. Crooked. Guy must have been in a hurry.

Jackson rang the bell. The air smelled of hydrangea. The one flowering bush near the door was a washed-out blue, a little garden stool sitting beside it as if someone here enjoyed the easy chaos of the undulating blooms. Still trimmed savagely, square, but better than the hedges.

Bees buzzed. No sounds from inside.

Petrosky reached for the knocker; it landed with a hollow *clunk*. He banged it a few more times for good measure.

The bees buzzed on. Somewhere in the distance, a car door slammed. Nothing more.

Petrosky sniffed. "You hear screams in there, Jackson?"

She shook her head. "Knock it off. You can't just go barreling in there and tell the brass you heard screaming."

"We're in pursuit of a suspicious fellow."

"A suspicious fellow? That's not a thing."

"Whatever he is, he's here," Petrosky said, gesturing to the car parked haphazardly in the drive. "The fact that he's not answering the door—"

"You don't answer your door either."

"I'm not a people person." Petrosky stepped down off the porch into the flower bed, edging toward the front window behind the hydrangea, branches scraping at his back through his jacket. He peered through the glass—six chairs upholstered in flowery fabric, a long oak table, and a three-pronged candelabra in the center, all of it steeped in shadow now that the sun had passed overhead and was easing down the back side of the house. "Maybe he's destroying evidence—we shouldn't let him get too far."

"And just what evidence do you think he has?" Jackson said from the porch. "There's nothing to suggest our suspect took souvenirs from Amos or any of the other victims, and what would he have brought back from overseas? A fucking scalp?"

Petrosky climbed out of the flowers and heaved his way back up to stand beside Jackson. "I've seen worse."

She shook her head. "We can't connect him to any crime...yet. We don't have grounds to search, and we definitely don't have grounds to arrest him—we can't even bring him in for questioning unless he agrees."

"We can strongly encourage it." Petrosky snatched up the garden seat from beneath the blue flowers. A bee buzzed by his ear, angry, then clearly thought better of it—it flitted away.

"I don't think you're supposed to stand on that."

Petrosky settled the tiny stool on the porch beneath the upper windows.

"If you fall and break your ass, I'm going to laugh all the way to the hospital."

He stepped onto the stool, tentative, but it held; then he climbed up, his hands braced on the door, and peered through the stained glass at a world turned red. Wood floors. Was that blood? No—just the glass. A dark towel or some other article of clothing lay crumpled in the foyer. A brief-case sat in the front hallway. Through an archway to the right of the foyer, he could see the corner of an oriental area rug; probably the living room. And on the floor just inside the living room entrance...

The bottom of a boot. Unmoving. His heart ratcheted up, heating his face.

"Got a foot," Petrosky said, stepping down. "Could be him or the wife—he's married, right?"

Jackson took his place, squinting through the stained glass window. "I can't see anything past the bottom of the boot; we don't know for sure there's a human attached to it." But when she jumped back down, her face was resigned. "But it's enough."

Jackson called it in. Petrosky stepped back and took a breath, lowering his shoulder, heart in his throat, preparing to ram the front door. Maybe he should jimmy it, that'd be easier, but it'd been way too long since he'd smashed his way into a building—the good old-fashioned way. Hopefully his heart could take it.

"Whoa, hang on." Jackson reached past him for the handle. It turned easily.

"Show off." Petrosky straightened. And raised his gun.

They slipped into house, Jackson to the left, Petrosky with his back against the right foyer wall. "Police!" But for the echo of his voice off the plaster, the house stayed silent, a weighty hush swallowing the remnants of his words. He sidled up the hall, closer to the living room, toward the shoe, his own sneakers squeaking like shy mice against the wood. From this angle, he could see the top of the boot—the blank space where a calf should have been.

Empty. He froze, listening. Collins would have heard the doorbell, the knocker, and them entering the foyer. He knew exactly where they were. But where was he?

Jackson's rubber soles tapped on the wood behind him —*thunk, thunk, thunk.*

He bent low, took a long, steady breath, and peered around the arch into the living room. He straightened. And re-holstered his weapon.

"Fuck," Jackson said, her voice barely above a whisper. She pulled out her cell.

Petrosky could still smell the musky stench of sweat and fear lingering in the air, thick and heavy. But that was still less pungent than the metallic stink of blood.

Vernon Collins was slouched in a straight-backed chair upholstered with those stupid little buttons, the white fabric glaringly bright against his blood-splattered skin— completely nude. Mouth open, lips painted ruby, eyes rolled back in his head, the whites spiderwebbed with vessels. The beige wall behind him was studded with bits of brain and bone. Thin streams of crimson trailed down the wall toward the floor—shiny and gelatinous and wet. It hadn't been long.

Beyond the boots that had been so carelessly kicked off at the living room entrance, a pair of khakis sat in a neat pile, the two leg holes still visible as if the man had pulled them down and simply stepped out. An undershirt, sweat stains beneath the pits, lay tossed across the back of the couch. "Forensics on the way?"

"Yeah." Jackson sighed. "You think he was our killer?"

"No."

She squinted at him. "We've both seen killers choose death over jail, and vets have much higher rates of suicide than the general population."

"I'm not saying he isn't guilty of those crimes in Iraq." Petrosky scanned the man's thighs, his legs dark with hair and speckled with blood. A jagged scar ran from kneecap to shin. "But I don't think our killer, Amos's killer, would give up so easily. Our suspect is traumatized, sure, but he has a higher purpose."

"A higher purpose like murder," she muttered.

"Or justice."

"Whatever helps you sleep at night." Jackson stepped closer to Collins's chair, scanning the wall behind him, then the blood-stained floor. "Why'd he take his pants off?"

"Like you've never seen a penis before."

"They're not usually so limp when I see them."

"Hey, we've got a dead rapist here, Jackson, show some goddamn respect." But he wasn't sorry Collins was dead, not if he was guilty of rape and murder in that far-away village; he was just irritated that they hadn't had the chance to interrogate him. That they hadn't caught Amos's killer.

"I'm serious, though," Jackson said. "Why bother getting naked?"

Petrosky squatted in front of Collins's khakis and pushed the back pocket open with his blade—saw the rectangle of metal and glass hidden beneath the cloth. Collins's phone. "Cleansing ritual, maybe. Stripping down to his most primal self?" He slipped the cell out and turned it on...stared at the fingerprint request on the screen. *Damn.* He brought the cell back to the body.

"His primal self? You've had too much therapy, Petrosky."

"That's probably true." He stooped and maneuvered the phone beneath Collins's thumb, edging it closer. Hopefully his hand was clean enough to—

Bingo. The thumbprint ID screen blinked off. Petrosky tapped on "Recent Calls." "Speaking of therapy... Collins got a few calls from the shrink," he said in response to Jackson's raised eyebrows. Cook had called Collins right after they'd left his office. Had the doctor called any of the others? They'd pull his phone records—maybe they'd find a number they didn't have yet, like that belonging to the elusive Rye Turner. "Between Cook's calls and this"—he gestured to Collins's shattered skull—"I think it's a good bet he's not an innocent man."

"So much for Cook having no contact with his service buddies." Jackson headed for the foyer. "I think we're alone— no sign of a struggle, and the wife's in real estate, so she should be out at work, but I'm going to poke around anyway while we wait for the ME."

"I fucking hate shrinks," Petrosky said again, mostly to himself. He peered at the weapon on the floor beneath Collins's dangling left hand, then at the single sheet of note-book paper behind his bare heel, stuck to the earth with congealing blood.

"I'm sorry."

Aren't we all, you rapist fuck. Aren't we all.

32

PETROSKY FROWNED out the window of Jackson's Escalade at the darkness beneath the willow trees. The cemetery was a glowing orange beacon behind them, the asphalt of the empty road painted gray with moonlight between the striations of shadow—same gray as the streaks in Linda's hair.

Call her.

No. He had more important things to worry about right now. So he sucked at relationships; then he'd die alone. But if he failed out here, someone else would die...violently. He couldn't accept that. Wouldn't take that risk. He knew too well how that guilt followed you, eating at your insides, festering until it destroyed your relationships...and everything else.

Petrosky sighed and leaned back in the SUV's cushy seat, brooding as he had been for the last thirty minutes. Pulling Cook's or Rose's phone records apparently required a warrant. Bureaucratic bullshit, bullshit that meant they'd never see those records; both Cook and Rose had alibis for the night of Amos's murder, so Petrosky didn't have grounds. He could ask Scott to try hacking into the records somehow, but unless one of them had called the killer, it was a waste of time anyway, and Petrosky couldn't see their killer befriending either of those assholes. The man who'd killed Amos was a vigilante, someone who thought he was saving women, the antithesis of a man whose wife would meekly stare while her husband was accused of rape. That left Rye Turner—and all they had was an expired driver's license. He could have been living anywhere in the world by now.

Could have been, if not for Justin Dubicki's positive ID. Petrosky and Jackson had made it to the soup kitchen just as they were closing up shop; unlike Eden Johansson, Dubicki had recognized Turner immediately, though he noted that the man's dark hair wasn't as neatly kept as it was in the driver's license photo—still short, but messier. *Duh.* Shaving with a razor wasn't the same as trying to cut your own hair with a rusty pair of sewing scissors, or whatever he might have found. Turner still hadn't been back to the soup kitchen —his usual biweekly meal had come and gone—which made sense. Turner was surely lying low after Amos's murder, if he hadn't already hightailed it out of Ash Park. Jackson seemed to think he had. So did Decantor. And the chief.

And yet, these streets pulled at Petrosky like a magnet. This fucker wasn't gone. He might have stopped, might have been medicated, maybe had found a way to repress his urges…but he wasn't finished. Petrosky was sure of that, just as he was certain this place held a special significance for their killer, the soft thick dark around the car calling to their suspect like a drug.

Jackson's eyes stayed on the windshield too, not staring into the night, but through it. Distracted. At least she was willing to humor him. She'd even passed a grease-soaked bag over the center console, the salty deliciousness wafting into his nostrils—egg rolls. But he'd shaken his head, hand on his belly. Something was wrong, something she wasn't saying.

"How's your boy?" Petrosky asked to break the tension that had been steadily building like humidity before a storm. Jackson had called to check on Lance twice while they were driving around today, and both times, she'd hung up looking more distressed than she'd been before she made the calls. It was hard enough leaving your child when they were able to function well in the world, but when your kids had a hard time…how did Jackson manage it?

"He's with my mother tonight." She sighed, but softly like she was trying to hide it. Her gaze remained focused beyond the windshield, on some far-off point in the dark. She reached into the bag for another egg roll.

Petrosky studied her profile in the dim light from the streetlamp up the block—the one near the alley where Layton had been attacked. "Is he—"

"Do you think our guy's out here now?"

Petrosky turned back to the windshield. Outside, everything remained hushed and still. "I don't know." He'd walked with Billie for almost an hour, and he hadn't seen a single car, police or otherwise—hadn't seen a single person. If their perp was smart, he was hiding in another city by now. But with no known associates, not one close friend or family member, this street was the only lead they had. "We'll take a walk around in a few. See what there is to see." *If there is anything.*

Petrosky adjusted himself in the seat. His tailbone ached, and the acid in his guts burned despite the pink shit he'd poured down his gullet. "Maybe we can find some folks on the neighboring streets who have met him. We've been here in the daytime, but there should be a different clientele once the sun goes down." And now they had a driver's license photo; hopefully someone had seen Turner. Or knew where he stayed. Because while Petrosky was aching to go door-to-door, blasting through shelters and tents trying to find their

suspect—anything besides sitting in a fucking car all night—
if they took the more aggressive route, the killer would catch
wind that they were coming well before they got to his
hidey-hole. This city was rife with abandoned buildings,
warehouses, back alleys, freeway underpasses—lots of places
for a well-trained soldier to sneak off to. "Too bad Collins
offed himself before we could get anything out of him,"
Petrosky said. Not that he'd been likely to have information
on Turner, but still.

Jackson wiped a bean sprout from her lip. "Yeah. Collins
kept in touch with Cook, though, so we'll bring him in
tomorrow."

Petrosky nodded. They might not be able to get Cook's
phone records, but Collins's wife had agreed to let them look
through her late husband's—the fact that Cook's was the last
phone call made to the dead man was more than enough to
bring him in for a little chat. "Let Decantor interrogate him."

"Decantor?" Her cheekbones shone in the moonlight that
bounced off the silver heating grates on the dashboard. "Why
Decantor?"

"I like the guy."

She rolled her eyes. "Fine, don't tell me."

It wasn't completely untrue; Decantor had grown on him
over the years, even helped him catch Morrison's killer, but it
was more than that. Cook was a pretentious bastard, with all
his little gleaming art pieces, his meticulous desk, the book-
case with his degrees—a perfectionist. By now, he'd know
Petrosky and Jackson were leads on the case, and that cocky
fuck wouldn't take kindly to being interrogated by someone
lower down the totem pole, even if Petrosky and Decantor
had the same rank. Maybe that would make Cook more
hostile.

And Decantor would take his ass apart.

In his mind's eye, Petrosky saw the shattered glass of

Cook's sculpture, the shards glittering on his wooden floor. His fancy office and his fancy fucking suit. Hiding such darkness.

The worst of humanity always hid in plain sight.

Which reminded him... "That Dunne bastard get whacked yet?" Petrosky asked.

Jackson shook her head. "Nothing going on at the care facility. Uniforms on rotating shifts, not a single sighting of Turner—ever. None of the staff have ever seen the others either; not Cook, Rose, Collins, or our good friend the general."

Petrosky harrumphed. All that shared trauma, and they'd just left Dunne in that room and forgotten about him. Just like their killer had, apparently. Maybe that wasn't shocking either; Dunne was already incapacitated, unable to hurt anyone else, and none of the other attacks were premeditated—it didn't take much planning to snap someone's neck, and there was no way the killer would know ahead of time where victims would be present. And all the others who had been with Turner in Iraq—Collins, Cook, Rose—they'd been right here in Michigan the whole time. They wouldn't have been difficult to find if their killer was cleaning up all the rapists of the world.

So what was he doing? Why here? And why start when he did? He hadn't killed anyone that they could find until two years after he'd returned home from Iraq, and then he'd stopped again for five more years. What had made him shift gears so suddenly? And what had brought him out of retirement to attack Amos last week?

Petrosky's gaze fell to the take-out sack in Jackson's lap. She caught him looking, and this time, he accepted one of the egg rolls—salty and so full of grease that it made his esophagus slippery. But it cleared his head. Maybe it had been a mistake to think this guy was just after vengeance, or even justice. Petrosky had thought he wanted to help—to save people after he'd seen so many die—but maybe their killer was just as guilty. Maybe he had killed and raped on orders and liked the murdering enough to keep it going stateside, a psychopath pretending to be delusional. Wouldn't be the first time a serial killer had tried to set up an insanity defense just in case.

Jackson wiped her hands on a paper napkin and twisted to set the bag on the floor of the backseat, but paused as she righted herself, eyes on the windshield.

Petrosky followed her gaze, squinting. *Acharya?* The journalist was striding up the opposite side of the street, moon silvering his already glossy hair. His high forehead gleamed in the light. "What the hell is this?" Petrosky said around a mouthful of fried dough. The man crossed the street without looking. "Jaywalking. Let's arrest him."

"You can't arrest everyone you don't like." But Jackson was frowning in the journalist's direction.

"Wait, I can't? What kind of shit job is this?"

Acharya kept his eyes on the ground, hands in his pockets. Perhaps he couldn't see them parked in the deep shadows of the willows near the cemetery entrance.

Then he made a beeline straight for them.

Petrosky bolted upright, glowering. "The hell is he—"

The back door opened, and the light flooded Petrosky's eyeballs. *Shit.* Since when did they leave the doors unlocked?

Jackson didn't even turn around. Nor, he realized, did she look shocked. Though her frown remained, her gaze was soft in the dome light's glare, her shoulders far more relaxed than his own—his whole back was rigid against the seat.

"Evening, Detectives." Acharya's smile glowed in the now fading light.

"Why the fuck are you here?" Petrosky barked.

Jackson's eyes remained fixed on the windshield. "I invited him."

"To a stakeout?" Sure, Petrosky had called Acharya earlier this week without discussing it with Jackson, but that was beside the point.

Jackson shrugged. "Well it's not really a—"

"I'm careful, Detective," Acharya said. "I know how to make sure I'm not followed."

Petrosky grunted and snatched one of the napkins from the top of the take-out bag, practically slapping Acharya's knee in the process. "Oh, so now you're a fucking ninja?"

"Only when I have to be." Acharya passed a folder to Jackson, but his dark eyes remained on Petrosky. "Did you like the article on Dunne?"

Hell yes. Petrosky plastered on a scowl. "It was okay. Did the job."

Acharya grinned. "It was better than okay. You owe me a coffee."

"Or pickles."

"Pickles?"

"They're better than coffee."

"You're not going to the right coffee shops, my friend."

"Jesus, you two." Jackson flipped open the folder. "Let's get on with it."

"Right." Acharya leaned over the console and pointed to the page Jackson was peering at, squinting in the little beam from her cellphone flashlight. "I used my sources to track down homeless veterans who might fit your description, all living within a five-mile radius of the cemetery."

Petrosky glanced at the sheet—less than a quarter of the page marked in scrawling blue ink. "Are these your very closest buddies? Or are your sources on another list?" Killers loved inside information. How crazy would it be if Turner was one of Acharya's sources?

"None of these men are people I've spoken to personally, and before you ask, none of my sources match your description."

"Where'd you get the names from again?"

"I never reveal—"

"Yeah, yeah." Petrosky waved the words away as if swatting a fly. "Didn't happen to get photos to go with these names, did you?"

"I wish."

Petrosky leaned back in his seat. "It's a list of names, but we already have his name, Acharya."

"Ah, but you don't. You have his social-security God-given Christian name. But half these folks out here, especially in this section of town...they don't go by that name. Most of them have something to hide." He snaked his hand over the console and tapped the page. "You're never going to find him looking for Rye Turner. But if you look for Peanut, or Wild Willie, or The Blowtorch..."

Acharya was right. *Fuck.* They should have thought of that. Hell, Billie had told him to call her "Lolly" until she'd been living next door for two weeks.

Petrosky glanced over again, squinting in the light from Jackson's phone. "Slippery Dick, eh? I'll let you take that one, Jackson." Though it did have a bit of a rape-y vibe. If only one of them called themselves General Vengeance.

Petrosky turned back to the windshield, staring out at the darkness, waiting for someone else to appear beneath the streetlight. Someone with a bull neck and the thick fingers of a killer.

33

THE SUV SAT PARKED in the gloom beneath the willows. He watched, crouching beyond the outside edge of the yellow streetlamp, the alley a lonely tunnel behind him. So many rustling leaves, so many shadows—so much darkness. Inside, his dark was deeper still.

Exhaustion tugged at the heavy base of his skull, where the nerves zipped and vibrated and sent little bolts of electricity down his spine. Every time he tried to rest, nightmares invaded his brain and tightened his throat, full of high-pitched screaming that seemed to come from a world beyond his own—a world he could only feel yet never fix. But even without the nightmares, he dared not close his eyes.

The enemy never slept. And so he must not.

He squinted at the vehicle. Anyone who stopped near the cemetery this time of night was suspicious. Those who stayed here, hiding, flashlight beams glinting in the dark, were all the more so. And another man had just entered the car—why? What were they planning?

"Are you coming, honey?" That low voice, slow as molasses. His hackles rose. But he saw no one else, just the shadows of those in the SUV, their little reading light bobbing, bobbing, bobbing.

"Where you goin', girl?"

His hands tingled, tendons tightening with anticipation, ears pricked and ready. Listening—listening to the rustling of the willow fronds and the subtle hum of conversation from the car. No, he shouldn't be able to hear it, he knew he shouldn't, but he felt it—they were talking. About him.

He inhaled the musty dark, and a salty tang hit his nose, like good corned beef. His mother used to make that for him as a child, the herbal, fatty, almost vinegary tang permeating the entire house. Now, that smell reminded him of sex, sweat mingling with salt and saliva and lubrication, the chlorine-y stink of completion. When had that smell changed so dramatically? And why?

"Right down here, just a little farther."

He startled, whirling to peer down the alley at his back, into the thick blackness that hung like a shroud over the road. He had a mission. And...someone was there.

A soldier—fatigues, buzzed scalp, heading away from where he crouched in the shadows, the man's weapon still slung across his back, and that voice whispering something...

"Be quiet, bitch, be quiet."

Iron clogged his sinuses. His mouth went dry. *No.*

The man's breathing hissed across the asphalt, the soldier's stance vaguely familiar...Dunne? Why did he know that name? Ah, from his dreams. That was where he knew the soldier from too, that tentative yet purposeful gait like a lion on the hunt—he had smelled of corned beef, had he not? No, that was someone else, someone else had smelled of salt and meat and...blood. He blinked, and the shadowed man vanished along with the sound of his breath.

"Be quiet, bitch. Be quiet, be quiet, be quiet."

The words echoed in his brain, and he bit his tongue to

keep from repeating them. *Crazy, I'm crazy.* But he couldn't help listening to that voice any more than he could help walking these streets—his feet moved on their own, dragging him down these alleys without his consent, even without his conscious thought.

But it wasn't his job to think.

The enemy. That's why he was here. Innocent people needed to know they were safe from the threat of enemy combatants, safe from anyone who might take their freedom along with their lives. They were all counting on him. DeLaney had said that.

DeLaney was right.

And in this place, where the enemy lurked, they needed him more than most.

He narrowed his eyes, crouched lower, and watched the SUV.

And waited.

Silent.

Like a good soldier.

34

ACHARYA LEFT after delivering his folder ninja-style. Petrosky and Jackson sat there for another hour, watching the dark and talking in hushed sentences about what they knew...and what they didn't. When they finally accepted that talking wasn't going to help any more than staring into the empty shadows, they scoured the streets. Back and forth behind the cemetery. Up and down the alley where Trina Layton had been attacked. Around and around and around the blocks surrounding their killer's hunting ground.

The street with the cemetery was uninhabited as if everyone was superstitious about sleeping so close to the dead. But just two blocks over, the rows of sleeping bags were as they'd been the day of the murder, though, in the dark, the sleepers looked like corpses, too.

They shook hands with the women in the doorways, knocked on tents, called out to the men in the cardboard boxes, Petrosky asking after his friend from the war—"Maybe he's known as Shaft, or Wild Willie, or The Blow-torch, now?" It wasn't a perfect solution—there was still a chance that their inquiries would get back to Turner if he was around—but canvassing was all they had. And they'd already been out here in the daytime.

Midnight passed. One o'clock. Petrosky's legs were leaden, his chest tight with exhaustion.

"Maybe we need to expand the search another few blocks," he muttered, turning down the alley behind the Ragdoll. Again. They'd been over these six blocks twice that night already, but…

Huh. He squinted at a dumpster halfway down the alley, the thin light of the streetlamp illuminating a wispy haze emerging over the rusted top lip.

Jackson stopped at his side. "Is that smoke?"

It was. A barely-there orange glow leaked from somewhere beyond his line of sight, and suddenly smoke was billowing out from behind the garbage container, as though someone had started a fire as a diversion. But then the smoke eased, revealing a vague shape: half a leg sticking out from behind the bottom of the dumpster. A sneaker, not a boot, but horrifyingly reminiscent of the scene at Collins's house. Probably not their guy—what covert soldier would be out sitting in an alley throwing smoke signals?—but you could never be certain.

"Hey, man, you okay?" Petrosky called. They approached up the alley, his hand on the weapon still hidden beneath his suit jacket. The smoke beyond the dumpster had thinned further still, but the man did not move, and then another cloud rose, tinted sickly yellow in the barely-there glow of the streetlamp at their backs. Their shoes clapped on the crumbling pavement and echoed back to them off the buildings: *cla-thunk-cla-thunk-cla-thunk.*

Petrosky poked his head around the corner of the dumpster. The man who gazed up at him was most definitely not Turner: blond beard to his clavicle, deep wrinkles like chasms across his forehead, e-cigarette in his dirty right hand. Those fucking things—more smoke than was prudent for any self-respecting tobacco lover, and far more dramatic than was necessary for anyone, like you were trying to call attention to your habit. This had to be...The Blowtorch?

The man released a plume of smoke from his lips that wafted into Petrosky's face. It smelled like fucking cookies. *What the hell?*

The man smiled, forehead creasing even deeper when he raised his eyebrows. "It's all good, brother."

"The way you were sending out smoke signals, I thought you might be lost."

He laughed, long and throaty. It was a good laugh. "Nah. I'm just hangin'." His eyes narrowed. "You guys cops?"

"Not tonight. Just out here looking for a friend of ours. Veteran. Served with me overseas."

"Aw, brother, there are a bunch of us out here."

"You know a lot of them?"

The man nodded slowly. "I'd say I do. Most of these folks...they come and go, don't bother talking. Head down, you know? But I've been out here for years, and I'd go crazy if I didn't get to run my mouth." He laughed heartily again, then squinted at Jackson like he couldn't quite see her, and he probably couldn't, at least not well in the dim light. The makeshift campfire the man had going near his knee was no bigger than his fist. The e-cig put out far more smoke.

"Have a seat, brother." The man sucked on the e-cigarette and released another sweet-smelling plume into the atmosphere.

Jackson met Petrosky's eyes, and he nodded—*I've got this*.

"I'll let you two talk while I hit the corner store," Jackson said. "You want anything?" Petrosky didn't like Jackson going off alone, not here, but Jackson was unlikely to be their killer's target. Besides, their guy had surely gone underground—if he was still here at all.

The man shook his head. "Nah, I just finished cookin' up a hot dog."

"Come on, Smokestack," Petrosky said. "On us."

This earned another laugh. "Well, when you put it that way, a burrito maybe?" He inhaled again, deeper this time, and sighed it back out in a vanilla-scented cloud. "Those things are better than sex."

Jackson snorted. "Then you're doing it all wrong."

The man cackled and waved as she headed off. "I like her, brother. I do."

Petrosky sat on the concrete beside him. "Where'd you do your time?"

"Vietnam. You?"

"Gulf."

He nodded. "Brutal shit, no matter where you go."

They sat in silence for a moment, the weight of that statement hanging in the air heavier than the muggy summer night. "You out here often?" Petrosky asked.

"Eh, sometimes—usually just when I need a moment to myself." He offered Petrosky the e-cig. Petrosky put it to his lips, inhaled deeply, and passed it back, trying like hell not to choke on the sweetness that had just invaded his lungs. If he wanted to taste sugar, he'd eat a goddamn donut.

"So maybe you know my friend Rye, that crazy bastard," Petrosky said, earning another chuckle from his new smoking buddy. "Ended up in Iraq until about seven years ago." Petrosky shifted; his ass was wet. Hopefully he'd sat in water, but he doubted there was any way he'd get that lucky.

"Rye? Never heard that name, man."

"Maybe he has a nickname? I've heard him talk about a few people out here. Are you The Blowtorch?"

The man laughed. "They call me Marvin. On account of me saying things are better than sex." He inhaled again, then slipped the e-cig into his front pocket. "*Sexual Healing*, get it?"

Marvin. Not even on Acharya's list. Then again, why would he be? Marvin had served well before the time Rye Turner was deployed.

"I have a picture." Petrosky pulled the driver's license photo from his jacket. "Rye's a big guy. Not real tall, but he's stocky as hell."

The man shrugged, frowning at the image.

Come on, give me something. "I heard he's out here walking a lot, but I haven't been able to find out where he lives. I'd sure like to find him, take him home."

Marvin met Petrosky's gaze. "You want to help him, eh, brother?"

"I do. I—"

Thud-thunk. Thud-thunk.

Petrosky froze and leaned back, peering past the dumpster toward the mouth of the alley. His shoulders relaxed. Just Jackson, carrying a bag bigger than their take-out sack; far more than burritos.

She handed it to Marvin, and the man's eyes widened. "Ma'am—"

"Don't thank me." Jackson shrugged, jerking her thumb at Petrosky. "I used this asshole's ATM."

Marvin guffawed. "Oh, I like her, brother." He laughed again. "I really, really do." He looked back at Petrosky. "I wish I could help you, but I don't know your guy. Maybe some of my friends do. If you know who he hangs with…"

"Slippery Dick?"

Marvin shook his head.

"Wild Willie?"

His face split in a grin. "Ah, you can find Willie up on Third. He sleeps under the overpass there, panhandles out on the highway…" His smile fell. "You're not going to arrest him, are ya?"

"Of course not," Petrosky said. "I'm just looking for my friend."

"Yeah, it's probably illegal to let me stay here with my fire, huh?"

"Vets gotta take care of our own," he said, and Marvin nodded. "Just don't light yourself on fire. I'm too old to carry your scorched ass out of here."

Another laugh. Petrosky couldn't help but smile back.

THEY FOUND Wild Willie that morning under the overpass, precisely where Marvin had said he would be. Not Turner. And he didn't know anything that might help them. They gave him the dozen bagels they'd brought from Rita's anyway, and a cup of coffee. Petrosky sat with him for a few minutes, listening to his apologies that he couldn't drink the coffee because of the sugar they'd added— diabetes. And he couldn't afford insulin. Coffee or death, what a fucking choice. Petrosky kept his eyes on Willie's face, trying not to glance at the dog tags still around the man's neck, at the dirt under his fingernails. The sores on his arms.

They were standing to leave when a woman wandered by —stocky, light hair, big green eyes ringed with deep purple. Younger than a lot of the folks out here, closer to Rye Turner's age. And the way she stared at them as she passed…

Petrosky left Jackson with Willie and followed the woman, Willie's refused coffee in his hand, and watched her climb into a tent with a busted flap.

He bent his face to the opening. "Hey there."

She looked up at him with suspicious eyes, brows furrowed, her mouth hard. "You with one of those church groups?"

"I'm just trying to find my friend." He offered her the coffee.

She stared. Crossed her arms. *Oh right*. Even in an upscale bar, women had to watch their drinks; the world was full of fuckheads.

Petrosky brought the coffee to his lips and took a deep swallow, then offered it again. This time, she took the cup, appraising him carefully as if she half expected him to pass out. When he didn't, she took a tiny, tentative sip, and he pulled Rye Turner's driver's license photo from his jacket.

"Yeah...he looks familiar." The girl—*woman*—peered past Petrosky to the spot where Jackson sat with Willie. The man was chewing on a bagel. Shit, were the bagels going to make his blood sugar go haywire too? Starve to death or diabetic coma—so many bullshit choices. "Cops, huh?" the woman said.

Petrosky nodded. "What's your name?"

Another glance at the bagels. "Jane."

As in Doe? Petrosky reached for his wallet and peeled off a ten. "What else can you tell me about this guy?"

She took the money the same way she'd taken the coffee —tentative. Untrusting. It made his heart hurt.

"I don't really know him, but I've seen him around." She touched the back of her head—was that a wince? "I think he stays at that big place over on Chilton."

Chilton. That was the warehouse district, lots of abandoned buildings, most of them huge. And that section of town was maybe six or seven blocks from the cemetery— probably one street past where he and Jackson had canvassed. Fucking figured.

"You know which building?"

"I think he said...on the corner?" She frowned. "Is he in trouble? Is he like...dangerous?"

Yes. But maybe not dangerous to her. "He's an old friend

of mine. I just need to make sure he's safe." She did not look convinced.

Petrosky softened his shoulders, aiming at nonchalant but probably failing. "Where'd you meet?"

She sipped the coffee, eyes on a spot behind his left arm as if she were trying to decide how much to tell him, or maybe trying to remember. It was disconcerting that he couldn't tell which. "He was out by the river once. Just standing. I thought he might be bathing."

"That what you were doing?"

She paused. Bit her lip. Nodded. "I had just finished when I saw him, got mad thinking he was watching. Lots of creeps out here, you know? But he kept staring at the water. It was like I wasn't even there." Seconds ticked past. She chewed harder on her lip—there was more there, more she wasn't saying. But if he pressed her too hard, she'd probably stop talking altogether.

"What happened next?" he said gently.

"I asked him if he was all right—he seemed almost catatonic." *Catatonic?* That was a fancy way of saying dazed. "And he said…"

Again, the silence stretched. "Jane?"

She swallowed hard. "He said that he'd had a nightmare, needed a place to clear his head. And there was a little fire—I think he was cooking something. Like…a small animal."

That explained how he was avoiding panhandling, why he showed up at the soup kitchen so infrequently—why no one knew him. "How did you figure out where he lived?"

Her nostrils flared, lips a tight line. She didn't want to tell him shit. He was opening his mouth to ask again when she said, "He was a nice guy, okay? I sat with him for a while. He talked about his place, how it didn't feel safe. And I saw him again this past Monday. In the street." She touched the back of her head as gingerly as she'd taken the cup—definitely wincing. "He...helped me."

Monday. His heart throbbed, fast, insistent. Two days after Amos's murder. Petrosky appraised her, but he couldn't see any injuries beneath her hair. "Were you attacked?"

"Not by him." Her voice had taken on a hard edge. "He scared the guy away." Scared him—but didn't kill him. Probably not for lack of trying. "I'm not going to talk about it, so don't even ask."

Petrosky could respect that. And she'd already given him what he needed. After Amos was killed, Rye Turner hadn't gone into hiding—hadn't left town. Most importantly, he hadn't stopped. He was going to keep pacing those streets until he found another would-be victim—and murdered someone else. "You're telling me about him, this man who saved you. Why?"

"Because." The coffee trembled in her hand. "He said the enemy was still out there—that he was going to find them. And I don't want him to get hurt." She dropped her gaze, and in that moment, she looked ten years older. *You don't feel safe either, do you?* "I know what that's like—the nightmares," she practically whispered. "Some of us never get to wake up."

Petrosky nodded, reached back into his wallet, and peeled off a fifty. *Amen, honey.*

35

CHILTON WAS quiet this time of day, but not dead—pigeons attacked sparse crumbs on the walk. As they got out of the car, a burly black man on a bicycle three sizes too small for him whizzed by wearing a knit cap and a bright pink Hello Kitty backpack.

"Well isn't he fabulous," Petrosky said approvingly. Or he had a daughter or a sister who needed her schoolwork. Either way, he liked the guy's face—honest. Unlike Cook and his stupid fucking rat 'stache.

"Let's hope the people inside are just as fabulous." Jackson craned her neck toward the building. A plastic bag skittered past them and dashed itself against a bush.

Nine stories of warehouse. Graffitied red brick. Most of the windows were gone, and any left intact were marred by spiderweb cracks that turned each square into a puzzle of glass triangles, any of them sharp enough to stab someone to death.

The inside didn't feel any friendlier, but at least it wasn't an apartment building where they'd have to go room to room—a realtor would say the warehouse boasted an open floor plan. Garbage on the floor, more graffiti on the walls, the stink of urine and shit in the air. All quiet. Most residents were likely out now—panhandling, seeing friends, even working jobs nearby. But the warehouse probably filled when the sun went down.

"Your friend from the overpass say what floor our guy hangs out on?"

Petrosky frowned. "I don't think she knew."

Jackson crept slowly into the marble-tiled lobby, weapon in hand, stepping carefully over the trash: rags, papers, little piles of torn cardboard charred from recent cooking fires. Used hypodermic needles. Was their guy an addict? Lots of veterans were—he still couldn't pass a liquor store without considering, for just a moment, wheeling into the lot and having a liquid dinner. But these days, the liquor cravings passed just as quickly. Unlike his tobacco addiction. Since his single hit off that vanilla-cookie e-cig, he'd been jonesing like a motherfucker.

Jackson hooked a left past the lobby, and Petrosky hustled to keep up. She was already halfway up the stairs to the second story before he put his hand on the rail.

"Step lightly," she hissed from somewhere in the blackness above him, then something that sounded like "with your fat ass," but Petrosky couldn't be sure. As he climbed the steps, he understood—the treads, surely supported by wooden beams, felt spongey and soft. He clicked on his cellphone flashlight and stuck it halfway into his pocket, one hand on the metal railing, one hand on the chipped brick, hoping one side or the other would hold. The stairwell brightened as he approached the door to the next level.

The second floor was in slightly better shape than the first. Less trash, for one thing, and far fewer piles of blackened kindling—you couldn't light a fire on the scarred wooden floors here, or you'd burn the place down, unlike the tiled lobby downstairs.

On the third floor, they found a young couple sleeping in the far corner on a pile of dirty blankets. They didn't even wake. Her leg was covered in track marks, paraphernalia scattered by her foot. The man was dark-haired and thin as a rail with tiny claw-like hands. Decidedly not Rye Turner.

He headed past Jackson for the stairwell and took the next flight two at a time—more effort, but fewer steps, and he was tired. Not just his legs, not just of this case, but tired of...all of it. The killing. Attacks on the innocent. All the fucking psychos.

On the fourth floor, the air was thick with weed. Better than that vanilla shit; at least you knew you were getting pot and not goddamn dessert. He followed the smoke trailing from behind one of the columns near the right side of the space and clicked off the cell light. "Police! Come out slowly." He raised his weapon.

Shuffling came from behind the pillar. Was the man crushing out the joint? Was he going for a weapon? At least Turner wouldn't be able to crank Petrosky's neck around if he came at him from the front.

From beyond the post came a strained whisper that was half cough: "I was just—"

"Show me your hands!" Petrosky called. Jackson stepped up behind him, weapon trained near the floor on the man's bare leg—the only body part he could see. Sitting cross-legged?

More shuffling, then hands poked out from behind the pillar, empty, thin fingers spread. Then bare arms covered in thick black hair. Then the rest of him. Dark curly hair every-fucking-where: pouring from his head, creeping over his back from behind the hem of his white tank top, around the overburdened waistband of his stained white shorts. The guy was a fucking yeti—and he wasn't their suspect.

The man turned to them, arms still in the air, a goddamn bush growing beneath each armpit. "Don't shoot, okay? You can arrest me or whatever, but don't shoot me. It's amaaaaazing outside." He smiled. His eyes glittered.

Petrosky lowered the weapon and shoved it back in the holster. *Fucking stoners.* "What's your name, sir?"

"Mike. But you can call me...well, call me whatever you want, really." He grinned. "Can I put my hands down?"

Petrosky glanced at Mike's shorts—boxers. Nowhere to keep a weapon unless he'd braided it into his back hair. "Yeah, you can lower your arms. Just keep your hands where we can see them."

"Right-o." Mike had glorious teeth for a homeless guy—white and straight and shiny. Was he new to the streets? If so, he was less likely to know their perp.

Petrosky pulled Turner's photo from his jacket. "You know this guy?"

"Of course!" Grin. "Why are you looking for Peanut?"

Jackson raised an eyebrow. Their killer's nickname was Peanut? How...anticlimactic.

"He's a friend of mine," Petrosky said slowly, giving the man time to process it through the haze of drugs. "I'm a little worried that he might have fallen in with some very bad guys." *Or that he is a very bad guy.*

Mike chuckled and shook his head, passing the photo back Petrosky's way. "Oh, there's no way Peanut knows any bad guys. He doesn't like bad guys *at all*. Stays far away from them."

"Sounds like you're talking from personal experience."

Mike's eyes clouded, just a little. But he nodded.

"Is Peanut here?" Jackson asked.

Mike shook his head again, but his eyes had lost their sparkle.

Weed and interrogations didn't mix. "When are you expecting him back?"

"Now, that's hard to say."

"Doesn't he live here?" Jane had been pretty convinced that Rye Turner lived in this building—had she been wrong?

Mike's brow furrowed. "Well...yes. But every once in a while, he has to get out a little."

Petrosky stepped closer, locking his gaze on Mike's. The man backed up. "You're going to have to be a little more specific, Mike."

Mike swallowed hard. "He gets...upset. Has these nightmares. And then...he takes off. But he always comes back." He glanced at Jackson, who had made her way to the corner behind Petrosky, scanning the floors, what looked like a blow-up mattress. She had far better eyesight than Petrosky these days—and preferred scouting to "talking to idiots."

Mike cocked his head in her direction. "Hey, lady, you tired? That's my bed, but you can nap there if you want. I'll wait outside."

Jackson ignored him and continued along the far wall, but Turner had probably taken everything he owned with him. If he'd owned anything to begin with.

"How long's he been gone for?"

Mike looked at the ceiling. "Hard to say. Every glorious day looks the same when you're as lucky as I am."

Luck? If this was luck, who would want it? "Was he here Saturday night?" When Mike frowned, he amended: "A week ago, Mike. And it rained the day before. Can you remember if maybe you saw him that day, the day after the thunderstorm?"

"Ah...that day." His eyes were glassy—was it from the

drugs, or was he trying not to cry? "That was the day he left. The last day he was here."

So he'd been gone since Amos's murder, or at least gone from this place. "Do you know where Rye...where Peanut goes when he leaves?"

Mike shrugged. "No idea, man. Like I said, he gets away, even from me."

Petrosky believed him. The guy had an honest face, but stoned as he was, he didn't seem capable of lying—why bother when the world was so amaaaaazing?

Mike grinned again. "We have a good thing going here; no one ever bothers us. Sometimes the cops go and raid the bottom floors, but not all the way up here, or on the roof— it's dangerous climbing. That's where we usually hang out at night. Watch the street."

Watch the street, huh? A vantage point? That would mean he might not be doing recon on foot; no wonder no one had seen him out strolling. "Will you show us?"

"Right-o." Mike glanced down. "Can I get my pants first?"

Like you need them, you've got a coat like a bear. But Petrosky nodded.

MIKE LED the way up the stairwell with a far-too-confident-in-the-floor gait, boards groaning beneath them, the sponginess he'd noticed earlier more pronounced until Petrosky felt certain the entire staircase was on the verge of collapse. Jackson had wisely elected to stay in Mike's makeshift flat— "Someone has to be alive to call a bus if the floor falls through." He'd never been more ready to escape onto a roof, but his back tensed once more when Mike ambled toward the roofline—not so much as a safety rail between them and the open air.

His stoned ass is going to wander right over the edge. "Hey, don't go near the side, okay, man?"

"I'm not going to fall." Mike sat down, still precariously close to the edge, but…better.

Petrosky made his way slowly toward Mike, peering at the roof beneath his feet to make sure he didn't trip on something and go careening to his death. He stopped just behind Mike's cross-legged form. Beyond the roof's edge, Mike's lonely pocket of city stretched, gray and brown brick, concrete, asphalt, the occasional biker or walker or car. And off to the right, in the distance…the cemetery. You couldn't really see much from here, just the uppermost parts of the giant willows, the iron top of the streetlight like a black dot, but maybe Turner had seen the movement of figures on the road. Maybe he wasn't doing recon at all—just sitting here with Mike the Stoner and waiting for someone to wander into his line of sight.

But that didn't make sense. Petrosky couldn't see the alley behind the Ragdoll from this vantage point—even the entrance was blocked by another building. And… He strained his ears, listening to the whisper of leaves and plastic bags, then the far-off bleat of a car horn, barely discernible over the whoosh of the breeze. Any cries for help would be whisked away by the wind or blocked by the myriad structures around them.

Petrosky turned to the man still sitting on the rooftop, staring out at the city like a hairy, stoned Buddha. "It's nice up here, Mike, I'll give you that." He waited for the guy to nod before he finished: "So how often did you guys sit out here?"

"Every night for four amazing years," Mike said, eyes still on the cityscape. "Watched the sun come up, usually."

Four years—that would mean Turner hadn't moved in

until after the Polluck and Layton attacks. "You sure about that time frame?"

No answer.

"Is four years ago…is that when he moved in?"

"Well, no." He jerked his head back then forth once, tiny little movements. "He started staying here on and off maybe five or six years ago."

"So he did live here five years ago?"

"Sure, sure. But he didn't start sitting up here with me until later." Mike kept his eyes on the city. "He used to take more walks. They helped with his nightmares."

There it is. Turner's nightmares must have been bad when he first came back from overseas, so he'd paced the streets instead of sleeping; he'd have come across both Layton and Polluck by chance.

Mike hacked, one low harsh smoker's cough, and it startled Petrosky out of his thoughts. "But he always came home after walking, even if it was the next afternoon," Mike said. His back had tightened.

"Home?"

A half smile. "It is what you make it." He swept an arm over the city like a king gesturing at his dominion. "And this…I mean, it can't get better than this, right?"

This guy had to be the happiest fucking person Petrosky had ever met; he might even like lemons. *He can probably teach me a thing or two. Not that I'd listen.*

Mike had turned back to the cityscape, his city, the best fucking place on earth from the way his shoulders had softened. "Peanut even had these binoculars…" He mimed the device by putting both hands to his eyes. "I told him he was going to get them stuck to his head if he didn't ease up." He laughed. "That's why I called him Peanut. The little circles around his eyes—they stayed even after he put the binoculars down, like little bruises, and one side was always worse than the other. Like that monocle Mr. Peanut wears." He laughed again.

Petrosky squinted out toward the cemetery once more—six blocks up? Seven? Maybe he'd seen Amos arrive at the cemetery from the rooftop; not a stretch with binoculars. And the fact that the cemetery was where he'd come upon Polluck raping his wife might have been enough to make Turner suspicious. Enough to trigger him into action.

Catching Polluck mid-attack would sure as shit bring back the trauma of walking through the village, scanning for enemies...who ended up being his own squad. He'd come upon Layton's attack the same way because he was out walking. Out doing recon in enemy territory—like a good soldier.

But Turner had gotten himself under control. He'd stopped pacing the streets at night, hadn't killed a single person that they could find between Layton and Amos—a span of five years. What had triggered his return? "Did Peanut's nightmares come back in the last couple weeks?"

Now Mike pursed his lips and shook his head slowly. "I don't think so." But his voice...tense, higher. He shuddered like a cold breeze had just whisked right up his hairy spine.

Petrosky wiped sweat from the back of his own neck. "But something happened, didn't it?"

The beeping of a car horn answered him. Then a breath of wind off the distant river. Mike shuddered again—trying not to think about something, or just trying not to say it?

"Did he see something from up here, Mike? Maybe he saw an attack down below?" They hadn't come across other reported rapes, but that didn't mean they hadn't happened; maybe Turner had seen a struggle and was unable to get there in time. Maybe Amos was a preemptive attack. Nothing worse than feeling as powerless as you had at your darkest points—nothing made a man more determined.

"It wasn't out there." Mike sighed and finally looked up at Petrosky. The happy glitter in his eyes had vanished.

Ah, fuck. "Was there an attack in here?"

Mike turned away, and Petrosky knelt at his side, his thighs aching, the old burns on the backs of his legs hot and itchy. "Who got attacked, Mike?"

Mike watched the city with shining eyes—not just the drugs.

"Did someone hurt you?" Male-on-male rape, even female-on-male sexual assaults, were less likely to be reported than male-on-female rape. It was hard enough to report as a woman, but men had different kinds of stigma— shame associated with their masculinity, or they started thinking their sexuality was under attack. Which was ridiculous. If someone raped you, it didn't make you gay any more than someone punching you made you the next ultimate fighting champ.

Mike nodded slowly.

"Did Turn…did Peanut see it?"

"He came back after. And he…he helped me." He sniffed. "Kept saying how sorry he was, as if he could have predicted something like that."

"When, Mike?"

"I dunno for sure." He swallowed hard. "Maybe it's been two weeks. Or three."

Fuck. That was what had triggered the attack on Amos. What had led to him casing the streets again. Turner must have felt his dereliction of duty had led to his friend being hurt.

"Did you consider pressing charges?" Petrosky said. "There's still—"

"They aren't going to do anything—I'm just a homeless guy. I think I'm pretty awesome, but…" Mike sighed. "It was dark anyhow. I don't think I could pick them out of a lineup."

"Did you get medical treatment?"

His silence was Petrosky's answer.

"I can take your statement here, Mike." He put his hand on the man's shoulder, and Mike jumped. Petrosky pulled his fingers back. "And if you want to, I can drive you up to Oaklawn. Make sure you get the care you need. You might need some stitches, some STD tests."

Mike shook his head and coughed. "This is ruining my buzz."

"Fair enough." Petrosky handed him his card. "We're going to be back, okay, Mike? Maybe you'll want to chat then?"

Mike shrugged.

"In the meantime, call me if Peanut comes back, but don't tell him we were here looking for him—he needs assistance with those nightmares, and I don't want to scare him off. Not everyone is comfortable accepting help."

And they all needed help sometimes. But the kind of help Petrosky needed wasn't a matter of nightmares or secrets. Turner was still out there, looking for his next victim. Patient. Stealthy.

Their only chance was to beat him at his own game.

36

"You're out of your fucking mind." Chief Carroll shook her head. "The kill sites are close to one another, but there's no reason to think he'll show up in the exact same spot. And just because you don't have leads on associates doesn't mean he didn't lure his victims, or the witnesses, out there in the first place."

Jackson stiffened beside him. Petrosky had to resist rolling his eyes. "Turner didn't lure Eden Johansson or Samuel Amos anywhere. Or Trina Layton. And Mrs. Polluck was literally dragged out there by her husb—"

"I'm just saying, how are you going to run a sting when you don't know if this guy is even here? Not a single person around the crime scenes has seen him since Amos's murder. If I were him, I'd be in the wind."

"Then what can it hurt?" Petrosky peered at the approaching dusk through the window behind the chief's increasingly angry frame. *Where are you tonight, asshole?* He did his best to keep his voice even. "Before, it was fine to wait, to canvass, to ask questions—it only made sense that he'd taken off, like any other killer would. But now we have new information, reason to think he's still out there, actively seeking another victim." Petrosky met her eyes. "I can get him, Chief. We can. Let us do this."

Carroll crossed her arms. "Convince me."

Jackson sat straighter. "We know for a fact that Turner was out on those streets two days after he killed Amos. He saved another woman in the same alley where Trina Layton was attacked."

"But no body this time? No one with a broken spine?"

Petrosky and Jackson exchanged a glance. "No," Petrosky said. "The witness thinks...maybe that guy ran off."

"But she doesn't know?" Carroll said incredulously. "How could she not—"

"She was hit in the head. Passed out." Petrosky couldn't be sure that was true, but from the way Jane had been touching her head, it seemed likely.

"We've got eyes on the place where he's been squatting," Jackson said, "but Turner hasn't been back since the attack on Amos. We think he's casing like he was doing after he caught Polluck down there."

"You mean after he murdered Polluck."

"Same difference," Petrosky said. "He saw that, kept walking the streets, came across Layton. Same thing happened overseas; he killed Ortiz in Iraq two months before he broke Dunne's neck. Now Amos and that other guy. He's obviously patient, willing to do recon until he believes the world is safe again." And one thing was certain: if he was finished with what he saw as his mission, he'd have gone home like he did before.

"I'm still not hearing a valid reason to put an officer in harm's way. Just because you don't think he'll show his face otherwise?" Carroll leaned toward him over the desk. "You already know where he lives. What he looks like. We have his picture plastered everywhere."

"And it's done *nothing*," Petrosky snapped. "We even have an officer posted at the soup kitchen; it's a fucking waste." Especially since Dubicki would call the second Turner showed. Dubicki's parole officer—a lovely woman with a soft voice and what sounded like a ready smile—had called Petrosky yesterday morning. Sounded like she'd put the fear of god into Dubicki. Or the fear of jail, which was at least as effective.

"We've doubled down on surveillance everywhere," Jackson said. "We need to do something more. He's going to kill someone else, it's only a matter of time."

"Or he'll go home, and we'll catch him there," Carroll said.

"Yeah, after he kills another innocent kid!" Petrosky's heel vibrated against the floor—*tap-tap-tap-tap-tap*. "Maybe this time it'll be the governor's son. Really put this place on the map."

"And just what do you think will happen if he kills one of our own?" Her voice had gone quiet. "This guy knows how to hide. He snuck out of the shadows and snapped the neck of a seasoned Marine, for god's sake."

"A Marine who was in the process of beating and raping his wife for the high crime of wanting to leave him," Jackson said.

"Fine. The victim was distracted. But that doesn't mean our officers aren't in danger." Carroll's teeth clenched—he could see the outline of the muscles along her jawline. "He has binoculars. Maybe he even has night vision. If you try to lure him out, he'll be able to see you well before—"

"He's a homeless vet living on a rooftop. He doesn't have boots let alone night vision." Carroll might actually be right on that—he shouldn't be able to afford binoculars either—but still. "He's going to come across another trigger. Another rape, or a couple of consenting adults like Amos and Johansson…those are the people who seek out privacy in the dark.

And that's where he's looking. If we try to set him up on the main road, under the streetlights, he'll bolt. We have to—"

"Stop, Petrosky. Stop. Give it a few more days, another news broadcast. Samuel Amos's father offered a substantial reward for information leading to his arrest. If someone sees him—"

"We're going in a fucking circle!" Petrosky slammed his fists onto the arms of his chair with a *thunk*. Jackson elbowed him, and he winced, hand on his ribs, then finished more softly, more slowly: "We can cover the city with cops, but there are more than enough places to hide. Buildings where he could be watching the streets. He knows how to stay off our radar—off *everyone's* radar. He's a ghost." *No. He's a soldier.* And they weren't going to see him until he wanted them to.

Or until they drew him out.

"We need to give him an incentive. We need to become the enemy he so desperately needs to defeat. And we need to do it with minimum police presence—any more than the bait and the backup and we'll lose him. He's not stupid."

"What you're proposing is a shoot and kill mission. But he's not going to come out in the open, is he? You won't have time to scream at him that you're the police." Her nostrils flared. "From the moment you see him coming out of the shadows, you'll have time to shoot, and that's exactly all."

Petrosky met her gaze. "We can do this, Chief."

Carroll narrowed her eyes. Disbelieving.

"We know what triggers him: Seeing what he perceives as an attack. We'll give him one, draw him out—he's probably moving slower than you think before he does any neck-breaking, watching the scene, assessing. And while he's distracted with his focus on the couple, we'll make sure that someone on our side is just as hidden as he is—and then we'll take him down."

"How can you be sure he'll show up?"

We can't. "So far, the cases have been spread out within a very small geographic area," Petrosky said. "A few blocks. The cemetery. We'll set up somewhere out behind Whispering Willows."

Carroll's jaw dropped. "You want to do this behind the cemetery? In the pitch dark? What about the building where he attacked Amos? At least that's near the light." Jackson turned to him, eyes wide. But Turner wasn't stupid. He wouldn't jump out into the light. And more than that, they knew the cemetery was a trigger in and of itself. Turner had attacked Amos there for doing nothing wrong. The cemetery made Turner careless—he'd made mistakes. The right mistake and he was finished.

"Sorry to say it, but my money's on him." Carroll sighed. "And you're willing to risk your neck for—"

"Actually, I'm willing to risk Decantor's neck."

Carroll's forehead wrinkled, her eyebrows in her hairline. "You want to run a sting and put another man's throat on the chopping block?"

"Not just any man. But I'd love to see Decantor's neck snapped like a wishbone."

"Not funny, Petrosky."

"It's a little funny." He blocked another sharp elbow with his forearm. Carroll stared like he'd completely lost his mind. But Decantor was a good cop; he'd helped Petrosky hunt down Morrison's killer. And as much as he harassed that Kardashian-loving fuck, he'd put his life in Decantor's hands, and in Jackson's. He just had to hope the feeling was mutual.

"It's the only way, Chief," Petrosky said, meeting Carroll's gaze. "Turner's a soldier. Like I was. And if we don't do this soon, we'll have someone else's blood on our hands."

Carroll watched him, maybe trying to decide if she could trust him. Finally, she blinked. And nodded.

37

"I CAN'T BELIEVE you're making me wear this," Jackson snapped, glaring down at her seatbelt...no, probably at her outfit. But she couldn't wear her suit or anything else that made her look like a cop.

"You're the one who picked it out this afternoon." His blood thrummed too fast, too hard in his veins. Out the front windshield, the dark shuddered with unseen things, impossible to tell which amorphous black shapes were mere shadow and which were living creatures, creeping through the gloom.

"Yeah, out of all the bullshit outfits in the lost-and-found locker." She tugged the hem of the shirt, but it barely made it to her navel. "You said you were bringing me something."

"I brought you that fancy skort thing with the gun pockets."

She sniffed. "It has rabbits on it."

"Agreed, rabbits suck," Petrosky said, but his throat was dry.

Jackson took a deep breath, still staring at her thighs. "At least they're baggy enough not to show everyone the junk in my trunk."

They both watched the willows sway in the night air. They'd parked a few blocks up from where they'd left the car last time, too far from the mouth of the alley for the light to reach. Even farther from the cemetery, which was where Decantor was heading at this moment—the path behind the cemetery where the darkness was thick enough to hide all of them. Where the man walking his dog hadn't even seen their suspect despite being mere feet away.

Where the killer could leap out of anywhere.

"You ready?" he asked.

She nodded. But when he turned her way, he could see her face was tight, her jaw muscles clenched even in the jaundiced glow from the SUV's dash lights.

"I've got you, okay? I'll be right here."

"He's not going to hurt me anyway," she said, her voice hollow.

"Decantor will be fine, too. I know how this guy thinks, I understand his—"

"Fucking hell, Petrosky, I don't need a pep talk! I know you have this thing for broken women, but I'm not one of your goddamn pet projects."

Whoa. He put his hands up in mock surrender. Maybe she and Decantor did have a thing going.

She sighed. "Okay, so I'm a little nervous." She unbuckled her seatbelt, took a deep breath, and opened the door. "See you out there."

"I see what you mean about the junky trunk!" he called.

She gave him the finger as she walked away.

TURNER HEARD the door slam from his position near the Ragdoll. He ducked behind the farthest dumpster, where the light did not reach—no one would see him here in the pitch black. And he'd hear the moment anyone entered the alley.

His muscles coiled, readying for action.

Like a good soldier. He was a good soldier.

He peered around the dumpster, down the alley toward Whispering Willows, in time to see a man with graying hair stride past. Holding something in his right hand. *Looking for trouble.*

"Be quiet, bitch," someone said, but that wasn't him, that had never been him. "Be quiet."

Turner followed the man, creeping up the alley, staying well hidden beneath the cover of night.

THE THUD of Petrosky's boots matched the steady throb of his heart as he marched into the thick velvet blackness of the weeping willows at the entrance to the cemetery. He stepped carefully over the curb. Through the gates. The scent of roses wafted into his nostrils, their perfume so thick and sweet it almost choked him.

Turner might see him, the way he had seen Simmons walking his dog, but out in the open, a man alone…the killer wouldn't consider him a threat. But the enemy, enemy soldiers —they would try to hide. That's who Turner was looking for.

If Petrosky was right. If he wasn't, Decantor was in trouble. Or he was.

Please let me be right.

Petrosky passed the mausoleum and knelt by the nearest tombstone. He set down the bouquet of flowers he carried and closed his eyes.

And listened—

—if Turner reaches Decantor before I can get there, Decantor's as good as dead—

—listened to the wind hissing over last year's leaves and through the fronds of willow—

—if Jackson tries to save him, Turner will kill her too—

A night bird screeched. Another answered.

They couldn't shoot in the dark—they'd risk hitting their own.

What else could they do?

Just wait in the shadows, the way any good soldier would. Decantor and Jackson were already waiting, minutes from something very good…or very bad.

Petrosky inhaled the rose scented air, quieting his heart, and made the sign of the cross.

TURNER WATCHED as the man in the cemetery knelt beside the gravestone. Henrietta Barrett—Turner knew every name on every stone in this cemetery by heart. She had died thirty years ago, age seven. Perhaps this man's sister. Or a child. You never forgot a child. Sometimes he heard the voices of women whispering about such things…and weeping horribly. Hallucinations—*crazy, crazy*. Still, he wept with them. In the night. In the dark.

"Where you goin', girl?" The voice was low. Thick like the night air. Horrifying.

The man mourning for poor Henrietta made the sign of the cross. Familiar. Did he live here, on the streets? No, too neat—clean. Perhaps he worked nearby? But no matter how he racked his brain, Turner could not place him.

He listened to the willows. Listened to the hiss of the

breeze. This man was no threat, not any more than those women were, crying in the dead of night.

Turner pulled his head back behind the tree and crept silently on.

PETROSKY HEARD the subtle hiss of leaves. Could have been the breeze, but it wasn't, and the hairs on the back of his neck vibrated in time with the *shh, shh, shh*ing from somewhere off to his left.

He stayed kneeling. Eyes closed. Listening. A needle pricked the base of his spine.

The hiss came again: Turner was on the move.

Petrosky opened his eyes, kept his gaze on the gravestone, but he heard it plainly: the whisk of grass that wasn't quite steady enough to be from the wind.

Farther away.

Farther.

Turner was heading for the back of the cemetery, and Petrosky now knew precisely which path he was taking— around the big center willow, behind the double grave of one of Ash Park's founding families where the deep shadows of the giant marble angels would hide their man from prying eyes. Then, crouching, hands and knees through the thick weeds on the south side; there, the tombstones were older and larger, from a time when you proved how much you loved someone by erecting a bigger piece of rock than the neighbors. Made for good hiding.

And then on to the willows at the far end of the cemetery. A straight shot to the darkness where Decantor and Jackson were.

Petrosky had cased the area this morning. Every possible path. And tonight, they only needed one.

Move.

Petrosky glanced into the dark beyond the tombstones, listening, waiting for Turner to be behind the statues, for his vision to be blocked by the—

Now.

Four steps, five, and then he was ducking into the shadows of his own path behind the mausoleum, the blackness the only armor he needed.

THE GRASS WAS cool and damp—wonderful against Turner's burning palms, but it didn't stop the heat from rising in his chest. Someone else was back there. Two of them, he'd heard their voices. Heard *her* voice.

Fiery daggers stabbed at his spine and released a cascade of oily sweat between his shoulder blades.

"Be quiet, bitch. Be quiet." Those words, clear as day, echoing through the cemetery. *The enemy.*

He reached the willow grove and slipped between the two largest trees, cloaked in the shadow of their long leafy fronds. Dark on the path—almost black. But he could see enough.

A man, a large man, arm around a much smaller woman. Walking. Almost to the shadow where no lights reached.

"Just a little farther, honey." Sweet as syrup. The big man put his arm lower on the woman's waist. Pulled her closer. The air smelled of salt.

"Be quiet, bitch. Be quiet."

Two steps to pure dark. Turner's hands clenched. Sweat poured down his back.

She pushed him away.

One step.

The enemy dragged the woman toward him. Toward the blackness.

She screamed.

Turner's vision went red.

THE DARK of the willows was all-consuming, a veil of blackness that stretched to eternity. But Petrosky had run every inch of the trails this morning; he knew where the last tendrils of the streetlight's glow reached, and where they didn't.

Jackson and Decantor stood at the edge of the subtle haze of orange, Decantor's hand on Jackson's waist, the other on her arm. Fifty feet into the dark was the fork in the road: one side edged back into the willows, the other toward the trip wire with the floodlight, carefully hidden in the deep blue-grass ten more feet down the way. When the lights flashed on, Decantor and Jackson would drop to the ground so Petrosky could get off a disabling shot before Turner hurt anyone. If all went well.

Jackson screamed once, Petrosky's signal to approach. His fingers twitched around the butt of his gun.

But something wasn't right. Turner had stopped muttering. And the eerie silence from the trees to his left was an empty kind of quiet, overridden by the hissing of Jackson's shoes against the gravelly dirt road. Why wasn't he approaching them? Why wasn't he...moving? He was supposed to be edging out of the willows now, creeping up on his prey.

Decantor pulled Jackson's arm. Pulled her toward the dark. Toward the edge of hell. Petrosky edged closer, forty feet away, shit, thirty-five, then—

Cshhhh-crackle. The clang of shattering glass. The world

went completely black as if some malevolent being had hit the off switch.

Petrosky blinked, blinked again, trying to force his eyes to adjust. No light, save the muted white of the moon—even Jackson and Decantor had stilled, momentarily stunned by the sudden dark. And in the black, the rustling of footsteps, approaching once more from the direction of the now broken streetlight. Fast. Too fast. *Too close.*

Petrosky's heart slammed against his ribs, bright, painful.

The willows whispered. Jackson's footsteps skittered and hissed, the leaves and the gravel a discordant symphony that grated on his ears and clawed at his spine. Then he heard it, so soft it might have been mistaken for rustling leaves if he'd been any farther away: "Be quiet, bitch, be quiet, be quiet." A haunting chant echoing through the velvet night. *He's coming.*

Even Petrosky's breath moved in slow motion.

But the swaying willows confused his eyes—moving shadows, the silhouette of a madman, or willow fronds pulled by the wind? The killer was hidden somewhere in the dark, but Jackson and Decantor stood illuminated by the silver haze of the moon: glowing targets. Should they run for it, run into the dark toward the trip wire? They were so far from the floodlights. *Just one step into the moonlight, fucker, just one.* Petrosky sidled closer, staying inside the black beneath the trees, almost hoping the guy would hear him and come after him instead.

"Be quiet, bitch, be quiet, be quiet."

Jackson whirled, scanning the surrounding trees, looking for the killer or maybe for Petrosky, Decantor still holding tight to her waist.

A louder rustling came from the undergrowth beneath the willows. "Be quiet, bitch, be quiet." Farther from Petrosky than he was seconds ago—Turner was closer to Jackson than Petrosky was to the killer, and his position...where was he going? Not on any known path, not anymore. "Be quiet, bitch, be quiet."

Too close. Out of time.

Rustling, hissing, a crackle, and then something was flying through the darkness behind Jackson, behind Decantor, in the pitch where Petrosky couldn't see. The world stopped. Jackson screamed, Decantor vanished, and the steady *thwack* of meat on meat hit Petrosky's ears. *Fuck, fuck, fuck.*

He stomped from the shadows, re-holstering his weapon. *"'Ana last aleadui!" I am not the enemy.*

The scuffling stopped. Then the man himself emerged from the blackness, Jackson's wrist now clamped in his fist, his shoulders high and rigid. And his eyes…glassy. Confused.

He wasn't here at all—not in this moment, not in this country.

Jackson put her other hand on her pocket, where her gun was. Petrosky shook his head and put his hands in the air. *"Ymknny musaeidatuha." I can help her.* He didn't know if Turner knew what that meant, but Billie had given him the idea. *You're not the bad guy—I'll just make sure whoever we meet knows that.* And Turner's enemies spoke English, so he might be less likely to attack someone speaking Arabic, even if Petrosky was an old white guy. *"Ymknny musaeidatuha,"* Petrosky repeated. *Where the hell is Decantor?*

Turner jolted as if he'd been hit with a mild electrical shock. His mouth moved, though no sound emerged: *Be quiet, bitch, be quiet, be quiet.*

Petrosky stepped closer, hands out at his sides in surrender. "Good soldiers save lives," he said. "But these people are innocent."

Behind Turner, a shadow stepped from the blackness and into the moonlight; steady gaze, mouth tight with concentration, gun trained on Turner's head. *Decantor, Jesus Christ.*

"Hands in the air," Decantor said. Low. Almost a whisper. Had Turner gotten to him, hurt his throat?

Turner froze, his jaw hard. Muscles coiled. Because they'd cornered him, and soldiers fought—they did not submit.

Turner dropped Jackson's wrist and whirled on Decantor, lunging, leaping through the air just as Petrosky reached for his own weapon—seconds, in seconds he'd have Decantor's head in his murderous hands. Petrosky raised his gun and fired, hitting Turner in the soft spot behind his knee. The killer kept moving. Jackson kicked out at Turner's shins, stopping his forward momentum and toppling Turner to his injured leg.

Turner screamed. "*'Ana last aleadui! 'Ana last aleadui!*"

Decantor shoved him onto his chest and buried his knee in the man's spine. Jackson reached for one flailing wrist, missed, and stepped on his hand instead. Turner howled, snuffling and spitting against the dirt.

Petrosky crept toward the man's head and knelt in the pebbly street. The spittle around Turner's mouth glittered in the moonlight.

"For what it's worth, I'd have done the same." Petrosky told him. "Ortiz deserved what he got."

Turner stared at Petrosky. His eyes filled. His big fists relaxed.

He looked much smaller in the light.

38

"Well, well, well, it looks like you survived, Decantor."

The big man grinned as he headed past Petrosky's desk in the bullpen and slid into his own chair. "Much to your chagrin."

Petrosky nodded. "Fair."

The man had taken a vacation after the sting—fun, not stress-related. Decantor had been the smartest option, and they'd both known it from the moment Petrosky called him; of course Decantor had wanted to bring Turner down, but his height had really given them an advantage. Turner was strong, stocky, but he wasn't nearly as tall—so long as Decantor managed to stay upright, Turner would have been forced to jump, and it was much harder to crack someone's spine when your feet were dangling. As it was, Turner had lost purchase in the dark and ended up with Jackson's arm instead.

Petrosky rubbed the now healed scratches on his arm. He hadn't even felt them three weeks ago, the branches grating against his flesh, but as soon as he'd put Turner in a cell, the pain had brightened, angry and raw.

Jackson plopped into the chair beside him. Again.

"Don't you have a desk, Jackson?" Why did all his partners have boundary issues? At least his friends knew when to keep their distance. Maybe a little too well. He should go visit George after work, celebrate the man's miraculous recovery...from the common cold. The illness had passed just as George had promised. Maybe he should call Linda too. Or maybe not.

Jackson stretched her legs and propped one foot on the corner of his desk. "Yours is so much comfier." She handed Petrosky a cup—not shitty precinct coffee, or shitty frilly coffee house coffee. Rita's.

He cocked his head. "You sucking up for something?"

"Actually, no. It's from Acharya. Met him at the diner to give him part two of his exclusive." She sighed and set her own cup beside his. "He also wants to put Turner's story out there—an exposé, I guess."

Turner had been talking to the DA while they prepared the charges against him, but he'd be talking to the jailhouse shrink soon enough—he'd been hearing voices almost constantly since returning from overseas, though Turner believed they were just hallucinations. He'd been unable to hold down a job because of his tendency to repeat the words from his flashbacks. That, and his urge to suddenly wander off.

"Imagine going through life thinking the voices you hear are hallucinations instead of real memories—flashbacks," Jackson said. "Thinking you're insane when you're really just traumatized."

"He's still pretty insane." The flashbacks were triggering... what had the shrink called it? Some kind of fugue state. Turner said he didn't remember hurting anyone either, the same way he claimed not to recall his time in Iraq. Whatever had happened there had been firmly repressed...until now.

Maybe the right meds and the right doctors would be able to help him out—too bad he had to go to jail to get the help he needed. Too bad Samuel Amos had lost his life because of it. It was all too familiar. So many cases of undiagnosed or untreated mental illnesses, especially in soldiers. They were a stubborn bunch, but there was also a huge stigma around mental illness—no one wanted to seek help and be seen as weak, or worse, get blacklisted. How long had Petrosky himself been an alcoholic before he put the Jack Daniel's aside? How many more years before he'd forget Joey's exploding head? Probably never. But it'd surely ease again; he'd had years where he hadn't considered it at all. And in this line of work, there would always be more memories, memories that would take the place of the things he'd seen in wartime. Things even more horrific.

Petrosky took a long swallow from the Rita's cup—bitter. Delicious. "Is Acharya going to save some of that exposé shit for DeLaney?"

She smiled—better spirits than in weeks past. Petrosky still didn't know the specifics on whatever had been stressing her out, but when he'd stopped by the house, Lance had seemed fine, played video games with him like usual...and he'd eaten all Petrosky's cheese puffs. But that was okay. Lance was a growing boy, and Petrosky was only growing sideways. "Yep," Jackson said now. "Acharya's going to drag DeLaney through publicity hell."

Good man. Acharya was definitely getting pickles—he'd earned them. But maybe he'd send them in the mail, make sure they were smashed up a little. Didn't want the journalist getting cocky.

"He's waiting to see how it shakes out," Jackson was saying. "Not sure what will stick, but they've called up charges on the entire squad, all the way up to the general. DeLaney's claiming he wasn't aware of any wrongdoing, that he only suspected Cook might have hurt women unnecessarily, but that the raid on the village was warranted."

"We'll let the military sort it out." And if they didn't do it right...*we'll watch Cook and DeLaney and all the others like the criminals they are*. They were bound to fuck up again. Rose had already been arrested, and they'd gotten his soon-to-be ex-wife out of that prissy shit-hole where he'd abused her. Maybe she'd find her voice again. Time would tell. Even Babcock was getting his due: it looked like he was going to lose his shield and have to pay back the money he'd taken from Amos. He wouldn't serve time, but at least Petrosky wouldn't have to look at his stupid face anymore.

"Acharya says he's writing a book about the case." Jackson sipped her coffee, the sunlight glinting off her necklace—was that new? "Oh, and he wants to know if he can quote you."

"Fuck no," Petrosky said. "I don't want to be in any book." But he'd buy it. He'd probably buy two. Especially since Acharya had gotten Samuel Amos's father to donate his reward money to the homeless people who'd helped them locate Turner. *Sexual Healing* Marvin had laughed so hard Petrosky had seen his tonsils. Even Stoner Mike had agreed to get medical care. And Jane...he'd taken Billie with him to talk to her, and then he'd driven them both back to the house next door. Turned out, Jane liked dogs too. Lucky for her.

"Hey, meathead!"

Petrosky looked over at Decantor, approaching now from his desk. "You talking to me, you Kardashian-loving fuck?"

Decantor reached for Petrosky's phone receiver—jabbed it with his index. It slid back onto the hook. "It can't just look like it's on the hook, it has to actually be on the hook."

Jackson frowned at the phone over the top lip of her coffee cup. "What'd you do to the chief this time?"

Petrosky shrugged. But surely a tongue lashing was warranted for something.

"It's not the chief," Decantor said. "It's a case. And this kid...there's something you need to see."

A kid. Petrosky glanced at Jackson, whose gaze had wandered to her own desktop behind him. To the photo she kept on the top. Her boys.

Of course.

Had to be a fucking kid.

**Can't wait for more? Petrosky's not done yet!
Get *IMPOSTER*, the next book in the Ash Park series,
at MEGHANOFLYNN.COM.**

"Dark and twisty... a masterful procedural that explores identity and family secrets, *Imposter* is as surprising as it is addictive. A must-read!"
~*Bestselling Author Wendy Heard*

IMPOSTER

AN ASH PARK NOVEL

**A kidnapped child. A detective on the edge.
And a suicide that's anything but.**

CHAPTER 1

DEATH. It was an impossibly loud thing, an eerie, high-pitched silence that dominated even the chattering people on the sidewalk just outside. He could feel it weighting his shoulders. He could taste it, sweet and metallic on his tongue and overlaid with the musty stink of shit. He'd seen hundreds of bodies, and every one still hit him in the gut—especially when the deceased was a child.

Petrosky stopped near the middle of the living room, a room like any other in the neighborhood save for the corpse hanging from the living room rafter. The boy couldn't be more than fifteen—skinny, his black workout shorts bagging off his bony hips, a fake-faded green T-shirt draping his shoulders like a poncho. His slight frame made it worse, somehow, as if the universe was actively attacking the vulnerable. And his head... Thick dark hair, half-slitted brown eyes now marred with broken blood vessels that made him look like he might at any moment start crying crimson tears.

Poor kid. "Who found him?" Petrosky glanced at the slippery pile of bodily fluids—mostly the kid's intestinal contents—now congealing on the floor beneath the boy's bare toes. Petrosky's own stomach clenched, hot and achy.

"Parents," Jackson said, kneeling near the floor to the right of the body, far outside the dark puddle. She'd been here half an hour, but Petrosky's partner was still crisp and pressed like she'd just stepped out of a "How to Detective" manual: tailored gray suit, sensible shoes, her tight black curls shorn close to the scalp, even shorter than his own thinning salt-and-pepper locks. He peered down at the floor where Jackson was looking. Was that a tiny scrape in the gleaming wood? But no, these floors had scrapes all over— "hand-scraped hardwoods," that was what his neighbor, Billie, had called them when she was jokingly trying to convince him to install them at her place. Petrosky thought the fashionably beat-up boards were as strange a fad as faded clothing.

Jackson straightened. "Parents and the younger brother came home this morning from a two-day visit with Mom's sister in Lansing. Figured he'd be okay alone for a couple nights, but..." She shrugged, mouth relaxed, face blank— professional. But her dark eyes were as tight as Petrosky's shoulders.

A breeze tickled his neck, and he turned toward the buzz of voices filtering in from the yard, like the clucking of hens —louder now. "Was the window open when you got here?"

Detroit and the surrounding metropolis were always muggy in August, but this week Ash Park had been especially sticky even out here in the historic district. He couldn't see anyone leaving the window open overnight.

"Yeah. One of the first responders opened it because of the..." She gestured to the sheen of nastiness on the floor. A white L-shaped couch stood behind the puddle—behind the swinging body. Not a single gooey drop on it. At least the kid hadn't still been kicking when he'd shit himself. The beige wingback he'd probably stepped off of—his last fully conscious act—wasn't so lucky; it lay upended, two of its wooden legs slimed with fluids. As were the boy's legs, the flesh around the heels stained purple, his toes stiff, drips of black and brown dried in fetid streaks from beneath the edge of his workout shorts to the bottom of his soles. But he could still see the port-wine birthmark on one pale, white thigh, deep reddish-brown and stark against his otherwise graying flesh. "Judging by the blood settling and the rigor, it's been less than twenty-four hours—probably last night, early this morning."

Jackson nodded. "We'll know for sure once the ME gets here."

Petrosky grunted assent, his eyes on the kid's face. His neck. Usually, hanging victims had moments of instinctive defensiveness once the suffocation began in earnest—a struggle against the ligature. Most had claw marks on their throat.

But not this boy. The child exhibited the expected bruising around the rope itself, lines of angry blue-black, but none of the claw-like scraping Petrosky had anticipated. *Huh.* Had he taken something to dull the pain before he put his head through the noose and stepped off that chair?

The clucking sound came again, from outside: the droning of voices. The neighbors? Sounded like more than the few horrified middle-aged women he'd seen loitering on the sidewalk—the kind who looked like they should have Chihuahuas in their purses. But with a case like this, there would be strangers out there soon enough, prying into every little crevice like scavenger birds tearing at a decomposing raccoon. "Where's the family now?"

"They're with friends a few houses down—the neighbor was rounding them up when I got here. That guy didn't see or hear anything unusual, not that you'd expect him to."

Right—suicide was often a silent affair. Like depression. Petrosky nodded, but he could not drag his gaze to his partner's face. The kid's bloody eyes. The purple line on his neck. The breeze sighed, and Petrosky got a nose full of shit—shit and death. You never got used to that. Never. He coughed.

"You dying, old man?" Her voice echoed off the curved wooden staircase to his right. The beige curtains on the bay windows at the far end and the plush white carpet on the exposed second story landing absorbed the hiss of his breath, but not the sounds of the room.

"Not today." *Probably*. But he'd give his left testicle for a jar of VapoRub—not like he was using them for much else at the moment. He finally pulled his eyes from the kid and peered up at the rope instead, new rope from the shiny braid. How long had the boy struggled before giving up? Maybe Petrosky didn't want to know. "What about Scott?"

"On his way. I already told the officers outside that no one enters this room but Scott and the ME."

Good. Evan Scott was the best forensic guy they had, still practically a kid, but a genius kid. Petrosky squinted one last time at the rafters, following the rope over the beam, then to the wooden banister where it was secured, then turned back to the body. A deeply purple tongue protruded from between the boy's lips, so swollen it didn't look like it should ever have fit into his mouth.

"Goddammit," Jackson muttered from the far side of the room, behind the couch, her hand on one of the floor-to-ceiling curtains the color of Petrosky's pasty ass. She frowned through the slit she'd opened in the draperies. "We've got company."

Petrosky edged around the couch to peer over her shoulder at the backyard: lush grass surrounded by an eight-foot fence, and bordered on the inside with thick conifers and oaks, a glistening swimming pool in the middle. Over the top of the fence, someone's fat face appeared, but the man dropped when he met Petrosky's glare. If the lookie-loos thought they were going to climb over the fence into the backyard, they had another thing coming. And from the street...

On the other side of the room, the thickly curtained windows faced the driveway on the side of the house. Petrosky pulled one curtain back in time to see an older model Range Rover squeal up to the curb, back doors winging open before it was even parked. A man with a belly like a basketball under his sweater flung an enormous camera onto his shoulder and stepped onto the emerald lawn.

"Ah, the vultures are here." But he'd expected that. When a kid in an affluent neighborhood offed himself, they had to at least get a sound bite for the evening news. Or more than a sound bite, because it was *this* kid.

And suddenly everything was too loud, too vibrant. Little needles prickled at the base of his brain and tingled down his back and along his arms like a memory trying to slither from its prison. *Focus, Petrosky. No time for nonsense.* But that's what he'd told himself yesterday too. He cleared his throat. "You think Acharya's on his way?"

"If there's a story, he is. Guy went primetime after our last case." Jackson raised an eyebrow. "You *want* to talk to the journalists now?"

"Fuck no." Petrosky sniffed. "I was just curious."

Jackson dropped the curtain and sighed. "Let's go talk to the parents. We'll meet up with Scott and the ME later on today after they toss the bedroom—I don't have the stomach for it right now."

At least they didn't have to make the death notification. Those conversations always brought to mind the day he'd been on the receiving end, and Julie... His daughter had been about the same age as this boy when she'd died. When she'd been murdered. He swallowed hard.

"Why'd they call us?" Jackson said. "No ligature marks at the wrists or ankles, no additional bruising that would indicate a struggle—probably a standard suicide."

"It's a little more complicated than that." Petrosky let his gaze drift back to the body—that horribly purple tongue.

"Why?"

He finally met her eyes. "This is Gregory Boyle, the kidnapped and miraculously returned wonder boy."

GET *IMPOSTER* ON MEGHANOFLYNN.COM.

DEADLY WORDS

A BORN BAD NOVEL

THE NAME'S POPPY, Poppy Pratt, and I'm at your service, though I'll be the first to admit that I'm not always so agreeable.

It's in my nature I suppose, and always has been—that fire I keep hidden within me is in my blood. Dad says it's like air, like water, anything that sits there unnoticed until you don't have it anymore. I don't have a single reason to disbelieve him.

I think we're all one step from a storm if we don't get what we need, but I guess that makes it sound more intense than it is. You won't find maniacs here, frothing at the mouth —we aren't those people.

Maniac adjacent, maybe, but only if you believe the gossip around town. The gossip is not about us, though; it's never about us. It's about the "deserters"—the folks who leave this or any of the other nearby towns looking for something better. This is the kind of place people move on from—they find a job, they find love, they drive away as fast as they can. It's not a shock that anyone might up and disappear, so most of the gossips cluck their tongues, but they don't worry about the deserters. They don't know they should.

I know more than most people. I can read the high school books, even if I'm not allowed to in my elementary classes, and the education I get at home…well, that's a different kind of smart.

I rest my elbows on the railing of our narrow back porch, the wood already wet, little slivers embedding themselves in my forearms. I like the way it feels, damp and prickly—like *something. Thrashy.* I made that word up when I was smaller to describe the way some things get through your defenses against your will, stabbing at your soft spots. I don't think my father likes the word much. That's why he bought me a dictionary, then a thesaurus. He doesn't like anything he's on the outside of, and here, in this house, the things you don't know can be dangerous.

I press my arms harder against the wood, letting the slivers prick, letting them stab—*thrashy, thrashy, thrashy.* Acres of glistening grass stare back at me. Beyond the green, the sky cuts the horizon with a wound of deep indigo that looks like a mark left by a good whipping. I wouldn't know from personal experience—my father would *never* hit me—but almost every other child I know bears the scars of their parents' rage. It's no wonder people leave here.

The wood of the shed is damp, too, I can tell by the darker color along the slab. What little remains of twilight glows against the west-facing boards and paints the roses that bloom around the building with a grayed blush of color. The single window is a hazy black.

The wind brushes silky fingers through my hair, but there's electricity in the clouds tonight—not just rain. We're going to get a storm. Just as well—it happens all the time down here in Alabama, one hurricane after another some years—but this'll be a soupy wet trek toward a flood, and that's worse than the wind. Torrential rains took out our shed one year, the water rising over the concrete slab, picking up the lower boards like it was going to lift the thing clean off like a newfangled Noah's Ark. I stood in the doorway, Dad's arm warm at my side, and imagined myself climbing aboard, my blond curls like corkscrews in the breeze, setting sail for somewhere else. Anywhere else.

That was a bad year. Until we rebuilt the shed. That's the thing about life, about all things that fall apart, that crumble under pressure: they can't stay crumbled. Not when they're up against me. Nature gave me glue, too, and I don't break easy.

I blink. The light in the shed goes on, and the glass of the single window glares at me from the other side of the yard, the path to the shed glowing a hazy reddish-orange. Tepid. Watered-down.

It still looks like blood.

THE JILTED

A NOVEL

Abram Shepherd, present day

The man writhes, his body twisting against the mattress, fists clenched, face shadowed beneath the low-hanging beams of the roofline. His olive-skinned chest seeps blood from wounds I cannot heal. He licks his lips like a nervous animal, and then cries out, high and piercing, as if someone were running him through with a blade, such a guttural incantation it sounds almost inhuman. And it may be, for who's to say what is mortal and what is not? From the moment humans emerged from Earth's womb, we have carried a thread of sharpness within us, a fury that expands when we allow even the slightest hint of that agitation to catch our gaze. Because we focus there, you know, fascinated by the wickedness we see laid bare like the flesh of a lover.

That madness becomes our own. And soon it is all we see.

I clench my pipe harder between my teeth, the smoke circling my head like an herbal fog.

The man's eyes snap open and focus—for an instant only —but in that moment I see his humanity concentrated there, fixed in that tiny glint of light around the iris. "Please, Father …" he croaks in a strong Spanish accent, and his head snaps back, his spine contorts—"Father, save me, help me"—and then his words degenerate into glottal, hopeless blubbering. "Perdóname, Padre, perdóname."

Forgive me, Father, forgive me.

I cough once, trying to clear the putrid, meaty stench from the back of my throat, but it remains despite the smoke from my pipe, the air heavy as the cross around my neck. Perhaps if I truly wore the Roman collar as I'd once intended, I would be better equipped to fight this. But even if I were a priest, no one is remarkable enough to be granted forgiveness; my deeds here are but a physical prayer of repentance.

The man moans, froth forming at his lips and dripping down his cheek to the bed like the ooze of raw egg white. I have seen this surrender before, oh so many times, but they do not all go so easily; the skin on my left leg still burns with my most recent wound. *Helen.* She fought harder than most, crying out in prayer as she fled over the lawn, red scarf flying behind her like blood spurting from a neck wound. Afterward, I could almost feel the quivering nerves beneath her flesh as if they were mine, the sharp agony as The Dark bound her in coils of hate that tore her soul from her body and dragged it to a place I cannot begin to name. It was over quickly, as endings so often are, and though I hurled my prayers into the night, I was soon alone, my only response the bitter howl of the wind.

The man bucks off the mattress now, spraying spittle against the pillow, wetting the stained green blanket. It will not be long. He has gone so much faster than the others, perhaps because the evil is thicker since Helen was taken; I can feel the violence in the air, seeping from The Dark like pollutants into a water supply.

I can practically hear the good doctor, my only friend, whispering, "You're obsessed, Mr. Shepherd. Delusional." The doctor would tell me I should stop this madness. "Go back to your wife," he'd say. But I've spent far too much of my life ignoring my calling—the past looms full of abandoned things, wasted moments I could have used more wisely.

The man's arms and legs still, though his chest heaves with the rapid inhales of a panting dog—much too fast. Then he screams again, loud and long, and this time it is wholly and poignantly human, and my own humanity responds with a painful tightening of my rib cage. Staring at the glitter in his wild eyes, watching him go from madness, to horror, and back, my heart vibrates with such savage intensity I think it might stop altogether; I fight against this, for I am not ready to be tossed into the fiery pits with my ancestors. I know what they did—I found the journals in this old house, hidden beneath a floorboard, the pages tattered and worn. How I wish I had not read them. Because now I see fully the wickedness I am up against—see The Dark for what he is. He's been tormenting these grounds for eons, spreading malevolence like a virus, and far more will be sacrificed unless I find another strong enough to help me, someone who can lure The Dark out, so I might expel him from this place. And if I cannot weaken his hold here, I will not have the slightest chance of salvation.

The doctor may believe he can ease my burden, soften the pain of the cancer, but he cannot ease the suffering of my soul—he does not believe there is anything to fear. But he will believe. Soon he will see it too.

I can feel The Dark even now in the coldness whirling around me, though there is no open window, no earthly source for such a breeze. The man in the bed shudders then stills, his breath a thin wheeze, his shirt covered in crimson, so steeped in his own pain he cannot not see beyond the tip of his nose. So many exorcisms, and every one ends in defeat. I still hear those lost souls crying sometimes—or the wails of angels, admonishing me for my failures. Or perhaps that is my own soul, crying out in the night, reminding me that my faith is not strong enough to heal anyone.

Yet healing is not the goal. Expelling The Dark requires far more unusual methods than exorcism or mere summoning; and something far more dangerous. The demons here must be allowed to roam free and all those near will feel their presence even if they are not perceptive enough to identify that barbarous clawing at the base of their spine. I do not know what it will do to those who are able to see the evil. Perhaps they'll go mad with it, too.

I sit on the edge of the bed, and the man's eyes snap open, the fear reflected there deeper and more harrowing than the malignancy that tightens the air around us, the breeze suddenly hot as campfire smoke. The Dark is messing with us, trying to confuse me. It will not work.

"The Light or The Dark?" I ask him.

"The Light, The Light …" Blood bubbles between his lips. I press a rosary into his hand—his mother's, his most prized possession, and it is the last bit of comfort I can offer. "Go now, my son."

"No, no, Padre, no … help … help …"

I lean close to his ear, whispering, the stink of his sweat ripe in my nostrils. "I cast thee out." He coughs, and his eyes flutter closed, still and silent as if in death. Then his back arches and he shrieks—even the walls vibrate with the intensity of his screams.

I spread my hands in the air above his forehead, his fevered skin already writhing, like a nest of snakes is wriggling beneath his flesh, and though my rings do not touch him, the skin sizzles—the smell of burning fat seeps into my sinuses. My wedding band, and Justine's band on my pinky, warm, the engraved crosses inside them brighter, hotter, than the rest. It does not matter that Justine no longer recognizes me—evil remains, but love lingers too, even if it is harder to spread.

I close my eyes, feeling the room shrink and expand, the entire house breathing with me. "I cast thee out," I whisper again. "Into The Light." I lean closer and whisper the final words, once, twice, thrice.

The man shudders. I lower my hands, the flesh on the young man's head still sizzling, burning, then extinguishing itself with a staccato sucking sound. My rings are still warm against my palm. And as the breath leaks from him in one final exhale, I feel it, the thread of insanity, the demon beneath his flesh, squirming at my nearness, gnashing its horrible teeth. I know precisely how to recognize it—I brought it here. And I will send it back.

The room seems to waver, contracting once as if birthing the evil from the atmosphere. Then it is over, the vestiges of spirit vanishing like the dew evaporating from the grass in the rays of dawn.

I push myself to standing, bones aching, and hobble to the window, to that pane of glass as perfectly round as the moon outside, and I am struck with a coldness in the gut, as if I've stepped into someone else's shoes. Is this what my ancestors saw looking out this window? Tonight I peer out at another world from the one I strode through this afternoon—the front yard is empty, the grass a dusky greenish-gray beneath the towering oak, and the earth is no longer sodden with spilled blood. But my heart hammers against my breastbone, and I see Helen's red scarf in my mind's eye, hear her screams in my ears, and the *snap* of her spine, see the way it appeared as though every bone in her body was being crunched to dust, blood spurting from the ruptured shell of her chest.

Then the scene returns to normal—quiet, gray-green, empty.

But it isn't really empty. I feel the energy there, lingering in the shadow of the porch, waiting for the next soul to be lured by the force that emanates from this place.

For every slight, there must come a balancing blow. Every dark deed done must be repaid in blood.

The girl, that unfortunate girl, red scarf billowing behind her, screaming, screaming … Helen saw the madness of this world, the evil that must be quelled. Everyone does.

But never soon enough.

GET *THE JILTED* ON MEGHANOFLYNN.COM.

"Relentless suspense that will leave
you questioning every element of reality."
~Bestselling Author *Wendy Heard*

PRAISE FOR BESTSELLING AUTHOR
MEGHAN O'FLYNN

"Creepy and haunting...fully immersive thrillers. The Ash Park series should be everyone's next binge-read."
~*NY Times Bestselling Author Andra Watkins*

"Full of complex, engaging characters and evocative detail, *Wicked Sharp* is a white-knuckle thrill ride. O'Flynn is a master storyteller."
~*Paul Austin Ardoin, USA Today Bestselling Author*

"Intense and suspenseful...captured me from the first chapter and held me enthralled until the final page."
~*Susan Sewell, Reader's Favorite*

"Visceral, fearless, and addictive, this series will keep you on the edge of your seat."
~*Bestselling Author Mandi Castle*

"Cunning, delightfully disturbing, and addictive, the Ash Park series is an expertly written labyrinth of twisted, unpredictable awesomeness!"
~*Award-winning Author Beth Teliho*

Recall

"Dark, gritty, and raw, O'Flynn's work will take your mind prisoner and keep you awake far into the morning hours."
~Bestselling Author Kristen Mae

"From the feverishly surreal to the downright demented, O'Flynn takes you on a twisted journey through the deepest and darkest corners of the human mind."
~Bestselling Author Mary Widdicks

"With unbearable tension and gripping, thought-provoking storytelling, O'Flynn explores fear in all the best—and creepiest—ways. Masterful psychological thrillers replete with staggering, unpredictable twists."
~Bestselling Author Wendy Heard

"Nobody writes with such compelling and entrancing prose as O'Flynn. The perfectly executed twists and expertly crafted web woven into this serial killer series will captivate you. Born Bad is chilling, twisted, heart-pounding suspense that kept me guessing all the way up to the jaw-dropping conclusion. This is my new favorite thriller series."
~Bestselling Author Emerald O'Brien

LEARN MORE AT MEGHANOFLYNN.COM

Learn more about Meghan's novels on
https://meghanoflynn.com

ABOUT THE AUTHOR

With books deemed "visceral, haunting, and fully immersive" (*New York Times bestseller, Andra Watkins*), Meghan O'Flynn has made her mark on the thriller genre. Meghan is a clinical therapist who draws her character inspiration from her knowledge of the human psyche. She is the bestselling author of gritty crime novels and serial killer thrillers, all of which take readers on the dark, gripping, and unputdownable journey for which Meghan is notorious. Learn more at https://meghanoflynn.com! While you're there, join Meghan's reader group, and get a **FREE SHORT STORY** just for signing up.

Want to connect with Meghan?
https://meghanoflynn.com

Made in the USA
Monee, IL
21 November 2024

70763117R10176